Aquasaurus

Other works by Ernie Lee

Professional Texts and Workbooks

Contracting for Control and Disposal of Hazardous Materials, 1993, Southwest Logistics Institute (out of print)

Public Procurement Professions, 6 vol. Published by: University of Texas, Extended Learning program, 1997, 1998 (reprint) (out of print)

Risk Management for Buyers e-Group & Associates, Extended Learning program, Training Module, 2012 (reprint) (out of print)

Analysis Techniques for Buyers, e-Group & Associates, Extended Learning program, Training Module, 2013 (reprint) (out of print)

Economics for Buyers, e-Group & Associates, Extended Learning program, Training Module, 2013 (reprint) (out of print)

The Ring of Gyges, Ethics When No One is Watching, e-Group & Associates, Extended Learning program, Training Module, 2013 (reprint) (out of print)

Poetry

The Bard of the Blanco, Aim-Hi Publishing, Canyon Lake, Texas 2016
ISBN: 978-0-997128-1-3

Aquasaurus

by

ERNIE LEE

AIM-HI PUBLISHING

Aim-Hi Publishing
1542 Lakeside Dr. West
Canyon Lake, Texas 78133
Publisher's Catalog-in-Publication Data
Names: Lee, Ernest (Ernie), 1946 - ; cover illustration: Trif Andrei _________
Title: Aquasaurus / by Ernie Lee
Description: Aim-Hi Publishing LLC, 2016. | Summary: An oil fracking operator in S. Texas sets off an earthquake that unleashes a previously thought extinct species of crocodile.
Identifiers:
Library of Congress Control Number: 2016900264

ISBN 978-0-9971284-0-6 (Trade paperback)
Subjects: Fear – Fiction. | Crocodiles – Fiction. | Oil Fracking – Fiction. | Disasters – Earthquakes – Fiction.
Third edition: May 2018

For my wife, the woman who says she loves me more than her jewelry,

DONNA KAYE DUKES
MARCRUM   LEE

<u>Acknowledgements:</u>

There is much more to writing a book than a good story, and putting sentences and paragraphs down on paper. This book is the product of several people who helped me put it together in a readable form. I would especially like to thank the following:

Ron Eisenbrey, **Ron Hathaway**, and **Robert Carpenter**, who suffered through extremely rough concept ideas and drafts for this story.
Billy James Wall, who gave me encouragement to finish this story.
Maria Elena Alvarado, who proofed and edited the first drafts.
Carrie Fredericks, who proofed and gave valuable feedback on middle drafts.
In addition, especially, **Sandra Gayle Young**, who edited the final version.

Without your help, support, and assistance I could not have completed this book. My heartfelt thanks goes to each of you.

The author's goal is to give away <u>**2,016**</u> copies of *this book* to **Cancer Fighters**. If you or someone you know is currently fighting cancer, or has survived a cancer fight, please go to <u>www.ernieleepoetry.com</u> and sign up on the website. Then send a personal message to Ernie Lee (contact button at top of webpage) with the <u>name, details, type of device (e-Pub, Kindle, .pdf, or other) and contact information of your nominee</u>. A copy of this book will be provided to the nominee in your name, free of charge. For details on the number of books distributed to date, please check the **Writing+is+Giving** page on the website. Your purchase of a book on Amazon, Barnes & Noble, or your favorite outlet helps pay for this campaign.

Chapter 1

Dark is more than the absence of light – more than nothingness. Dark, in its final form, moves from perception to chilling reality. That indescribable, untouchable 'thing' you feel in the dark … is the dark. You cannot touch it; it touches you. It fondles you with cold icy fingers as frigid as the dark side of the moon. Not just black, it is blacker than black. It presses all around you and steals your breath away. It squeezes you into something microscopic. It sucks all awareness into a void that is empty and lifeless. If you opened a light in this dark, it would appear as the gleaming blade of light slicing through the dark like a razor-sharp knife that slowly turns edgewise until it shrinks into a tiny sliver before disappearing in the voluminous, overwhelming dark.

Though it seems empty and lifeless, you know that it is not. You know with absolute certainty that you are not alone in this dark. You cannot see it, but it is there… stalking … waiting. This is not the certainty you felt when you knew something dwelt in your closet that did not know how to open doors. Nor is it the certainty when you knew something lurked beneath your bed. Those childish, irrational, illogical certainties have paled and receded with youth and time. This certainty does not recede; it advances. It breathes in the relentless dark. It moves with slow, sucking sounds. It nears. It breathes your air.

She had left the light on again, which irritated Jesse Perrine to no end. He had been seeing Rita for a little over a year now, and he seriously could not understand the obsession she had of always leaving a light on. At first, it was sexy and refreshing. Most women want the lights off when they make love. Not Rita. Sometimes, she even drifted to sleep without turning off the lamp next to her bed. Jesse would invariably wake up in the middle of the night, harsh light interrupting his peaceful dreams, and he would have to go all the way around the bed to turn the damn light off. It was a minor irritant, but it was continuous. Every night!

And those sounds she made in her sleep! Almost like crying. Moans and sudden sharp breaths. One night it sounded like she had an air leak. She was huffing and puffing as if she were struggling to blow up a balloon and was losing the battle. He half expected to wake up to find her flat as a pancake! Flat was one thing, Rita Martin was not. She had strong arms and legs of an athlete. She was toned and muscled except in places where she was supposed to be soft. All the good places.

As he padded across the room, barefoot, to the bathroom, he looked at her as she slept and decided she was worth it. She was 'the one'. Only he was not sure if he was 'the one' for her. If it meant that he had to spend a lifetime getting up in the middle of the night to turn a light off, he guessed he would adjust to it in time. Right now, they did not live together, so it did not matter much. From the lights-on thing and the restless dreams, he knew something was bothering her. Something bad. Something deep she did not – or could not – discuss. He also knew better than to ask. Every time he mentioned it,

she would either, deny anything was wrong, or change
the subject by launching into her favorite diversion –
trying to convince him to transfer from Texas State to
UTSA.

When he came out of the bathroom, she was
sitting in the middle of the bed putting on her makeup.
Music was playing on the clock radio; a recent hit they
both liked. Rita said "Morning, baby!" playfully leering
at his half-zipped jeans. He looked down self-
consciously and hiked them up. "Aw, you teaser!" she
pouted. "You give me a little peek, and then cover up!
Are you sure you aren't a male stripper?" she teasingly
asked. The song 'I'm So Fancy' was playing, so Jesse
playfully grabbed the decorative bedpost and used it like
a stripper pole. Jesse was no stripper, though he had the
body of one. His moves were clumsy and comical, and
Rita delighted in his impulsive antics. He was still
dancing to 'Fancy' when the song ended and 'Shake It
Off!' came on. Jesse stopped dancing and pretended to
be upset the song had changed. "Damn! Just when I was
halfway to Tokyo!"

"Shake it off, baby!" Rita encouraged. "Shake it
off!"

Jesse gamely picked up a hairbrush from the bed
and danced around singing the lyrics to the song about
cruising and not being able to stop moving. Jesse, with
his long black hair flying looked to Rita like a big black
sheep dog! Rita screamed and jumped out of bed
laughing hard and running toward the bathroom. "Stop!
You're gonna make me pee!" Jesse was still singing and
prancing around when she came out and stood in the
doorway to watch. She stuck out her sexy lower lip,
slowly shook her head, and gave him a playful thumbs-
down. Jesse was unfazed, "Haters gonna hate, hate,

hate…" he sang. Rita joined in, "Fakers gonna fake, fake, fake..." They collapsed on the bed laughing. He wrapped her in his arms and kissed her. "You know I gotta go," he moaned into her neck. It was a mistake. He knew it as soon as it left his mouth.

"You don't **have** to – you **want** to." Rita wasn't laughing anymore.

"What do you mean? We talked about this over and over. It's Spring Break. You know I've had plans to go into Honey Creek cave for over a year," he reminded. "And, you have plans to go to Enchanted Rock! You've got to get Katie ready to go to Colorado this summer."

"I know. But I was holding out hope that you might give up the cave trip, and go with us." Her mood abruptly changed as she sat upright again. "It's alright – don't worry about it. It's fine," she said quickly. Jesse knew when she said that, things were far from fine.

Desperate that they not part on a bad note, he offered, "Look. When I get back next week, maybe we can … talk about me transferring to UTSA next semester."

"Really? Baby!" She beamed and grabbed him; pulling him tight to her. Then she pushed him away with a suspicious look on her face. "You're not just saying that are you? You're serious?"

"Sure," he said. "But right now, I've got to go! I'll be late. Professor Morrison has already threatened to lock the classroom door! I can't be late again."

"If you moved to UTSA…" she began.

"Yeah, yeah, yeah, I know! We could sleep in and not have to fight traffic to get to school. You're right. But right now I've gotta go." He slipped into his shoes, pulled on a t-shirt, "I'll see you in a couple of days when we get back from the cave." He headed toward the door, picking up his backpack along the way. He looked back over his shoulder and gave her his most dazzling smile and a wink. She pouted and blew him a kiss, and then he was gone.

Clint Marshall stood with his thumbs hooked in his belt. He was not pleased. Under a blistering Texas sun, the soaring skeleton of an oilrig shimmered and played in the reflection on the lenses of his dark aviator glasses. His foreman, Hugh Shipmann, stood nearby kicking a scuffed boot against a chunk of flakey limestone.

"Well, it ain't good enough," Clint barked.

Hugh squinted at his boss. In his best cowboy voice he said, "We're squeezing the lime for all it's worth, Hoss. Crew is spent. We been pumping fluids 16-7 for two weeks straight. Mamma Earth just won't give up the juice."

Clint ignored his feeble attempt to sound like a Texan as he unscrewed a bottle of water and took a drink, swishing the water around as if he had a bad taste in his mouth. He spat it out. "Well, we better figure out something. If the numbers don't go up, we got big problems. The S-wave and the SedLogs say the crude is down there. SpecA and mud logs both look good. Oil is in the hole. If we can't pump it out, that's on us. Where is Hootie?"

"Called out sick."

"Called out sick? What the hell is that? You mean called 'in' sick?" Clint grumbled. "You Yankee boys drive me nuts! Sick from what? He better be bleeding, broke, or on fire!" Clint pulled a long draw on his water bottle.

"Said he had anal glaucoma," Hugh grinned.

Clint interrupted his drink, tilting his head forward to avoid spilling on his starched shirt. The bottle made a popping sound as he pulled it way from his lips, and water dripped on his hand. "Anal what? What the hell is anal glaucoma?" he asked as he shook the water from his hand.

"Said he couldn't see his ass coming to work today!" Hugh clinched his jaw and tried hard not to laugh.

Clint was not amused. "Well, you get his butt in here by 10 o'clock or he's gonna see my boot fitting him for a monocle. I'm flyin' down to Houston at two, and I better go with some answers -- or a plan! If we have to pull pipe on this job; we're all out on the street."

Hugh's browed wrinkled as he tried to talk Texan again, "Well, we keep on keeping on and hope we break up whatever is down there blocking the flow."

"Keepin'-on-keepin'-on ain't getting it done! I'm thinking we need something extra," Clint growled.

"What have you got in mind, Hoss?"

"I don't know – somethin'! Maybe we need a new method." He paused, "Maybe Pawson's," Clint mused, almost to himself.

Hugh sucked his lips tight to his teeth to keep from smiling. It was no laughing matter. He fixed his boss' eyes with a dead serious look and released the pressure on his lips with an audible snick. "Pawson's hasn't been approved," he said, knowing Clint already knew.

"Well, I can't think of a better well to do some field-testing on. Can you?"

"Yeah," Hugh nodded. "One somewhere in South America!"

Clint turned and walked back to his truck. "Well, we ain't in South America!" He flung what was left of his water bottle against the light cart on his way past. Water dripped off the side of the yellow machine. "Anal glaucoma!" he muttered to himself.

Professor Tom Morrison sipped his coffee and watched his gathering students. God he hated teaching! He wished he were anywhere but in this classroom. He hated kids almost as much as he hated teaching! Zombies! Drugged-out, fogged-out, burned-out, boozed-out, zoned-out zombies! Moreover, eight o'clock classes were the absolute worst! Later, when they went into the field for research in 100-plus-degree-heat, they'd be grateful for an early class. But right now all they wanted to do was sleep, except for one; and she wanted to go to bed. Better watch out for that one, Tom thought. Trouble. Whatever! This was the last class before Spring Break. He would be free for a whole two weeks. He could not wait to get away to the outback in the Florida 'Glades, and no students to bother with! They would all gather like zombies on the beaches, partying like there was no tomorrow.

Tom launched into his Earth Sciences lesson plan. "Let's talk today about something that threatens to have a lasting impact on global biological and environmental health, especially here in South Texas. The frickin' oil business! Oops! I mean the **fracking** oil business." He paused for their laughter.

"Due to world-wide uber-dependence on fossilized fuels, demand for petroleum has increased exponentially. Here in America, volatile prices and the cost of importing oil have spurred new processes for getting oil from shale deposits unreachable only a few years past. Hydraulic fracturing – or hydro fracking – or just plain fracking, is one way to get at those sources of natural gas and petroleum. It can even be used to produce water, but it makes for extremely expensive water." Tom explained shale sediments could hold large amounts of gas, water, and oil in tiny pores of the rock deep underground. "So does Limestone, but it is harder to crack than shale. Granite and marble are even harder. Drilling deep within the earth, the drillers inject a fluid mixture of water, sand, and chemicals into the well under pressure. These chemicals and the high pressure will weaken the shale rock and fracture it – thus the name. The fractures seep oil and gas into the well, which they pump to the surface. Old style oil wells were vertical, but fracking most often uses lateral lines branching out horizontally through the field. Gravity drains the freed oil and gas into the well channel more efficiently." Tom drew a picture on a white board illustrating his lecture as he talked.

"More oil here at home equals higher profits, more jobs for workers, lower cost to us at the pump for gasoline, and less dependency on volatile political systems abroad. So, what's the problem?" he asked.

Tom explained over 600 chemicals go into the oil fracking fluid, all of them toxic, some of them potentially deadly. He went over the list which included formaldehyde, lead, mercury, hydrochloric acid, radium, uranium, to name a few – all hazardous and all pollutants. Tom talked about the carcinogens and toxic chemicals that, once released into the ground water, can become dangerous to large populations. Not only was there the huge human risk, but the damage to animals and the environment was tremendous. The fracking method uses an extraordinary amount of water, which they haul to the oil well site in tanker trucks, putting pressure on supply, increasing the risk to traffic and public safety, and causing great damage to area roads and bridges. Some small South Texas communities simply cannot keep up with the increased costs.

In addition, a measurable increase of detectable tremors has occurred in recent years. Some suggest fracking might be contributing to the instability of underground geological structures. Jesse's eyes came up, as he stopped reading the text on his cell phone and listened closely. Tom continued, "There have been more tremors in Texas in the last two years alone than the previous one hundred." Tom interrupted his lecture and pointed his stir stick toward Jesse Perrine, the terminally late one, who had his hand in the air. "Mr. Perrine?" How refreshing. A zombie with a question.

"Is that … just a localized effect? I mean, only around the drilling sites?"

"Only if you consider Texas and Oklahoma and every fracking state from here to Pennsylvania, local," Morrison answered to renewed laughter. These kids love the word, 'fracking'. "Everywhere the technique is used, an increase in earth movement and subsidence, including cave-ins and sink holes, have been detected. The environmental impact has been immeasurable. Vital habitat is being irreparably damaged. We may not know the true cost for years to come."

Tom ended his lecture by stating the oil and gas industry has long been fully aware of the dangers and the risks. "Nevertheless, big oil, and big profits mean huge political contributions. The high price of oil makes it financially more attractive for oil companies to pump rather than work towards developing renewable sources of energy that have less impact on the environment. Demand for wind and solar power energy has increased some, but not enough to offset the growth in demand for petroleum produced energy. Texas now leads the nation in wind-produced electric energy, but it is not enough. Profits drive energy; and as long as the profit is in petroleum, the emphasis will remain on pumping. Despite the risks to public health, the damage to infrastructure and natural systems, the waste of already scarce water resources, the polluting spills, the huge number of industrial accidents, and injuries – including deaths, the oil drillers just shake it off!"

"Class dismissed. Wake up and get out of here! Enjoy your fracking Spring Break. See you next week!" he laughed.

Texas State University campus in San Marcos is an idyllic setting. It is an awesome paradise of crystal-clear water, warm weather, leafy green trees, and blue-eyed blondes adorning every rock ledge bordering the slow moving river. People have lived around the nearby springs for 12,000 years. Deep beneath the campus, the aquifer bubbles, drips, and flows through cracks, holes, and natural limestone caverns. The limestone rock naturally filters the pure, transparent water, which feeds San Marcos Springs, Comal Springs further south, and an immeasurable number of other springs, streams, and rivers around the edges bordering the Texas hill country. The underground system is teeming with life. It is the subterranean home of thousands of aquatic and terrestrial animals. Salamanders, blind catfish, crayfish, darters, snakes, and all types of aquatic animals thrive in the constant eighty-two degree water. Many connecting caverns, alternately dry or wet depending upon the water table, are also home to birds, gigantic rats, shrews, spiders, beetles, and millions of bats.

A connected system of underground pools, known as the Edwards Aquifer, wraps around the edge of the hill country. This vast aquifer runs some 250 miles from near Brackettville, through San Antonio, then northward toward Austin and Waco. It is unknown how large these subterranean systems are. Water monitors maintain test wells to measure the aquifer's rise and fall, which have never gone dry – even during the worst drought conditions on record. Some might compare the aquifer to a large underground lake. It has been suggested that if the aquifer were on the surface, it might be an inland sea some three hundred miles long. Some scientists estimate it would be so large that it would have tides and waves. At the least, it would be as large as one of the Great Lakes.

Deep underground, wet walls glisten in the dank darkness, and water drips from the ceiling making unceasing echoes. There, in the deep, deep darkness – blacker than any night, a large alligator-like creature slides from a semi-dry ledge into the brackish water. The scaly reptile is slimy and moss colored, and reeks of rotted meat. It is hungry. Hunting. Suspended in the water, it is motionless in total darkness. Thousands of years of adaptation allow it to maneuver in the boundless gloom – much like the way night-vision technology operates. It gathers and amplifies tiny fragments of ambient and low spectrum infrared light. Combined with thermal imaging, like snakes, the creature can "see" in total darkness. It floats with its eyes barely above the water line. The eyes and the bulla, which contain sensory organs, are normally the only thing visible on the surface. Huge webbed, clawed feet provide balance and stability. The claws are long and as sharp as knives. A long encrusted tail, swings slowly from side to side giving it a slight forward motion, barely rippling the water. As it swims into fresher water, hundreds of fish, detecting its presence, scurry away from the massive predator. The beast begins to emit a low purr. The sound is inaudible to humans. The animal becomes invisible to the fish. The reptile knows now only its movements can reveal its presence. The silvery fish swim back and surround the floating leviathan, unaware the creature is not a moss-covered rock. The small darters and minnows feed off its skin as they would on algae covered cave walls. It waits. The predator waits to feed – silently, motionless, undetectable – it waits to feed.

A dark cloud of bats fifty-feet wide are coming through the channel toward their roost, which lies beyond the creature. They swirl and swoop along the glossy cave walls, using sonar to avoid collisions. Conditioned by eons of time, they know they will be able to "see" any potential threat in time to avoid disaster. They do not know of the stealth capabilities of the submerged beast whose low-pitched humming disrupts their sonar signals. The bats fly nearer and nearer over the concealed, undetected predator. They swirl and flit along jagged cliff walls a hundred feet high, then dive steeply to skim the surface of the dark water snagging mosquitoes and water bugs as they zoom past, breaking formation, feeding, then reforming into their cloudlike swarm. Closer and closer they come.

Exploding from the murky water, the predator's crocodilian maw, gaping wide, engulfs the cloud of surprised bats. The jaws snare a huge segment of the moving cloud, fifteen feet wide, which disappears inside the creature's massive mouth. Splashing back into the water the massive animal twists and turns, and churns the water, devouring hundreds of bats in huge snaps and chomps. The sounds of water roiling, wings flapping, and bones crunching fill the cavern. Gyrating and turning in the water, the creature scrapes against ancient ragged limestone outcroppings, tearing a length of skin from its side, which hangs loosely and trails behind the left rear leg. It is an unnoticed minor wound to the animal. Merely a nick. In the melee, the small flap of skin flakes off and bobs in the water nearby along with pieces of wings and dozens of dead or dying bats. Some bats escape, flying through the huge serrated teeth, as the huge beast continues to chew and grind prey with huge snaps of it toothy jaws. Foamy, red-flicked water sloshes across the cavern in huge waves washing from side to side like in a gruesome bathtub.

The surviving bats regroup and fly onward to their roosts while the creature subsides into the deep, dark, unfathomable water. Resting now, an opaque flap of skin slowly slides over the dead, yellowish eyes. The low-pitched sonic hum ceases, and darter fish dash swim near in metallic flashes to peck at the bloody entrails hanging from the sides of the great grinning mouth. Echoes of dripping water are again the only sound. Fed now, it sleeps within the deep, dreadful, dark cavern.

Chapter 2

A long line of busses stretched southward down San Jacinto Boulevard. There must have been fifty of every known make and color. An equal number were stacked along Trinity Street pointing north. The government buildings of Austin reflected against a gray sky in multiple windshields as April winds rippled the banners hanging from the sides of the large vehicles. There were banners of all sizes and shapes and colors. They danced and flapped in the strong spring gusts like the happy, colorful kites over Zilker Park. The Audubon Society, Sierra Club, Environmental Trust, and Green Peace; all were represented; even the Humane Society was there. Local activists were visibly present like Save Our Springs (SOS), Austin Environmental Protection Society, Wildlife Conservation, the Nature Conservancy, and Friends groups of various state and national parks from all over Texas. You name it; they were in the crowd. Even the lunatic fringe groups were marching in their "Keep Austin Weird" tie-dyed t-shirts.

Thousands of people filled the chill, damp streets around the capitol for the rally, which the activists organized to protest big oil influence and to defeat the oil fracking bill, which the Texas Legislature was now debating. There were people of every age, shape, and description; preppies, geeks, business professionals, longhaired hippies, yuppies, tree huggers, yindies, nerds, beards, bicyclers, and biker gangs. They were all there. Every sub-culture from freak to new age were mingled and competing for space. Everyone seemed to be carrying signs or banners or wearing message t-shirts and some covered all three bases. One even sported a bumper sticker on his butt, and the familiar recycle logo etched into his hair.

A large stage to accommodate the speakers was set up in front of the Capitol at the head of Congress Avenue. The crowd drowned out even the loudspeaker system. Everyone yelled and waved signs, trying to get the attention of several hundred media people covering the event. News teams had parked their satellite trucks and communications vans on Lavaca Street to the west. NBC, ABC, CBS, Fox News, CNN, and every major and independent news media known was present. Today, Good Morning America – even Oprah! Radio stations were even more prevalent than the TV trucks. Large electric and communications cables stretched across streets and sidewalks up and down Congress and across 11th Street. Austin had not seen this kind of coverage since the misty night George Bush won the presidential nomination, only to have it yanked from his grasp when Florida could not be determined.

Representative Sara Hughes watched the unfolding scene from the third floor legislative law library inside the Capitol building. She prayed her son Cody was not out there in that mob. In these last days before Spring Break, she felt sure he was still on campus in San Marcos, thirty miles south. The large plate glass window normally gave a breathtaking view of Congress Avenue all the way to the Colorado River. Today, thousands of milling people obstructed that glorious view. She could see people crossing the bat bridge on foot ten blocks away. Cops had the streets blocked off for the protesters. First came the motorcyclists with their loud roars that echoed off the huge capitol building.

Then the bicyclists came pedaling along, filling the wide avenue from curb to curb. They were weaving from side to side in unison like some synchronized, wheeled ballet. Behind came the foot marchers, carrying their banners and signs. It was quite a spectacle.

Sara was a first year representative from the district that seemed to get the most interest and criticism from these protesters. She opposed the bill they were against and had even attached several riders to the bill in an effort to regulate the drilling companies and require greater environmental controls. The House had shot down all of her suggestions on the floor, removed them from the calendar, or greatly watered them down in committee. She was frustrated.

"Look at that, Pokey!" she said to Pablo. "Have you ever seen anything like that before?"

Representative Pablo "Pokey" Marin was her mentor and trusted confidant. From the moment of her election, he had stepped forward to "take her under his wing" as he often said. He lived in the next county west of her district and Sara and her parents had known him for years. He had been an elected official for most of his life now and was a fixture in Austin for some twenty years. He currently held the Vice-Chair of the Environmental Commission. He would be Chair, but the Democrats were not in power. Republicans had run Texas for a very long time and it seemed they would stay in power for the near future. Regardless, Pokey was entrenched, and no one in his district would dream of a challenge. They would certainly lose. Besides, almost everyone loved Pokey. Even the oilmen.

"Not since George left," he said. "Not even when Perry wanted to build a toll road all the way across Texas."

"All those voters down there against the bill and it still moves forward. I don't get it," she shook her head.

"All those people!" he emphasized. "Some of them are voters; some of them are just hell raisers out for a good time to shake the old establishment tree. Voters have a short memory, Sara. By the time elections come around, they won't even remember they were here. Every naysayer in Texas is out there. The CAVE people we call 'em, 'Citizens-Against-Virtually-Everything'!" he laughed.

"That's still a lot of votes down there," she mused, clicking her front tooth with a fingernail.

"What are you worried about? Ninety-nine percent of them are not from your district anyway; and those who are, love you to death. You are the environmental queen," he laughed, stressing the word queen. "You've introduced fifteen environmental bills this first session, and amended this one they hate so much, at least a dozen times."

"Fat lot of good it's done me," she grumbled. "Everyone one of them beat to death right out of the gate. I haven't accomplished a single thing up here."

"Nonsense!" he said. "You've got your name out there. Everyone respects you and knows what you stand for. Most of them agree with you even if they won't admit it. You've made a tremendous showing for your first lap. We all know the evils of big oil, every last one of us. You bring it to their attention without rubbing their noses in it. I couldn't do that. They'd have me cleaning cattle stalls at the livestock auction back home if I introduced any of those bills. You can get away with it."

It was true. She also knew Pokey and his staff had written three-quarters of the bills she had introduced. He had sponsored or endorsed all those, along with the ones she had written herself. He was a true ally, but she also knew about politicians. He was not going to stick his neck out if he did not have to. He was teaching her that there were more ways than one to skin a cat! Nevertheless, she sometimes felt like the cat. Of all the many ways to get your point across and to get your objectives met, direct confrontation is rarely one of them. So, he let her carry the bills, and he signed off on them and got them into committee. Once it reached that stage, he had no more control than she did; but he did have a lot more influence. She respected and trusted Pokey; but on more than one occasion, she felt he had stuck her out on the end of a meat stick to measure public opinion. She repeated to herself often that it was all part of paying her dues. No one would go after a first term rookie representative. Hell! She might not even be here next term anyway! Pokey was in it for the long haul. He could be Speaker of the House if the elections ever turned.

"Maybe I should go down and talk to them" she mused.

"Are you crazy?" he shouted. "They'd tear you to pieces. They don't know who you are. They don't know if you are the good guy or the bad – and they don't care! They are looking for trouble. Every nut case and weirdo this side of the Sabine is down there! You can't talk to them! They'd never hear you. Even the speakers on the platform can't be heard above this din. Even if they could, they wouldn't listen. What would you say anyway? The bill is going to pass without the safeguards they want, and there ain't a damn thing you or I can do about it."

Clint circled his Cessna over Hobby Airport. He noticed the company logo painted on the hangar roof had changed again. In place of the old Aggie maroon HNH Oil, the company had painted a new logo. The top part was bright green over an ocean blue bottom; with a big white swoosh across the middle. 'I guess we aren't Aggies anymore,' Clint thought. The Board must have bought in to all this environmental consciousness crap. He glided in and taxied to the company hangar. The limo idled nearby, waiting. The ground crew took over the plane as he climbed inside the plush, cool car for the ride downtown to the Petroleum Building. Darla was waiting in his outer office.

"Get dressed. You are on the agenda for four thirty. Your reports are in the green folders on your desk." Same green as the new logo.

"Well, hello to you too" he teased. "Miss me?" Clint handed her his satchel. "Put these in my folder and make a copy for each seat."

"I always miss you, honey." Dara Dunn called everyone honey. She made it sound sincere. Clint pulled off his flight jacket, unclipped his phone from his belt, and handed them to Darla. "There are four pictures of the well head here. Print in color, full size sheets for the folders."

In his inner office, he stripped to his underwear and threw his jeans and shirt over the back of a leather sofa. He moved into the bathroom and turned on the shower. Testing the water, he stripped off his underwear and stepped inside. When he stepped out, he saw Darla had left fresh underclothes for him on the valet. He put on his shorts and used the sink to shave. After shaving, he ran a comb through his hair. Was he grayer today? He could swear he was. He pushed his face closer to the mirror and ran his fingers through his hair, spreading it out and looking for gray. He saw Darla come in behind him with a fresh shirt and tie in her hand. She could hardly miss what he was doing.

"You look great, honey. You aren't getting older; you're getting better! Damn your blue eyes!" she laughed.

"Oh yeah? Well, I'm sure not getting any younger!"

"I'd still do ya!" she quipped with a smile.

Clint laughed. "Yeah? What if I didn't have two dimes to rub together? Would you do me then?" he asked.

"Well…" she drew it out long with doubt in her tone, "Yeah! At least once!" she laughed.

"Once is about all I could afford!" he shot back, knowing she would not be offended.

She threw his fresh shirt in his face and left the room. He pulled on his shirt, tied the tie, and stepped into his pants. He took fresh socks and shined shoes from his closet then sat on the couch to put them on. When he was finished, moved over to his desk and inspected the folders Darla had assembled for him.

"It's all there. In order," she said as she swept into the room.

He stuffed the folders into a leather portfolio and headed for the door. Darla was ready with his suit jacket. He shrugged into the jacket and turned to face her. She reached out to adjust his tie, and inspected him head to toe. He was ready.

He walked the long walnut-paneled hallway to the boardroom with Darla close behind. The executive secretary sat outside the paneled office. When she saw them coming, she stood and opened the huge oak double doors. Darla took a seat near the door on a tall stool that gave her a clear line-of-sight to Clint so she could be ready for anything he might need. The board meeting was in recess. Clint went around the table in the richly paneled room greeting, shaking hands, and touching the shoulders of various directors until TJ called the meeting back to order.

As Darla distributed the folders, Clint circled the large glossy conference table, where a dozen directors reclined in their seats. Clint sank into the expensive armchair on the left side of the table. He knew his spot. TJ Howlett, seated at the head of the table, the second "H" in HNH, looked at Clint over the top of his reader glasses and nodded at him. Behind TJ, the impressive skyline of Houston spread across the floor-to-ceiling plate glass windows. TJ was clearly in charge, being the majority shareholder.

"Clint is here now, just on time. Clint, you have the floor," TJ gestured.

Clint looked around the big table at the balding, pot-bellied men who controlled his present and his future. He did not like any of them very much, but he knew they held the keys to the checkbook. They were an aging group of lawyers, finance men, bankers, and business executives – not a single woman at the table. The only decent oilmen among them were TJ and Mr. Nobles, the "N" in HNH. They had to be appeased at all times and Clint played the ultimate appeaser; regardless of how he personally felt about their capabilities and their intelligence sometimes, Clint catered to each one as if they were favored uncles.

"Gentlemen, I have prepared written reports for each of you concerning the Dilley Chalk #2 Project. I've just come in from the field, and I apologize for the fact some of these reports were not given to you in advance. You have seen the numbers. I know you have kept track of this project; and as you are no doubt quite aware, they do not look good. Despite promising science, a huge granite dome is blocking our hole; and we haven't been able to get through the barrier to reach the reserve that we know is there. We've increased the fracking pressure 30% but still haven't broken through."

"What's your yield?" Phillip Nobles broke in.

Clint knew Nobles was fully aware of the yield. It was his way of getting the fact that the well was under-producing on the table.

"Hundred barrels a day … nearly."

"Not even covering your nut," the old man stated the obvious, shaking his gray head.

Clint did not take the bait, and launched back into his presentation. "The results of tests show us we are right on top of a huge reserve. We know we can't get to it with the technology we have at our disposal right now. This field is huge, stretching all the way from Karnes County to Uvalde. We are right on top of it, and no one knows it's down there but us. We're negotiating leases to every acre between Karnes City and Rio Medina. Once it comes in, this hole will pump a thousand a day for seven years running at least."

"If it comes in." Nobles interjected.

Clint fingered the alligator skin portfolio. He slowly traced between the nodules running across the great animal's back, which now covered the surface of his case. The contrast of smooth leather and the rough square mounds of the skin were striking. His fingers traced the narrow isles between the raised knobs. He knew he was in danger of losing this project. "This granite structure is at least a hundred yards thick and a thousand feet deep, blocking the path to the oil. Granite is not supposed to be down there; but it is. Normal fracking methods are probably not going to break this formation up," he finally said. "The only option, except one, is to move the hole again. If we do that, we are looking at six months at least and the possibility someone else will discover the reserve. If word gets out about this pool, the cost of those leases will skyrocket, and someone else is going to poke a straw into our oil field. Gentlemen, this reserve is bigger than anything ever hit in Texas! It's bigger than anything Saudi has. And it is sweet, sweet crude with practically zero Sulphur content, unlike west Texas crude that needs CAT cracking. We get past this rock; we've got a gusher! All we'll have to do is pump it out. There's a pool of oil down there three counties wide."

TJ frowned. "What's the other option?"

Clint took his time with the answer; then he slowly stood. "Pawson's Bitter Pill."

The men erupted in noise and chaos as everyone talked at once. TJ finally had to gavel the meeting to order. He glared at Clint as the noise, laughter, and hoots gradually died. Clint heard them all. Everyone had something to say across the conference table, "Damndest thing I ever heard of!" "That boy is crazy!" "Can't do it! No way!"

TJ got the meeting back to order as Clint sat back in his seat. "You know we don't have State approval on that method. It's never been proven or tried, except in the lab. TNRCC will never ok it," Nobles said.

"It's cheaper to ask than to move a hole," Clint snapped. "We can ask, or we can just do it! It's better to ask forgiveness than for permission sometimes …" he started to say but the table erupted in protests again. They rose from their seats, shouted "No!", and sat down again. It looked like the wave at a football game. Negative comments of all kinds filled the air as everyone tried to talk at once. "They will pull our permits!" "We'll never drill again!" "The fines will bankrupt us!" "We'll be finished as a company!" "We'll all go to jail!"

Once TJ had restored order again, he pointed his fancy fountain pen at Clint. "No. You keep fracking within the confines of your permit; and if you don't break through in two weeks, you move the hole. All agreed?" he looked around the table.

They all agreed. Clint gathered his portfolio and left the room as TJ moved to adjourn the meeting. It was a long walk back down the dark paneled hall. "You ok?" Darla whispered once. "No." was all Clint could reply.

Back in his inner office, Clint changed back into his jeans and boots. Darla put her head in the doorway. "He wants to see you." Clint grabbed his flight jacket and fedora and headed toward TJ's office, telling Darla goodbye as he went through the door. She was on the phone, but she waved at him as he left. She arched her eyes asking if he wanted her to accompany. Clint shook his head 'no' and she returned to her call. "Crap!" muttered Clint. 'I guess I deserve this butt-chewing' he thought to himself.

Clint entered the inner office of the CEO and found TJ sitting behind his huge desk. The yellow-hued evening sun over Houston cast Clint's shadow on the rough stone walls of TJ's inner office. The shadow made Clint look like Indiana Jones in the "Temple of Doom." "Sit down!" he barked. "What the hell are you thinking, putting that idea out there like that? You should have cleared it through me first!"

Clint could only say, "I was desperate."

"Son, we are all desperate." The old man said in a calmer voice, "Clint, there are some things you just don't know." TJ updated him on inside politics of HNH. TJ's father, Wilson Howlett, would not be getting any better. The Alzheimer's had spread so fast there hadn't been time to plan properly. Finances had not been taken care of, proxies had not been issued, the will had not been updated, and a thousand things had been left undone. The rapid progress of the disease had taken them all by surprise. Financially the company was in good shape. However, if the courts declared the old man incompetent, or if he died, things would change drastically in the management of the company. Right now, the ownership split was 60-40, with the Howletts controlling the 60%. Wilson Howlett and Phillip Nobles had been partners since the 1940's. Right out of A&M. They had gone to the Permian Basin with Bush. They began splitting everything 50-50 from the very start. Partners all the way. However, Phillip got into some trouble back in 1950-something and sold 10% of the company back to Wilson. The bond between the men went back over half a century – to the days when a man's word meant something. Later, over the objections of Nobles, Wilson gave that 10% to TJ when he graduated from A&M. It had caused some bitter feelings between the old friends. Now TJ wanted to buy the rest of Phillip's interest; but he did not have the money. What Nobles did not know – what no one but TJ, his wife, and the attorneys knew – was that when the old man died, the will called for a split of Wilson's fifty percent to be divided two ways. Half of it went to TJ and his mother, which TJ would naturally control; but the other half went to Phillip. If that happened, the numbers would then be 65-35 in favor of Nobles. "See the problem?" TJ gazed out the window at the sinking yellow sun.

Clint did see the problem very clearly. TJ would no longer control the company. TJ picked up a remote control and turned on a radio sound system. He raised the volume, and came around his desk. He sat in the chair next to Clint, inching it closer. He spoke quietly and softly. "Clint, I need this well to come in because I need the revenue to buy out Phillip. It has to happen soon. Dad's not going to last long, I'm afraid. I need you to get me that oil."

"I'll do the best I can…" Clint started.

"Son." TJ shook his head slowly. "The best you can ain't good enough." TJ stressed in obvious overtones, "It needs to happen." TJ looked Clint meaningfully in the eyes. "Do you hear what I am saying?" It was clear that TJ was trying to tell Clint to go ahead without actually saying the words.

"When Dilley hits, won't Nobles get his forty percent of it anyway?" Clint asked.

"No." TJ locked eyes with Clint and paused for a few seconds. "He won't."

Clint shook his head not understanding. It made no sense. TJ spoke quietly, "Clint, HNH doesn't own the Dilley Chalk project – they never have. HNH only has a fixed price maintenance, operation, and administrative agreement. No stock," the older man grinned.

"Who owns it then?"

"Rio Frio Oil Company," TJ said in a matter-of-fact tone.

A smile of awareness spread across Clint's face. "And you own Rio Frio?"

"Lock, stock, and barrel!" TJ laughed aloud. HNH and Nobles won't get a cent more than they already get."

TJ slid his arm around Clint's shoulder. He lowered his voice again, "Son, you do what you have to do," he said in a fatherly tone. "You take care of me, and I'll take care of you – just like always."

"You can count on it," Clint promised.

"I am counting on it, son." TJ pulled a thick white envelope from his desk and handed it to Clint.

"What's this?"

"Twenty-five percent of Rio Frio. It's yours." Clint was speechless.

TJ now spoke with more authority. "OK! From this point on, no communications about this with me whatsoever! No e-mails, no phone calls, no faxes, no twitters, no nothing! You don't even tell your crew that I know anything. You got it?" Clint nodded his head. "If you get caught, you are on your own. I know nothing. Understood?"

"Yes, sir."

"You just went rogue. I'll take that story to my grave! You roll big; you win big. You lose; you're out of the oil business forever. You might even go to prison. You have to trust me to take care of you, and your little girl. You do trust me, don't you Clint?" he asked.

"Yes, sir."

TJ stood, his hands on his aching back, as he stretched stiff joints. "Go get us that oil!" He turned the music off with the remote and sat down behind his huge walnut desk. TJ quietly watched, as Indiana Jones grew smaller on his office wall.

Chapter 3

At exactly 4:15 a.m., Hootie Johnson slipped on his lightweight nylon hoodie and quietly crept out of his trailer. A light mist was falling, but it was not cold. He silently walked through the sleeping man camp, passed by his truck, and strolled to the edge of the highway. He turned east and walked a quarter mile along the shoulder of Texas 85. When he reached the Pump House Bar, he went around the side of the wooden lap-and-gap building. The place had closed for the night with only the Lone Star neon beer signs shining inside. Hector always kept one naked yellow bulb lit above the back door. He went along the side parking lot, dodging puddles, and stood beneath a mesquite tree in the dark. He wrinkled his nose at the smell of urine, and weighed the option of moving up on Hector's porch. Clint had told him to stay out of sight, so he stayed where he was.

After a few minutes, a Frio County Sheriff's black-and-white cruiser turned off the highway into the gravel parking lot. The tires made a crunchy sound as they rolled across the caliche driveway. The deputy shined his spotlight at the front door, then made a U-turn, and pulled back onto the highway. A short way down Texas 85, the cruiser turned left onto FM 1583 and headed north toward the interstate. Hootie had stayed under the tree, unseen. He laughed aloud, "Now ain't that special? Didn't even see me."

It was not long before Clint's truck pulled into the Pump House parking lot. It was a big red 4x4. The big Hemi motor idled while Clint waited with the lights off. Exhaust curled from the tailpipe in the damp night air. Hootie considered staying under the tree until they found him or started cussing, but something about the way this all came down made him walk out and climb into the back passenger seat of the crew cab. He closed the door, and Clint flipped the headlights on and pulled back out onto Highway 85, heading further east.

"You just missed the Sheriff," Hootie said as he looked at the other occupants. Hugh sat in the front passenger seat. Carl Kline, Hootie's counterpart who supervised the night shift, occupied the back seat behind Clint, who drove.

"Did he see you?" Clint asked over his shoulder.

"No. You told me to stay out of sight. He buzzed the parking lot and left."

"Which way?"

"North toward I-35," Hootie answered.

Clint nodded and drove east for a few miles past the gate at their regular site entrance, then turned right onto a gravel road edging the far perimeter. Hootie realized Jim Gunderson was not in the group. He did not ask why. He sensed it was not the time to be asking questions or cutting up.

Clint pulled the truck around on a little hillock overlooking Dilley Chalk #2. The pale yellow lights flickered from the derrick tower, fighting weakly against the murky night. He killed the engine and cut the lights. The men sat quietly in the dark for a few minutes. Hootie could hear the cicadas in the acacia trees with their ceaseless racket. Hugh pushed a door button, slid down his window, and lit a cigarette. The flame from his lighter illuminated the side of his face as he shielded the flame from the wind. He offered the pack around, but no one wanted a smoke. Marlboros. Hugh blew a stream of gray smoke through his open window into the foggy night. He held the lit cigarette outside the car window. Kline spit Copenhagen into a Dixie cup. 'Nasty!' thought Hootie. For a minute no one spoke. They sat and waited.

'This is it,' Hootie thought. 'They are pulling us off this job.' Three or four men would stay on to do the shutdown, but he would have to lay-off the rest of the crew. In his mind, Hootie began to compile a list of who would be leaving and who would stay. It was never easy. It was the worst part of the job.

Clint slipped off his seat belt and twisted around in his seat to face his passengers. It was so dark you could barely make out his features. Hugh stared out the window into the black night, holding his cigarette outside the window. "They gave us two weeks. If we can't break through by then, we're done."

Hootie breathed a small sigh of relief. They would have a small stay of execution, but they would be able to keep a full crew for at least a couple more weeks. It was inevitable the lay-off would come then. Hootie doubted anything would break the hard rock barricade that blocked the oil.

Clint rubbed his forehead as he talked. "You can tell the men that if they feel like they need to sign-on somewhere else, they got time to find something. Don't let everyone leave; retain a shut-down crew." The next thing he said got Hootie's attention. "Starting today, I want you to stop pumping fluids; just maintain the hole. Put your two helpers on pump duty and standby and send everyone else on a 3-day turn-around with pay. I want everyone back here, sober, on Tuesday."

Hootie almost blurted, "Who are you, and what have you done with Clint?" but stopped himself in time. He looked at Kline who had scrunched his right cheek nearly to his earlobe. What? We have two weeks to break through that rock, and we're taking a 3-day weekend? What's up with that? Hootie waited for an answer. It never came. No one asked anything. Are we giving up? It was a foregone conclusion the well was lost, but Hootie had never known Clint to give up two weeks early.

"By Wednesday, I want a dry empty hole." Hugh snapped his head around from the window and stared at Clint in the gloom. Clint locked his eyes on Hugh's in a kind of nocturnal stare-down. Keeping his eyes on Hugh, Clint kept talking, "I want a head with a ten-inch valve, and an eight-inch injection port placed on the well by then." Hugh lost the glare-down, turned back to the window, and disgustedly flipped his cigarette out into the wet grass. Not one single man in the truck had the guts to ask, "What are you putting down that hole, Clint?" Hootie could not imagine, but now he knew why Gunderson was not with them.

The State of Texas requires each drilling operation to have a licensed geologist on site during drilling operations. Jim Gunderson was that person. He worked for HNH but reported directly to the corporate safety officer, Paul Strickland. Jim was watchful and alert. Most roughnecks did not like Jim because it looked like he was a loafer. To the workers it seemed he stood around all day doing nothing. He and Clint had gone head-to-head a few times; but for the most part, Jim kept out of the way. Jim had the reputation of being bull-headed and he had shut down more than one job in his career because of safety issues. He would not back off when he knew he was right. Clint would not back off

– ever! Jim was difficult and confrontational, knowing he could call headquarters anytime he needed Paul to back him up.

Clint kept looking at the back of Hugh's head. "Tell the crew there will be a delivery from an outfit in Laredo on Monday. It will be marked for Rio Frio Oil Company. Keep it out of sight and lock it up in the pump shed – unopened!" Hootie and Kline looked at each other. "And, keep Gunderson away from it. If he sees it being delivered, tell him it's a shipment for Rio Frio, and we're holding it for pick-up for a friend of mine."

"Anyone have any questions?" Clint asked. You could tell by the tone of his voice that he did not want any. No one spoke. "From this point on, you don't see nothing; you don't know nothing. Don't be speculating on anything; don't be talking among yourselves, or asking questions about anything that might happen. Understood?"

He is saying, 'Ask me no questions, and I'll tell you no lies,' thought Hootie. Despite the restriction on speculation, Hootie's mind raced wildly. What in the hell could be in that shipment? If he puts some kind of explosive down that hole, it will blow the casing right out of the well. That would be crazy! Clint was many things but crazy was not one of them. Acid? What kind of acid is going to eat through a gazillion tons of granite?

"Good!" The meeting was over. Clint started the engine, and drove down the hill to the back gate of the oil site. Hugh got out to open the gate and locked it after the truck went through. He waved them on and walked the rest of the way back to the rig alone. Hootie got out of the truck and watched Clint drive out the front gate to take Kline back to his trailer in the man camp. Hootie looked at Hugh coming toward him in the dawn twilight. Neither man spoke; then Hugh shook his head and walked toward the trailer office. It was clear that whatever was going on, Hugh did not agree. Hootie watched him slowly climb the little wooden steps. Hootie went about his morning pump checks.

Rita unwrapped a granola bar, and stuffed a huge chunk in her cheek. She sat down on the rock next to Katie. Like schoolgirls sitting on a bus bench, they swung their legs back and forth and side-to-side in the morning air. What a beautiful day. The blue Texas sky spread above them like a downy blanket. The April sun was warm but not too hot. It was a perfect day to be out in the open.

Katie looked off into the far horizon of the Texas hill country. The view was gorgeous with the hillsides tinted blue and red by the famous bluebonnets and Indian paintbrushes. "So. What are we doing for spring break?" she asked Rita.

"You know." Rita answered, "We're coming back out here to Enchanted Rock for a couple of days. You've got about five or six more climbs to get qualified at level five."

"A lot of the girls are going to South Padre for the break. Big party. Why don't we go?"

"Oooh… too rich for my blood," Rita shook her head. "I can barely afford next semester, let alone running off to South Padre for spring break."

"Forgedaboutit! Daddy's got a plane. Remember? He'll fly us down there. And, once you get there, you can bunk with me. Drinks are free! Lots of boys … lots of beach … lots of everything – evvvverything!" Katie's left eye arched as she stretched out the last 'everything' in the deepest voice she could manage.

Rita laughed. "Thank you, but no. That's sweet. Besides, I couldn't go off without Jesse knowing."

"What? You need a kitchen pass? You are a married woman now and didn't tell me?" Katie teased.

Rita frowned at her. "No! Of course not. But, Jesse wouldn't know where I was; he'd be worried."

"So? Tell him."

"Can't. He's with Jake and Cody down in a cave somewhere. He and his cave buddies are working on a mapping system way back in Honey Creek Cave. He's probably twenty miles back in there with no cell phone signal. He won't be back until next Friday."

"Wow! That sounds like Jesse. Always in over his head!" she laughed. "Why didn't you go with him?"

"Are you crazy? Me in a cave? No way! I wouldn't go down in that hole if you paid me!"

"Afraid of the dark?" Katie teased.

"No." She always denied it although it was a well-known secret among her friends. It was a sensitive subject.

"Then why do you always leave the bathroom light on? All night long."

"I just forgot to turn it off; that's all!" Katie could see from the flushed red cheeks that she was getting a rise out of Rita. She gloated inwardly, but she did not really want to make her friend mad. "I don't leave it on every night. Besides, it may have been you that forgot to turn it off when you stayed over last week."

Katie nodded her head knowingly. "I drove by your place the other night, and it was on again." Not wanting a full-blown argument, Katie quickly switched back to the previous subject. She knew she had pushed far enough. "Why don't you come with me? We'll be back Saturday. Leave Jesse a note or send him an e-mail. He'll get it when he comes out."

"No. Better not. Besides, you agreed to come to Enchanted Rock with me! If we don't get you qualified you won't be able to climb with us this summer. You'll be stuck on the ground." Rita reminded her friend. "Remember? We'll go out there this afternoon, camp out, and make s'mores, and sing around the campfire…"

"Ohhhh! Just like Girl Scouts!" Katie laughed, bouncing up and down.

"Whoa, girl! Careful there," Rita said as she grabbed Katie's arm and stopped her from bouncing. "Well, we can camp out and do s'mores – no singing. Promise."

Katie laughed and held out her hands palms up. "Let's see," Katie jiggled her left hand. "You." She moved her right hand up and down, "South Padre." She moved her hands back and forth in a juggling pantomime.

Rita laughed, "OK. I get it. It's not a hard choice."

"Ok," Katie relented. "I don't want to miss the Colorado trip," Katie said reluctantly, "so we'll got out there in the wilderness and climb rocks. Hey! I'm seeing Dad tonight at Sholtz Beer Garden in Austin. You gotta come with me! We'll go on to Enchanted Rock from there." Katie stood and offered her hand to assist Rita to her feet.

"Sure, why not?"

"Jesse really went twenty miles back in a cave?" Katie asked.

"It's a big cave. Jesse thinks it may run all the way to Mexico." Rita stuck the last of the granola bar between her teeth and grasped Katie's hand.

"Boys and their crazy toys! What makes them want to risk their necks doing the stupidest things?" With a grunt, Katie pulled Rita to her feet.

The effort caused Rita to bite down on the granola bar, causing a large chunk to tumble across her chest. The girls stood on a narrow ledge barely eight inches wide. "Three-hour rule?" Katie quipped as they watched it fall. The chunk of granola fell between Rita's shoes and into a deep canyon two hundred feet below.

"Well, we better finish up," Rita laughed, "if we're meeting your Dad at six. We still have a ways to climb to reach the top."

The girls resumed their ascent of the sheer rock canyon face. From a distance, they looked like tiny specks on a great towering rock wall.

Under the tall limbs of a bald cypress tree, Jake Hew finished inventorying the contents of his drag bag. He crossed everything off against a laminated checklist. The forty-pound waterproof bag would have to contain everything he would need for the next six days. He had learned the hard way, if you leave something behind you do without until you get back to civilization. Nearby, Cody Hughes and Jesse Perrine were doing the same. Not only would each man carry his own personal gear, but each also shouldered the weight of an equal share of common goods the entire team would need for the survey. If you forgot one of those items, you would never hear the end of it. A mile down and ten miles back inside a cave, your team members can become really testy and really blunt, really fast.

Another reason for checking your bag was to make sure no one of the party had rocked you. Secretly slipping a heavy rock into your bag so you had to drag it to the end of the tunnel was a favorite trick cavers loved to play on the rookies. The main body of the team, fifteen spelunkers or so, had entered the cave the day before. Now Jesse and his friends were hurrying to catch them at the base camp rendezvous before the main party left to begin the twenty-mile death-march back to the newly found TC passage in the most remote part of the cave. The main party would not wait long. If they could not join the main team before they left base camp, Jesse and his friends would have to abort their adventure and come back out.

Honey Creek Cave is the longest known cave in Texas. It stretches under the southern rim of the Hill Country and extends some twenty miles, possibly further. The cave was undeveloped and still being explored and surveyed. The thousands of openings in the cave walls, called leads, connect to other passages, thought to go even farther back. Some believe this vast underground system connects with the huge cave systems in New Mexico and as far as old Mexico. The expedition intended to chart an unexplored passageway a quarter-mile above the end of the known cave.

You do not simply walk in to Honey Creek Cave. The entrance is a few feet beneath the surface of the Guadalupe River. You have to swim; or more accurately, dive. You can do it without scuba gear, but no one recommends doing that. Most cavers use small mini-scuba tanks and swim goggles. The best swimmers just wing it and submarine through. It is not a long swim, only twenty yards or so, before the cave opens and the ceiling rises. Once in, there is plenty of air. Sometimes, it is not possible to enter the cave at all because the current coming out of the spring into the river is far too strong. Because of the hardship of entering, another caving group is planning to drill a well to use as an entrance on the riverbank and then insert cavers into the main passage using a large boom and a wench. The site is on private land, which makes access and improvements even more difficult. Had the entrance been a quarter-mile west it would have been on Guadalupe State Park property. You could forget a well entrance on state property. Luckily, the owner is supportive of organized cavers who behave themselves. In payment, they help him with repairs around the ranch and especially during hay-baling season. It is a win-win for them all.

Jesse was to enter first. He slipped into the water. It was a cold, late spring, but not so bad that they would need wet suits. Jesse spat into his mask and rubbed it around the lenses to prevent fogging. He washed the mouthpiece off in the river to get it wet, turned on his air, and then wrapped his lips around the rubber. With a nod, he flipped on his light, sank into the water, and searched for the opening to the cave. They were right on top of it. He swam twenty yards through the opening and surfaced.

It was awesome inside the dank, dark cavern. The sound of rushing water filled the void. His light flickered across wet cavern walls. He could see the ceiling about fifteen feet above. He swam over to the side of the dark room where he knew a partially submerged ledge would allow him to stand with water only up to his chest. He was waiting when Cody popped to the surface. He helped Cody pull his bag onto a dry shelf at the base of the cave wall. Then, they got the idea it would be funny if they switched off their lights before Jake surfaced. They waited for a few minutes in the dark. No Jake.

Jake Hew had been a caver longer than both Jesse and Cody combined. Jake knew his way around, and was very familiar with Honey Creek. Jake loved playing jokes on new cavers. Underwater, without lights, Jake swam an additional twenty yards until he knew he was well beyond Jesse and Cody. He had cut off his air supply so the bubbles would not give him away, and surfaced as silently as he could. Sure enough, Jesse and Cody were giggling in the dark like girls at a slumber party as they waited for him to come up. It was pitch black; but from the sounds they were making, he knew exactly where they were. They did not know where he was. He quietly inched open the nylon zipper on his bag and pulled out his rubber water moccasin. This was going to be so great!

Soon, he heard Cody ask Jesse if maybe something had happened. Should they go back to look for Jake? Jesse shushed him quiet. After a little while, Jesse turned on his light and flashed it toward the submerged entrance. Perfect. Now they would be able to see it. Jake could clearly see them in the arc of light. Jesse focused his attention on the entrance. He did not swing his light around to reveal Jake standing only a few yards away. "He should be up by now," Jesse's voice echoed off the sodden cave walls in the dim light.

At that precise moment, Jake tossed the wet, slimy, fake snake into the pool of light in front of the two cavers. As expected, Cody let out a scream which the rest of the team probably heard in base camp a couple of miles away." It was so satisfying.

"At least they know we're coming now," laughed Jake.

Chapter 4

Clint took a taxi from the Laredo airport to a building on Zaragoza Street off South Santa Ursula. It was a squat building only a few blocks from the Mexican border stained with black mold. Plaster was peeling off the outside walls and there was no sign to identify the business. There was no visible indication that the building was occupied. No street number identified the address at all; nevertheless, Clint knew he was at the right place. He had been here many times before. The place was a satellite office of LarTex Supply. Specialty supplies. "Here," Clint told the cab driver, indicating he should park at the curb next to a short iron fence. Clint took a small plastic black and silver bag from the seat and told the driver to wait. "You got 30 minutes!" the driver muttered. Clint knew the driver would be gone in ten. He walked across a narrow, dirty street lined with boarded-up buildings. Clint knocked on a door located between two windows enclosed with burglar bars and strung with a nest of white cobwebs. Half a block away, a Miller 64 beer truck blocked the street. Two men were stacking beer cases on a two-wheeled dolly.

After a moment, the heavy wooden door swung open from the inside. Clint stepped into a darkened room. Beams of sunlight slanted through the boarded up windows and Clint could see minute pieces of lint and dust floating in the small beams of light leaking through the nail holes. Some kind of ranchero music was faintly playing behind a green wooden door leading to another room. The green paint curled and peeling. A few dusty, plastic chairs sat under the plywood-covered windows and a long counter ran across the center of the room. No one had swept the room since the last century. Whoever opened the door was nowhere in sight. Clint wiped off one dusty chair and sat. He knew someone watched his every move, and probably taped recorded it too.

After a while, the green door swung open and a man with a heavy black mustache came out of the back room. Mondo Morales was a Tejano who used the street name Chango. Clint recognized him even in the dim light. Chango and Clint had done business many times before. Whenever Clint needed something on the "down-low," he went to Chango. Chango could be trusted – if the money was right. "Clint Marshall! ¿Como estas? How you been, cabrón?"

Clint stood and accepted the extended hand from across the counter. He knew better than to go around, knowing that Chango probably kept a sawed-off under the counter. Chango slipped past his hand and grasped Clint's forearm and pulled him even closer in a near embrace, as Clint replied, "Bien, gracias."

Chango turned him loose and asked, "Want a beer?" Without waiting for an answer, he yelled over his shoulder, "Dos cervezas, Paco! Por favor!" Clint placed the plastic bag on the counter.

Chango was all smiles. "¿Que es esto?" He stepped back a step or two, admiring the bag.

"Spurs championship hat from last year. You know, it's just a cheap knock-off. You may not want to wear it," Clint laughed.

Chango grabbed the bag and ripped it open like a kid on Christmas morning. He pulled out the hat. He checked the NBA logo, and saw that it was not a knock-off at all. "Nonsense! I love it!" He put the hat on his head, making sure the official label was showing. "Man! The white one too, with the NBA trophy! Gracias amigo!"

"Look inside," Clint prompted.

Chango pulled the hat off and looked inside the brim. "¡No mames!" His eyes showed his astonishment. "Paco! Ven!" He shouted. He showed the autographed hat to Paco who entered and placed two sweaty bottles of Dos Equis on the counter. "Manu Ginóbili, man!" He slapped Paco's hand away when he reached out to touch the hat. Chango jerked the hat back. "Stop pendejo! Get your sweaty hands away! Don't touch." He carefully placed the hat back in the bag and turned back to Clint.

"Muchas gracias, amigo! Me alegra mucho! Gracias."

"De nada," Clint shrugged.

Chango looked at Clint sideways, and a huge toothy grin took over his face. "I know you, Clint. You want something. You don't come down here just to give me Ginóbili's hat."

"Quiero algo." Clint admitted.

"¿Que desea?"

Clint pulled a folded piece of paper out of his jacket pocket and watched Chango's eyes grow larger than when he saw the hat. He whistled and then cursed in Tex-Mex. "What you gonna do, Mijo, invade Honduras? Damn!"

"You can get it?"

"Si! But … man! Willie Pete?" Chango cocked his head and looked at Clint sideways. "What you gonna do with Willie Pete?"

"I've got a dump pit I need to burn out."

"Dump pit? A kilo? And thermite, too? ¡Que pasa?" Chango gave Clint a knowing look as he stretched the 'pasa' as far as it would go. Then suddenly, the smile disappeared from his face. "And don't give me no dump pit bullshit!"

"Seriously! Ship it to me at this address. Be sure to mark it for Rio Frio Oil Company just like the note says."

Chango shook his head no a few times and then flashed a big toothy 'I-got-you-now' grin "Rio Frio been out of business four years, dude."

"I know. I bought it. I'm going to wildcat a well for myself and I need that pit gone. I need the stuff by Monday – on the DL, man."

"Man!" Chango stretched it out long. "Why don't you just ask for coke, or somebody's head in a bag? Now I gotta file paperwork, placard a truck, and make a manifest! All that shit draws attention. You know that. No way around it. They watch the roads close now because of the coyotes. They stop me without a permit; we both go to jail. It's gonna cost you, man."

Clint laid a Jourdanton State Bank envelope on the counter. Chango took the envelope and peeked inside at a stack of bills. He closed the flap and stuffed the envelope into the bag.

Clint turned back toward the door. "No later than Monday" he called on his way to the door. "Address is in the note. Don't be late."

Chango scratched his head as he studied the note, "Ok, culero! Orale!"

Scholz Beer Garten in downtown Austin has been open since 1866. It is the oldest establishment in Texas. Picturesque and rustic, the historic bar attracts an eclectic crowd from practically everywhere. It is a cultural crossroads. University students hang out with politicians from the nearby capitol building. Cowboys, bikers, old hippies, and millennials from 6th Street hang out there for beer and barbeque. You never know what you will see there. One day it may be the Governor, the next day it might be a transvestite drummer from a rock band. The day of Longhorn games, you cannot get near the place. It is a typical primitive Texas tavern with cement floors and rough wooden picnic tables stained with beer and bar-b-que sauce. The rambling restaurant winds around the street corner and out onto a beer garden on the back patio. If Texas had a physical home, Scholz's would be the place.

Katie and Rita sat at an open table on the patio, and decided to split a schnitzel. It was far too much food for one person. Katie kept her eye on the door, watching for her dad. The girls each sipped a Lone Star long neck. "This is the perfect hangout," Katie yelled over the crowd nose. "Everyone thinks we're from UT. They will never guess we were from San Antonio if we don't tell them. You can even use your real name! They'll be looking all over UT campus for us!" she laughed.

Rita laughed and pointed at the big UTSA roadrunner logo on Katie's t-shirt. "Damn! I forgot! Guess we'll have to use our fake names after all."

Rita pointed at Katie, "I'm going to be Linda this time! You always get to be Linda! It's my turn." Katie shrugged and Rita took a sip of beer. Suddenly, a tall, dark-haired boy came out of the crowd and called to Katie. "Hey! Linda!" Rita spat beer across the slats in the wooden tabletop.

He pointed at Katie's t-shirt. "Hey! I thought you was at UT! That's why I couldn't find you anywhere!" he grinned. Suddenly, everything was funny to Rita. She could not stop laughing.

"Uh, … transferred." Katie thought quickly. Rita wiped beer from her chin and tried to stop laughing behind her hand.

"Bummer! I know the feeling. I think, after this semester, I'm transferring to Houston myself! Mind if I sit down?" He was already squeezing into the seat.

"Actually," Katie pretended to be sad, "it's a bad time. We are waiting on my dad who should be here in just a few. Why don't we catch you later down on 6th Street?"

"K. We'll be at the RoofTop pretty much all night. The band, Titty Bingo is playing! There will be a group of us up there. Come join us."

"That's a plan! See you there," Katie said. He eyed Rita up and down. "Hello, I'm Bob."

Before Rita could introduce herself, Katie interrupted, "This is my friend, Linda." Rita spat beer again narrowly missing Bob's outstretched hand. He quickly pulled it back, wiping it on his jeans. "Don't mind her, she's drunk. She has trouble holding her beer,"

Bob nodded and laughed with them, looking from one to the other. "No shit," he paused. "No shit? Two Lindas?" He bent and gave Katie Linda an awkward hug before disappearing into the crowd. "See you Lindas on the RoofTop! Laters!" He called back over his shoulder.

Katie watched him leave then looked at Rita. "Really? I can't take you anywhere."

"He was cute," Rita teased, tongue in cheek. "So is that guy over there." She pointed. "He's not bad for an old man. Look at that butt in those Wranglers!"

Katie turned to follow the pointing finger. "Rita! That's my dad!" She called out, "Dad! Over here!"

Katie stood as her father folded her in his arms. He pushed Katie to arms-length and looked at her lovingly. "Just look at you. I've missed you sweetheart."

Katie turned him around, "Dad, I want you to meet my best friend, Rita Martin." Rita looked up into the bluest eyes she had ever seen.

"Hello, Rita, I'm Clint Marshall."

After being in hip-deep cave water for most of a mile, they climbed out onto the stone ledge. The cave ceiling finally rose higher and a dry passage led off into the distance. Glad to be out of the water, they took off their wet river shoes and slapped them against the rock. The flat shelf lay before a large shaft opening leading onward, while cold, clear water gushed out from underneath the shelf. "Mostly dry from here on out," Jake reported as they dug towels out of their bags and dried off.

After a short break, they moved further into the darkened tunnel. Their LED lights barely lit the long rocky corridor. The footing was smooth but the corridor wound downwards on a slant, taking them deeper and deeper into the cave. The air was dank and stale and smelled of mildew. After a couple of miles, the floor became rough and broken with shards of limestone and shattered cave formations. They sat by a small pool for another rest. The dark pool was flush against a high wall on their right, with jagged rocks jutting out over the edge of the water. They passed around some chocolate and switched off all their lights but one to save battery power.

Cody remarked on how dark it was, so Jake switched on his light and laid it on the cave floor next to him. The beam skipped across the surface of the little pool that now looked slightly greenish in the gloom. Jake began telling Cody how caving used to be before LEDs, back when cavers used Carbide. Many still do, because the Carbide gives off a little heat in the constant sixty-eight degree cave. Cody sat listening, staring at the little pool, mainly because there was nothing else to look at.

"Why does it rise and fall like that?" he wanted to know.

"What rises and falls?"

"The water in that pool."

Jesse and Jake switched on their lights and looked at the water, then at each other. Something was causing the water to rise and fall. "A lead!" they said simultaneously. Nothing was feeding the pool, so there had to be an underwater lead to another cavern. They peered deep into the murky green pool looking for an opening. Jake took off his shoes and dry socks and slipped into the cold water, feeling around the sides. He looked at Jesse, "I think I found it with my foot. It's about three feet down."

Jake sank beneath the surface. After a few seconds, he came up spitting water. "It's down there. It's big enough to get into, but I don't know how far in it goes. It could narrow out or end at the wall. There's no way of telling, but I've got a plan." He pulled himself half out of the water and pulled his bag to the edge. He drug out his iPad and a miniature battery-operated submarine. Mounted on the little submarine was a GoPro camera. "I knew this would come in handy."

Jesse booted the iPad and turned on the mobile Wi-Fi while Jake got back into the water with the boat. Jake adjusted the camera and switched on the on-board light. Soon they were getting a picture on the tablet screen. Jake stood in waist-deep water and took back the tablet. He controlled the sub with the iPad, swimming the little boat around the pool for a few seconds. Then he hit the record icon and put the sub into a dive. Jesse and Cody watched as the scene unfolded on the tiny screen.

The hole was exactly where Jake located it. They watched as the little boat maneuvered through the channel. It was only a little more than fifteen feet back into the tunnel when Jake surfaced the little craft. The camera showed the ceiling was high up the wall. "We got air on the other side," he grinned. "Lots of it!"

Jake remotely ran the little sub in circles around the open space on the other side when suddenly the iPad screen flickered and went black. Jake turned white. "My boat!"

He tossed the iPad to Cody. "I'm going after it."

"Not by yourself. Hold up!" Jesse shouted before Jake could dive.

Jesse hooked a safety rope around his waist and tossed the end to Cody. He did the same for Jake. "Three tugs means pull us back through that hole! Otherwise, just keep the slack out of the line. We'll be back." He jumped into the water with Jake.

They dove beneath the surface and went through the lead single file. On the other side, they surfaced and looked around the new cavern. Their lights did little to illuminate the huge space. "This place is huge!" They shined light across the surface of the water but they did not see a floating boat.

"Where's my sub?" There was no sign of the little submarine. Jake dove beneath the surface but soon came back up. "I can't find it. It's too dark down there!"

"Well, let's go back. We'll chart this lead and make a report," Jesse offered.

As the boys neared the entrance, Jesse was about to swim through the hole when Jake grabbed his arm. "Wait!" Jake yelled. "I feel something! Jesse! Something's got me!" he gulped and went under!

Jesse peered into the dark water where Jake had disappeared. There was no way to see more than a few inches below the surface. He was ready to make a rescue dive when Jake bobbed back up again. "Damn you! Stop screwing around! You scared the hell out of me!"

"Something is wrapped around my leg. Something heavy. It was dragging me down!"

"What? Are you messing with me?"

"No! I don't know what it is, but it's heavy! It feels like a tarp or something." Jake was flailing around trying to untangle his legs. "Help me get it up!" Finally, they pulled up the corner of something that looked like a piece of tarpaulin, except it did not have grommets. "What the hell is this?" he asked.

Jesse looked at it. "Beats me! Maybe we weren't the first ones in here. Someone got in here through a different lead. Maybe they left a tarp or a tent. We'll haul it out for trash." As Jake ranted about cavers who left junk in caves, Jesse untied his line and secured it around a corner of the cloth. "Who would bring a tent into a cave anyway?" Jesse asked, not expecting an answer.

Jake carped about losing his sub and the camera. "That gear cost me a couple of hundred bucks!" Jesse gave the line three tugs, and Cody, on the other side of the wall, reeled the tarp through the narrow hole. The canvas appeared to be about five feet long. Jesse swam through after it. When he surfaced on the other side, Jesse helped Cody pull the thing out of the water onto the bank. Then Cody went back to his position and reeled in the slack from Jake's line as he swam toward them through the narrow passage. Cody looped the rope around his shoulder and elbow as he pulled.

Jesse examined the strange tarp. Suddenly, Cody shouted, "Jesse. He stopped!" Jesse could see no that no more slack was coming on the line. Jesse believed Jake was hung up somewhere in the tunnel. He told Cody, "Pull him out hard! Quick!"

Cody took another grip on the line and pulled as hard as he could. All of a sudden, he was jerked face-first into the sharp rocky wall. He dropped the coils of rope and immediately fell into the water. The coils of rope streaked out in a whipping sound like the line from a fishing reel. Jesse jumped in and grabbed Cody before he sank and pulled him to the side. His face was a bloody mess, and he was out cold. Jesse was struggling to get Cody out of the water when Jake popped up.

"Man! You ain't gonna believe this!" Jake shouted.

"Shut up, and help me get him out of the water!"

Blood dripped from deep cuts on Cody's ruined face, and hung from his nose in thick, stringy clots. Blood was even coming from his ears. Jake helped Jesse get Cody out of the water onto the bank. "What happened?"

"What happened?" Jesse yelled. "Hell, he got jerked into the rocks face-first is what happened! You and your stupid jokes!"

The boys worked quickly to stop the bleeding. Some of Cody's front teeth were cracked. His nose was obviously broken. A huge gash ran across his cheek. The worse part was a visible indention nearly the size of a golf ball on Cody's forehead. "I think his skull may be cracked. We have to get him out of here. He needs a doctor!" Jesse grimly stated.

They cleaned and bandaged Cody as best they could; using what was in their first aid kit. The cold pack help staunch the bleeding nose. Cody kept fading

in and out of consciousness. His vital signs stabilized
but were weak. They discussed how to carry Cody out of
the cave. Jake drug the tarp over and spread it out.
"Let's use this." They placed Cody on the canvas; and
with a tight grip on each end, they began to move Cody
toward the entrance of Honey Creek Cave.

Chapter 5

It was full dark by the time Rita and Kate got to their campsite at Enchanted Rock Park. They pitched a tent and inflated their air mattresses. Even though it was warm for early April, they lit a small fire and sat talking in the flickering light while staring into the glowing embers. After an hour talk dwindled off, and they settled in for the night; each to her own thoughts. Fireflies were already blinking their green and yellow lights among the trees, foretelling an early summer. Toward the east, lightning flickered low across the horizon, randomly lighting the dark, granite dome towering above them. At least if it rained, Rita thought, they would still be able to climb the granite rock. If they were in Palo Duro, they would have to postpone because of the sandstone and clay formations. Granite on the other hand, dried out quickly and did not flake off or become sticky. The cupped moon briefly broke through the heavy clouds and tilted downward. Pouring water, Rita thought. Rain tonight. The soft glow of the moon bathed the granite dome in a fleshy pink color. It looked like the head of an old, bald man in the creamy moonlight.

"You never told me your dad was a hottie!" Rita teased as she crawled into her sleeping bag.

"Shut up! Yuck! That's so gross!" Katie groaned.

"Well, he is! And those eyes!"

"Shut up! Damn! Hey! Where's those s'mores you promised?" Katie questioned.

"We'll do it tomorrow. It's late. Besides, it's going to rain." Rita yawned and turned over as lightning flickered and the sound of distant thunder rolled in the Texas night.

Rita's thoughts turned to Jesse. What is he doing right now? Down in a cave like that, it must be very dark. All concept of day or night would disappear. There is only the dark. All awareness of time and distance withers away. No dimensions exist in the deep dark. Light disambiguates while darkness confounds and confuses the mind. Light has straight edges like a razor-sharp knife, when turned sideways it gives a brief flash and then shrinks to a thin sharp edge before disappearing from sight. The gloom robs spatial discernment. It is difficult to measure that which cannot be seen; so distance and size become disconnected from conscious awareness. Space in a cube needs three points of reference – three dimensions. A sphere only needs two. Dark reduces the awareness of space to a single dimension – like the thin, gleaming line of the edge of a knife blade.

Darkness covers like a blanket. Without coordinates of space and time, position becomes immeasurable. In outer space, 'up' and 'down' do not exist. In the black deep dark, sight evaporates. Time, if not a dimension, also ceases to be. In the dark, all you are … is all you are. You float in a one-dimensional plane, on a razor's edge, with no awareness of time or space. Vulnerability skulks into your subconscious like a furtive thing, a relic of when man was prey for creatures roaming the night. Nervousness creeps into sweaty hands; palpitations begin to disrupt heart rhythms; and nausea rises in the upper chest, caught up in a survival response ingrained in our psyches since the beginning of time. Like a boa constrictor, it covers you and presses in on your body like a heavy weight. It mounts you; and you are powerless to resist.

Imagination overcomes reason. Things, which you know are present, become figments of your mind; and, things that do not exist become too real. Darkness grips you in a stranglehold, squeezes the life from your lungs, and uses fantasy to evoke threats from forgotten memories and dreams into a reality of here and now. The air thickens and becomes velvet. Dark matter exists. It does! And like the three stages of water, the deep dark evolves from a gas-like fog forming all around you. In the blink of an eye, it morphs into a liquid that flows like ink. Finally, it turns into an ice-cold solid, which clots your blood and freezes movement. The black eats everything in its path. Everything in the black dissolves as if it were never there. It is as if the universe has yet to begin; or never was.

Sounds, however faint, become magnified and intensified. Faint sounds give a hint of direction. Noises can recede or fall away, or they can come closer, and closer – and closer. You realize something is in the dark with you. With a dragging, sucking sound it moves nearer. From a distance comes sobbing, a frail animal cry. It is terrifying, but it gives you some relief, because it is, at least, a direction – until you realize it is your own weeping. A stench fills your nostrils, and turns your stomach. Wet, fetid breath flushes your face as its putrid mouth opens wide with flashing jagged teeth!

"Rita! Wake up! You're moaning in your sleep!"

Rita opened her eyes to see the darkened form of her friend against the nylon tent ceiling, as lightning flashed behind her silhouetted form. Katie softly wiped the tears from Rita's cheeks. "It was only a dream, honey."

Katie looked at her friend with eyes opened wide. "Jesse's in trouble," Rita gasped.

It was slow going, getting Cody to the cave entrance. When they got to the rock shelf, Jake took out four large garbage bags and filled them with air. He tied them around the rough tarp they had used to drag and carry Cody thus far. They packed their dry socks and shoes into their waterproof bags and slipped on their river shoes, then gently pulled Cody's tarp into the water with them. The buoyant air-filled bags helped keep Cody afloat. Soon, they arrived at the deep pool leading out of the cavern.

"What do we do now?" Jesse asked. "He can't take a mouthpiece from a regulator; his mouth is wrecked! If we take him underwater, he'll drown."

Jake tied a lead rope to their three gear bags while figuring out what to do. "We'll use one of these trash bags. You go out first and pull the gear through. Once you are in the river, give me three tugs on the rope. I'll deflate all the bags except for one to use as a breathing bag for Cody. Then I'll tug twice, and you pull us out. Don't waste any time pulling us through either."

Jesse nodded, strapped on his air tank, and popped in the mouthpiece. He took the rope tied to gear bags and a rope tied to Cody's float, and he went under. The ropes fed out between his fingers as he swam through the tunnel. Finally, he bobbed up in the river current outside. It was night, and the stream flowed faster than when they had entered the cave. There must have been a rainstorm while they were underground. Taking off his mask and tank, Jesse threw them onto the riverbank. After he pulled the gear bags through, and threw them on the bank, he gave three stout tugs on Jake's rope.

When Jake felt Jesse tug the rope, he untied one bag from the corner of the tarp. Cody was still unconscious; his breath was shallow and labored. It was good. Maybe that way Cody would not be fighting the bag. However, the thin, raspy breaths worried him. Jake took masking tape and placed the air-filled bag over Cody's head. Jake wrapped the masking tape around Cody's neck as tight as he could without cutting off his breath. "I'm sorry, buddy." He quickly deflated the flotation bags, and tugged the rope twice.

Cody and Jake sank beneath the water, the plastic bag billowing. Jake could feel them being pulled through the tunnel and out of the cave. Pull fast, Jesse! Don't stop! Jake came to the surface within three feet of Jesse. They reached deep and pulled Cody up out of the water. Jake ripped off the impromptu breathing bag and sighed in relief to see Cody still breathing.

Jesse and Jake gripped the corners of the tarp and waded up the muddy riverbank past cypress knees and thick tree trunks. They had parked the Jeep a hundred yards up a small rocky path. They hauled Cody through the dark until they reached Jesse's old Jeep. Jake opened the driver's door, took the keys out from under the mat, and unlocked the back hatch door. Together, they hoisted Cody and the tarp into the back compartment. Jake checked Cody's vital signs again while Jesse retrieved the equipment they had left on the bank. Not bothering to coil the ropes or stow the gear, Jesse threw everything into the back seat as Jake got behind the wheel. Jesse jumped into the back seat to be able to check on Cody as they drove. The Jeep jerked and bounced toward the main road.

The boys drove through the early morning toward the hospital in San Marcos, forty miles away. San Antonio was just as far, so it did not make much difference which way they went. Besides, the local hospital would probably already have Cody's medical records. It was 4:30 in the morning, when they pulled into the emergency entrance of Central Texas Medical Center. Jake kept the Jeep running while Jesse ran inside and quickly returned with a nurse pushing a gurney. Jake came around and helped lift Cody off the tarp onto the blue-sheeted gurney. Jesse went with the nurse to provide information while Jake turned off the ignition, and slumped into the driver's seat, exhausted. When Jake opened his eyes again, pre-dawn had begun, and Jesse was still inside. The inside of the jeep reeked.

Jake went around back, raised the hatch, and pulled the huge canvas out of the car. It was definitely where the stench came from. The thing was folded over and bunched at the corners where they had roped it off for handholds. He dragged the tarp out of the Jeep onto the paved parking lot. In the light, it now appeared to be a huge hide as big as a sail. It looked like an animal skin. It looked like alligator. He traced the bumps and valley with his finger.

"What the heck is that?" Jesse asked from behind, causing Jake to jump in fright.

"That? That is what we used to pull Cody out of the. This thing is huge!" The boys got on their knees and crawled across the surface to get a better look. It was undoubtedly a skin of some sort; maybe a huge lizard or a crocodile hide.

Jesse and Jake looked at each other in amazement. "How did it get in the cave?"

"How is Cody?" Jake asked.

"He's real bad. They are going to call his parents. Jake, he's had a bad concussion. He's not conscious. He may not make it. They can't seem to wake him up. He's got all kinds of tubes and stuff coming out of him." The boys stood solemnly as they absorbed the gravity of Cody's medical condition.

Jesse looked down at the hide. "This is definitely alligator! See these bumps and ridges? Or a crocodile."

"Can you imagine how big this thing must be? There are no crocodiles this big that I ever heard about," said Jake, "and they don't live in caves. What do you want to do with it? We can haul it to the dumpster over there. The damn thing stinks!"

"Let's find out what it is, for sure." Jesse offered.

"How?"

"We'll call Professor Morrison."

Tom jolted awake and snatched his buzzing cell phone off the nightstand before it could wake the dark-haired curvy form sleeping next to him.

"Who is this, and what do you want?"

"Professor Morrison, this is Jesse Perrine."

"It's Spring Break, man!" Tom wailed into the phone and started to hang up.

"Sir! Wait… don't hang up."

Tom put the phone back to his ear. "What is it?"

"We found something in Honey Creek Cave. You need to see this."

"What is it?" Tom repeated, irritated.

"We don't know. It looks like a skin of some kind; but it's huge. How big is the biggest alligator ever recorded?"

"Some 15 feet long and half a ton."

"We've got a piece of skin about half that long, and it's only a fragment, not the whole alligator."

Tom sat upright in bed and looked at his watch. "Where are you?" It was time for his morning bike ride anyway, so he might as well get up.

Tom arrived at the hospital parking lot within five minutes. Dressed in shorts and sandals, he peddled a mountain bike. The three got on hands and knees and crawled slowly across the hide. "You guys weren't kidding. Where did you get this?"

"We drug it out of a cave." They told Morrison the whole story.

"Guys, I don't know what this is. If it is crocodilian, it beats any record I know. Crocs and alligators are ectothermic, meaning they have to lie in the sun to warm themselves. A cave is usually too cool for them. There are some cave crocs in Madagascar, but none in the US as far as I know."

"What do they eat?"

Tom spoke as he examined the hide. "Anything and everything. The ones in Madagascar even eat bats and all the little creatures that feed on bat guano. Large

creatures can sometimes subsist on tiny food sources."
He got to his feet. "Let's get this over to my place."

They loaded the hide back into the Jeep and hauled it up Tom's driveway, a quarter-mile away. Tom placed two sawhorses several feet apart and laid a couple of planks across them. Then he spread the hide on the makeshift table. It hung over the sides and draped onto the cement floor. Tom wiped his hands on his shorts and looked closer, "That was one big crocodile!"

Paco would not make the old pickup go faster than fifty. He drove a classic step-side GMC, painted lime green with bright yellow wheels with an apple red interior. The bed had a polished oak floor. The truck was worth more than Paco made in a year. He had inherited it from his father, and he took care to keep it up, at great expense. It was the only thing of value he owned.

He did not usually drive this truck on deliveries. But afterwards he was going to see his brother in Port Lavaca. He planned to drop the box off at Dilley, and then go west to Kennedy, before heading south to his brother's house. It was not far out of the way, and Chango paid good money for the delivery. It was enough to pay for the whole trip.

He had to keep stopping to retrieve the orange sign, which blew off the back of the truck every few miles. The sign read, "Class 4 Explosives." The law required the sign. Paco had fixed the plastic sign to a narrow wooden slat, which he stuck into a stake hole on the pickup bed. Chango had wanted to tape it to the back window, but Paco would not let him. The little slat would be good enough.

He pulled into the I-35 checkpoint at Encinal, halfway to Cotulla, and waited in line. He was glad he had started early, because the truck had no air conditioning, and it was already hot. He waited behind several cars and a tour bus lined up in front of him. When it was finally his turn, the agent looked under his truck, and looked at the small wooden box in the bed. The officer saw the placard but did not say anything. They were looking for illegals and drugs. Paco had neither.

The agent came to the driver's window and held out his hand. Paco surrendered his driver's license and registration. Paco could almost read the documents in the officer's sunglasses, as another agent circled the truck with a drug dog. "Where are you going?"

"Dilley. Making a delivery; then to Port Lavaca to see my brother," Paco told him. "…who lives there," he added on the end.

"Do you have any weapons?"

"No."

"What about that sign that says volatile chemicals? Are you carrying chemicals?"

"Si!"

"Why?"

"I told you. Making a delivery for my boss to an oil field in Dilley." Paco handed him the DOT manifest and the delivery order, along with his hazardous cargo permit. The load was properly fastened and tied-down, and the truck displayed the required placard. The agent asked him to get out of his truck anyway. "What's in the box?"

"I don't know. A shipment! I never look. I just carry the box to where it goes, man."

"I want to see the packing slip so I can compare it to the manifest," the officer said.

Paco shrugged and climbed up onto the running board. With his pocketknife, he slit the small plastic envelope on the side the crate, and pulled out the folded paper. He handed the pink slip across the truck bed to the officer standing on the running board on the other side of the truck. Paco did not like people standing on the running board, but he said nothing. The officer read the packing list and handed it back to Paco, who slipped it into his left shirt pocket.

The agent tapped the box with his nightstick. "Ay-yi-yi!" Paco yelled. The agent jumped back so quickly, his foot slipped off the running board. His feet hit the ground as the edge of the baton caught the top of the pickup sideboard and conked him on the head. The impact knocked his sunglasses sideways, and his hat fell on the ground. Paco laughed to himself as the officers huddled nearby discussing what they should do next. Finding no reason to hold Paco, they waved him through the checkpoint. When Paco got to the outskirts of Cotulla, a highway patrol cruiser fell in behind, and followed him all the way into Dilley. Paco turned east on Texas 85 and was relieved to see the black and white keep going north.

Paco passed up the place a couple of times before he found the locked gate marked with a small sign reading HNH Oil Company, Dilley Chalk # 2. This is where he was supposed to drop off the box. There was a pickup parked near the office trailer. He honked his horn for someone to let him in.

Hootie looked out from the office window and saw the green truck. "What the hell?" He went out to the road to open the gate. The truck drove through before he could stop it, and drove up and parked near the office trailer. Hootie walked up behind, admiring the truck, as the driver got out of his seat.

"Hey! Man! Sorry, we're not hiring today."

"I got a delivery for Rio Frio," Paco said, handing him the freight bill. "Sign here."

"You're supposed to be here Monday. This is Sunday! You are just lucky I'm here this morning." Hootie looked at the papers. Everything checked out. He helped Paco unload the box and they carefully placed it on the office porch. He signed the receipt and Paco got back into his truck. "You always make deliveries in a cherry, '55 GMC?" Hootie asked.

Paco shrugged, "It was on my way, man."

Hootie shook his head and admired the truck. "Man! It would be a shame to blow this fine pickup all to hell and back!"

"Truck? What about me, man?" Paco laughed.

Hootie could not help but like the man. "What's your name? Come on, I'll buy you a beer at the Pump House."

"Gracias, but no," Paco shook his head. "I saw that place coming in. It's back toward Dilley. I gotta go east to Kennedy. Maybe another time, but gracias."

After locking the box in the pump house, Hootie followed Paco out to the road, and locked the gate behind him as the pickup turned east. Hootie turned west and watched in his rear view mirror as the green truck

kicked up dust, and rambled out of sight down 85.
"Damndest explosive delivery truck I ever saw,"
laughed Hootie, as the sounds of Conjunto music faded
into the distance and dust flew up from under the
yellow-rimmed tires.

Paco drove five miles before he suddenly
remembered the packing slip in his shirt pocket.
"Caramba!" he grumbled, and made a U-turn to drive
back to the well site. When he arrived at the gate, the
oilman was nowhere in sight. He honked but no one was
around to let him through. After a few minutes, he got
out of his truck and taped the pink packing slip to the
aluminum gate. He backed out onto the highway and
went on his way, singing along with Ramon Ayala to
'La Casa de Madera'. The pink paper fluttered in the
warm Texas breeze.

Chapter 6

After they left Morrison's garage, Jake was at a loss. "Now what?" he asked, "Go back to Honey Creek? We missed the main party for sure now."

"No. I want to stay close to town in case Cody gets worse. I think I'll go out to Fredericksburg. Rita and the crew are out there on Enchanted Rock. They're going to climb a 5-11 out there this week. She thinks you and I are still at the cave."

"Is Katie out there with her?"

"I don't know. Probably. She is supposed to be getting qualified for level five. Katie has a few more climbs to do before she can go on the Colorado trip this summer. It's Spring Break, so this is the perfect time to get her practice climbs in. But she may have gone to Port A, or somewhere to see her folks. I don't know. What are you going to do?" For the first time he could remember, Jesse felt disconnected with Jake. Right now, he did not care if Jake came or not.

"I'll go with you, if you don't mind."

After grabbing breakfast and coffee, they drove out of town on RM 12. They drove west, admiring the sweeping Texas Hill Country scenery. At the cutoff to Wimberley, the road turned west and became Texas 32. They pulled into a roadside park at a place called the Devil's Backbone, and looked at canyon walls across a chain link fence. The Balcones Fault had formed rocky, stair-stepped slopes, like little balconies, which gave the fault its name. Across the canyons, they could see a purplish haze laying like a ragged coverlet on the hills. Locusts were buzzing so loud in the trees; they had to raise their voices to hear each other. These cliffs were flop compared to the ones they had been climbing, but Jesse made a note to check them out again one day. They were too short to base-jump. Jesse liked the name, Devil's Backbone; it sounded rad. It would not be very challenging, though. Maybe they could run the bikes off the cliffs or something – that'd be solid. They admired the view for several minutes before driving on, through the backroads of Texas. A little south of Blanco, they took Hwy 281 north.

They talked over the events of the past two days. Neither one brought up Cody. They wondered about the skin, discussed what it was, and what it might mean. They wondered if someone had left the pelt behind as a joke. Potholers love to play tricks on each other. They wondered if their team had reached the TC passage yet. They laughed at how different Professor Morrison looked in shorts.

"Man! I hate losing that submarine. The GoPro alone cost almost a hundred!"

Jesse felt the heat rise in his neck. "Camera? You are worried about a camera while Cody is laid up in a hospital bed? Damn! He wouldn't be racked up except for that damned submarine!"

Jake did not respond. He plugged his ear buds, and looked out his window and said nothing else as they drove. They located the campsite, but the girls were not in camp. They were out on the cliffs somewhere, Jesse guessed. With nothing else to do, and not wanting to talk to each other, they rolled out their sleeping bags under the shady cedar elm beside the tent, and fell fast asleep.

"What the hell is this?"

Clint looked up from his metal office desk. Jim Gunderson waived a pink sheet of paper around as if he was flagging down a train. "I don't know, Jim. What is it?" he calmly responded.

"It's a packing slip!"

"Well," Clint fake-laughed, "if you knew, why in the hell did you ask me?"

Jim thrust the paper toward Clint. Clint did not move to take the paper, and left Jim with his arm hanging out in space. Gunderson, unfazed by the snub, recited. "White Phosphorus? Thermite? What do we need this stuff for?"

Gunderson threw the packing list onto the desk. "Oh! That's a delivery we took for Rio Frio. See? It says Rio Frio on top. It's not even ours. We're holding it for them to pick up."

"Where is it?"

"I don't know. Maybe they came and got it."

Jim looked Clint in the eye. "I ain't believin' this! If you put that crap down that well, all hell is going to break loose! That stuff will burn forever! No telling what would happen!"

"What? I have no intention of doing anything like that. I told you. The shipment wasn't for us! We just held it for that other outfit."

"Rio Frio?"

"Rio Frio." Clint nodded.

Jim jutted his chin toward Clint and pronounced each word separately. "Who - the - hell - is - Rio - Frio?"

"I don't know, Jim!" Exasperated, Clint turned back toward his desk. "Go look them up and ask them. I just did a favor for a friend who asked me to hold an order for them until they could pick it up. That's all. I don't know what's in it or what it's for – and I don't give a rat's ass!"

"I'm not buying this, Marshall! I'm going to remind you right now! Officially, nothing goes in that well without my knowledge!"

Clint sighed long and deep. "Jim, we're pulling the bit on this job. Shuttin' it down. I'm writing the work order right now." He retrieved the order from his desk and handed it to Gunderson. It called for removal of the drill bit on Tuesday. "We're not drilling or fracking anymore, so your services here are no longer needed." Clint fixed Jim with a dead stare and did not try to soften the words. "Get off my well site!"

"This ain't the end of this!" Gunderson threw the work order back at Clint, turned and slammed out the door. Clint watched through the window. Gunderson stomped off the steps and slammed his truck door before Clint said to Hootie over his shoulder. "How'd he get that slip?"

Hootie shrugged, "I don't have a clue."

Clint kept his eyes on Gunderson's truck pulling out of the site, "Go get that box and move it to #1 in Cotulla. Hugh, change the work order! First thing tomorrow, when the crew comes back, split 'em into two teams. Leave the night crew here to pull the bit and cap this well. Take the day crew to Cotulla. I want that valve and injection port placed on #1 as soon as possible."

"You got it, boss."

"He's probably already got Strickland on his cell phone. Get that box out of here today. Now!"

Dr. Colton Bryan looked at his patient over the top of the blue medical clipboard. He had pushed his magnifiers down onto the bridge of his nose. "What do we know about him?" he asked the nurse taking Cody's blood pressure.

"Not much," the nurse said. "Came in through the ER early this morning. Before daylight. The kid who brought him in says he's a student here at Southwest – I mean Texas State – I'll never get used to that name change! His name is Cody Hughes. His friend said we probably have his records here, but we don't have anyone in the system under that name. The kid that brought him in is named Perrine. I've got his phone number here if we need it. This kid has never been in here for treatment. It's Sunday, so we can't check the college registrar until in the morning. Once we do, we can notify his parents. The Perrine kid said this one fell into a wall inside a cave somewhere. He and another friend hauled him here themselves instead of calling EMS – they should have called EMS."

"Did he fall into a cave, or did he fall while he was inside one?"

The nurse took the blue chart and recorded the blood pressure. The he flipped a page on the chart,

"From the admitting notes, he was inside a cave and fell face-first into a wall."

"Did it look suspicious at all? Any indication they may have beat him up?"

"No. The contusions seem to match what the kid said. All of the injuries are on the front or the side. Charge nurse said they pulled pieces of rock and dirt out of his hair and from the cuts. If he was beat up, they beat him with a rock. I don't think so though, notes say the kid who brought him in was pretty upset about it. He could have been injured some other way – maybe fell off his skateboard or something. I think the Perrine kid probably told the truth."

"That's the name of the kid who brought him in?"

"Jesse Perrine. Cell phone, but no other contact information."

"Drugs or alcohol?"

"Nope. Kid is clean."

"No wallet? No ID bracelet or anything."

"Not a thing. That Perrine kid reported his mother worked in Austin, but no one wrote down where," the nurse said as he wrote down Cody's temperature.

"Well, we can fall back on old faithful. Why don't you go Google him, and search Facebook too! All these kids have a Facebook page. If that fails we may have to call that Jesse kid and get more information."

Dr. Bryan took the chart back and looked closely at the young man lying in bed. He was hurt bad. He was breathing on his own, but barely. Unconscious. "What happened to you, Cody Hughes?" Poor kid looked like he was hit by a semi. If they could keep the swelling down in his head, he might make it. On his way across the hall, he placed the chart on the counter top, and asked the nurse. "Any luck?"

"Bingo! I think this is our kid!" Bryan came around and looked at the computer screen. The picture was a nice looking, blond haired young man. The kid in the bed across the hall was so banged up it was hard to recognize him from the picture on the computer. "His name is the same, and he goes to school here on campus." The nurse clicked on Cody's profile page. "Skater, mountain biker, bungee jumper – the kid was in to anything hazardous. No wonder the x-rays showed so many old injuries. From his medical profile, he looked like an abused child. No phone numbers, no address, no identifying information. I think we found the right Cody Hughes." Dr. Bryan went back around the counter. "What about parents?" he asked.

The nurse clicked the 'contacts' button on Cody's Facebook page and said, "Hey, doc! If this is the right kid, his mother is a Texas State Representative named Sara Hughes!"

"Find her! Get her down here."

When the girls returned to camp after their afternoon climb, they were surprised and excited to see Jesse and Jake. Rita had feared something had happened, so she was relieved to find Jesse uninjured. Jesse and Jake told them Cody was injured, and they had taken him to a San Marcos hospital. Cody was seriously hurt; they did not know how badly. They scratched plans to explore the cavern since they had missed the main party. "So, if it's all right," Jesse grinned, "we'll just hang out here with you two. Maybe we'll do some climbing too."

Neither Jake nor Jesse mentioned the skin they had found. Later, Jake and Katie drove the jeep into town to buy extra provisions for dinner. Jesse and Rita hiked through the shady trails beneath the great domed rock.

As they walked beneath the dusty Ash Junipers, Rita excitedly told him their climbing plans for the week. Katie had moved through a series of progressive climbs and was gaining proficiency. This morning they had completed a practice route called 'Chunky Tuna' rated a 5.5. It was an easy climb for Rita, but Katie struggled some. They scheduled 'Orange Peel' a 5.9 for the next day. If Katie passed that challenge, they planned to complete a final ascent; a 5.11 called 'False Determination', by Wednesday or Thursday. If Katie could become proficient at that level, they would be ready for some serious climbing this summer in Colorado. Jesse and Rita had made plans to go to Clear Creek Canyon in late June to tackle "Morning Glory' ascent. "Do you think Katie will be ready?" Jesse wondered.

"She'll go, even if she won't make the climb. What about Jake?"

"I don't know. He says he wants to go, but I'm having doubts about taking him along."

"Why?" Rita was shocked. "He's a good guy, and Katie likes him," she laughed. "Besides you need a climbing partner. If you guys are planning to free base the cliff, you can't do that alone. What's going on with you two? Jake's been your friend since high school. What's wrong?"

Jesse shook the questions off. "I don't know. Just having trust issues right now, I guess. We'll work it out."

"Trust issues?"

"He plays too much, pulling jokes and horsing around. He needs to get serious. People get hurt." Jesse would not say any more, so Rita let it go.

When they returned to camp, they gathered wood and made a fire. They watched the yellow fingers flick over and around oak limbs, as they waited for the coals to form into white-dusted, red embers. While they waited for dinner, Jesse showed Rita the maps he had made of Honey Creek cave. He excitedly told her about finding the new lead, and described the underwater swim needed to access the new chamber. The problem, he said, was maybe it was not a new chamber after all. Maybe someone had been in that section before, because someone left something behind. He described it as a tarp, or a piece of a tent. He told her it could be an animal skin, and they had turned it over to his professor who was checking it out.

Shortly, Jake and Rita slid up in the jeep and unloaded bags of food and beer. They sat in their nylon folding chairs and watched evening creep through the camp, as Jesse smeared mustard on pork chops. "Trust me! You'll like it!" he promised.

Fireflies winked on and off, flitting around in gathering dusk, as the smell of cooking meat scented the air. The pork chops were delicious, char-grilled to a golden brown. The mustard made a tan, light, crust on the meat. Along with the potatoes and bacon, the food quickly disappeared. They sat back and watched the stars come out. Remnants of light still lit the low-hanging clouds as darkness fell. It appeared as if someone had outlined the pale clouds in charcoal. Trees, boulders, and other tents became outlines, dissolved into black silhouettes against the dark blue evening sky. Small blue points of light were starting to become visible in the sky. They realized how good life was. How lucky they felt to be young, and able to enjoy life. As darkness fell, Jesse felt things could not be more perfect. Perfect did not last.

Jake brought up the elephant in the room. "Jesse, I know you think I did, but I didn't pull Cody into that wall."

Jesse sat upright in his chair. He could feel his anger rising, and the heat flush his cheeks. "Jake. I was there! I saw it, dude. You jerked him forward and he went into that wall face first. He didn't fall, man. He was pulled."

Katie and Rita looked at one another with mouths open and eyes wide. Katie was going to say something, but Rita put out her hand to quiet her. They needed to work this out on their own.

"So was I," retorted Jake.

"Of course you were there! What are you talking about?"

"I'm telling you I was jerked too!"

"What do you mean you were jerked? What does that mean?"

"Jesse, something is down in the cave," Jake insisted.

"What? Nothing can live down there. It's a cave!"

"I don't know. Maybe … maybe something like Morrison was talking about – like those crocs in Madagascar."

"Madagascar, but not in Texas! Even Morrison said it's too cold in caves for them."

Katie could hold it in no longer. "What are you guys talking about?"

"He's talking about that stinking thing we found in the cave," Jesse told her. "It looks like a piece of skin, like an alligator or something, way back in there where I showed you on the map. It's probably nothing. It's probably something someone left down there to scare someone. We were pulling the thing out when Cody got hurt."

Jake broke in, "Jesse, I don't know what it was, but something grabbed hold of me and jerked me back into the lead, man! I never felt such power before in my life! Something grabbed my leg and jerked me back down that tunnel!"

"Like what?" the girls asked in wide-eyed unison.

Jake paused before he answered. "Like maybe, whatever owned that piece of skin!" Jake stretched out his left leg toward Jesse, and slowly raised his pants leg to reveal a purple-yellow bruise around his upper calf. "Like maybe … whatever did this!"

Deep, down inside the earth, a wet, dark mass swims in black waters. Circling and twining around deeper pools, it hunts. Orbiting in ever decreasing arcs, the animal scans the water for any motion. Sensors in its bulla detect vibrations caused by any movement, however slight. Not perceiving anything moving through the dark water, the animal crawls out onto a wet, flat ledge bordering the immense pool deep inside the dark grotto. The pitch-black cave was no deterrent for the huge creature; it will detect anything that moves. Anything entering the cavern will soon be easily caught and eaten whole. Finding nothing suitable to eat on the dry shelf, it changes its tactics. Slowly and quietly, it slithers off the ledge and slides back into the water, leaving behind a slimy, wet trail.

It lies silently and motionless in a black pool. It waits. A low-pitched hum begins. Nearby, a catfish, almost two feet long and weighing forty pounds feeds among the rocks. It comes nearer and nearer to the unseen beast. Underwater and undetected, the creature opens its wide, jagged-tooth mouth and waits, gaping wide. It holds this open-mouthed position for several long minutes. Waiting. The fish swims near, feeding along the rocks. The catfish swims between the massive jaws; at that precise instant, the massive jaws snap together with a loud gnashing sound. The fish flops and struggles to get away. The creature drags the helpless fish into deeper water and begins to twist and turn in a torturous death roll, tearing huge chunks of flesh from the fish and swallowing them whole. The water roils and splashes as the massive creature tears the fish to bits. Water sloshes high upon the rocky ledge, and drains back into the water. Clouds of blood slowly spreads through the dark water, diluting to pink before finally disappearing altogether. Small darter fish quickly swim in; take quick pecking bites of the small bits of meat left from the creature's meal, as the water calms and subsids. In the cold dark, the creature rests, and the cavern is silent once again except for the echoes of dripping water.

Chapter 7

Jim Gunderson watched Paul Strickland pull into the gravel parking lot behind the Pump House Tavern. Paul was a heavy-set man, who served as Safety Officer for HNH Oil. He always joked that as a true safetyman he always wore both belt and suspenders. It always got a laugh. Paul loved a good laugh, but he always took his job seriously. One of his major faults however, was that Paul often changed his mind about things. Paul always agreed with the last person who talked to him. He formulated an action plan based that conversation until he ran into someone else, then Paul agreed with the new person, and changed the plan again. It was frustrating for everyone, but you soon learned to make sure you were always the last person to talk to Strickland; and then make sure no one else got to him before you did about whatever it was you needed to do. If someone slipped in behind you, you would have to start the whole process over again.

Paul flicked the unlock button on his door panel as Jim Gunderson slid into the passenger seat. "Paul, you didn't stop by the well site, did you?" Gunderson asked, trying to ascertain if Clint had already gotten to him.

"No. I drove here straight from Houston to pick you up, just like you said. Now do you want to tell me what is going on?"

"Yeah, I'll tell you." Jim paused for effect, "Paul, you know I always check things out before I jump don't you?"

"Yeah..." Paul responded, pensive and guarded.

"Well, I think we have big problems here. Problems that are going to bite us in the butt if we don't do something quick! I think you and I need to go to Austin and have the permit pulled on this site."

"What? Why do we need to go to Austin? We can do that right here; right now."

"Because I think top brass at HNH is in on it! TJ will over-rule us."

"What in Sam Hill are you talking about?"

"Clint is desperate. I think he's going to drop something into the well that is going to cause us problems – maybe get us banned."

"Noooo! Clint wouldn't do that, Jim. That's crazy. Why would he do that?"

"He wants that oil. He's tried twice to crack through that blockage down there. This is his second attempt, and now he still can't break through. Desperate men do desperate things, Paul! There is something going on at the site. No one is talking, but there is lots of whispering. Something about a secret method."

"Oh, that! No. Listen! Listen. Listen." Paul tried to placate his friend. "He is desperate, but he's not crazy," Strickland laughed. "Sure, he brought something up about an experimental method at the board meeting the other day, but they turned him down flat. He's not going to do anything off-the-wall. They told him no. Nobles was against this second well to begin with. And TJ… TJ gave him two weeks to break through, or pull the bit."

"Paul, Clint took a shipment yesterday, marked for some other outfit – Rio Frio Oil Company."

"So?"

"Rio Frio doesn't exist anymore! AND, the box contained white phosphorus and Thermite."

"What?" Paul's plump face lost its natural smile.

"I saw the packing slip myself. There is no good reason on God's green earth why he would need those chemicals in a fracking well."

Paul rubbed his chin as he listened to Jim continue, "I've got a 10:00 o'clock appointment with Sara Hughes this morning. You know her; she's the state rep for this area, and she's on the environmental commission. I want you to go up there with me when I talk to her. If you won't, I'll go myself."

"What if you're wrong? I still don't…"

"I'm not wrong! Look, I'll take full responsibility. All you have to do is be my wingman. Just be there. I'll do all the talking."

"If you are wrong, they'll fire us both."

"They'll fire me. In fact, they already have. Clint is getting ready to pull the bit two weeks early. I can't go back on-site. He told me to leave and not come back. If we don't do something, and he blows up that well – they'll fire us anyway."

An astonished Paul Strickland could only shake his head. "Why would Clint do that, unless he's giving up on hitting oil? It don't make sense Clint giving up two weeks early," he agreed. "That is odd." On the hundred-mile drive to Austin, Paul came up with every possible explanation he could think of. Jim did not buy any of them. By the time they got to the Austin city limits, Paul was as convinced as Jim was that something was wrong.

They waited outside Sara's office for several minutes. A couple of times Jim had to persuade Paul not to call headquarters. Jim had been down this road too many times before, and he knew that Paul was not to be trusted alone on the phone. One minute on the phone with TJ and this meeting was over, and they would be on the way back to Dilley. At 10:15, the secretary invited them in to Sara's office. Sara stood to meet them, shaking their hands and offering them a seat. Sara moved around her desk to the sofa to sit facing them, asking if they wanted coffee.

After the introductions, Jim jumped right in, "Ms. Hughes, we've got a serious problem down in Dilley, We believe the operator on Dilley Chalk #2 is going to go outside of his drilling and exploration permit, and create a dangerous situation – one that could greatly endanger public safety."

"Have you talked to your corporate office about this?" Sara asked.

"No, because we think they already know."

Jim launched into this indictment before Sara could fire off further questions. "Miss Hughes, have you ever heard of a man named Elmer Pawson?" Sara shook her head no. "Elmer Pawson was an ordinance expert for the Army, way back during Viet Nam. Elmer worked in a unit that developed weapons to deforest the heavy jungles over there – things like napalm and Agent Orange. His research was the primary science behind those weapons, including the use of white phosphorus, which NATO banned as a military weapon by international law. He did all this without a science background at all, and the big chemical companies jumped on it smelling huge profits. After the war, with no more jungles to burn down, he returned to his home out in Midland. Around that time, the oil industry had problems breaking through hard rock. Shale and limestone were no problem, but granite and marble, and the harder stones?" he made it sound like a question. "They were eating up drill bits and slowing down production. So Pawson got this idea that if he could heat up the rock formations deep inside the well, it would be easier to drill through them. The heat might even crack those hard rocks, allowing the drill to slice through like butter. So he designed a method he called the Bitter Pill. He used Thermite. The one thing, it's really hard to get Thermite to burn; but when it does burn, it burns really hot – really hot! Almost as hot as the surface of the sun. So, Pawson used white phosphorus as an igniting source."

"White phosphorus is extremely dangerous Miss Hughes, but it is not an explosive by itself – it's a pyrotechnic composition that gives off heat high enough to ignite the Thermite. White Phosphorus, by itself, it is an extremely volatile substance, and is a horrendous chemical when it touches human flesh. In the war, they called it Willie Pete. It burns until it runs out of oxygen, or consumes itself. Most recently, the Saddam Hussein regime used white phosphorus on his own people. There are stories of the Marines using it in Fallujah before we signed a treaty banning it as a weapon in 2009. These days, we mostly use it to illuminate the night sky over a battlefield. Ms. Hughes, this chemical is so dangerous, it can burn right through a person. If it gets on you, you can't get it off! Even those who try to help the victims, end up getting exposed themselves. This stuff creates a fire you can't extinguish with water! The only way to put out a white phosphorus fire is to deprive it of oxygen. It literally melts the skin right off a body, and then eats the bone. The Organization for the Prohibition of Chemical Weapons calls this substance the most inhumane chemical weapon in human history! As I said, in 2009, the United States signed a treaty prohibiting its use as a military weapon."

Paul raised his hand as if starting to speak, but Jim continued before he could interject, "So, Pawson took this stuff, and wrapped it in a canister of carbon disulfide and aluminum oxide. What he discovered was that the carbon disulfide evaporates, and then the white phosphorus bursts into flame. The white phosphorus burns and sets off the Thermite, and you have a fire that you can't put out. The main problem is in that trigger mechanism. The Thermite gets so hot, it strips oxygen molecules from the aluminum oxide, which provides the oxygen needed to feed the fire. It makes its own oxygen! You have a fire you can't put out!"

Jim pressed on, "It would be a *very* bad thing to drop a bunch of this into water. It would instantly vaporize a tremendous amount of water, and cause a steam explosion you cannot imagine. It would create steam hot enough to catch paper on fire! Luckily, before Pawson could test this method on oilrigs, which he would probably have never gotten approval for anyway, the technology for drill bits improved to the point where we could drill through practically any kind of rock if we approached it from the right angle. Pawson's idea was quickly forgotten – and so was he."

"So, what does this have to do with your problem, Mr. Gunderson?"

"I have reason to believe that one of the fracking operators south of San Antonio is about to use this method – very soon."

Sara looked at the men for a full thirty seconds in complete silence. Then she pressed a button on her intercom. "June, please ask Pokey to step in here if he can. Tell him it's very important." She turned back to the HNH men.

"Gentlemen, I'm asking Representative Marin to sit in with us if you don't mind. He knows a lot about the oil business, and he's the Vice-chair of the State Environmental Commission."

Within ten minutes, Pokey arrived and introduced himself to Paul and Jim. Pokey sat in an overstuffed chair as he caught up on the earlier conversation. Pokey listened and then nodded, "I saw this stuff in Viet Nam. It is spooky stuff. I've seen guys burned so bad you couldn't even tell it was a human body you were looking at. It was just of lump of smoldering meat! And the damned stuff burns forever!"

"You mentioned you thought your company was aware of this plan, Mr. Gunderson. Why?" Sara prodded.

"I have no proof, Ms. Hughes, but from comments made by the operator and rumors on the site, it seems likely," he said solemnly. Jim was very convincing. "At a recent meeting of the company board of directors, the operator I told you about brought up the idea as a suggestion."

"There should be a record of that agenda item then," Pokey offered.

"There probably is," agreed Paul. "However, the board turned him down flat, and told him to stay within the limits of his operating permit. That's the official position of the company."

"But, you don't believe them?" Pokey raised his eyebrows.

"No. I do not." Jim said flatly.

"Why not, Mr. Strickland?" Sara probed.

"Yesterday, a delivery was made to the drilling site in Dilley. A kilo of Willie Pete and a kilo of Thermite were in that shipment."

"Do you have proof of that delivery, Mr. Strickland?"

"Yes. I saw the packing slip with my own eyes. They delivered it to a company that everyone thought was out of business, called Rio Frio Oil Company. The operator, Clint Marshall, stated he was receiving it for a friend." Jim looked from one to the other, "Ms. Hughes; Mr. Marin; there is no legitimate use for either of those chemicals in any drilling operation."

"Rio Frio?" Pokey mused. "I know that outfit. I thought they folded a few years ago."

"Well, they are still receiving shipments!" Jim pointed out. "Mr. Marin, we need to stop this before they blow half of south Texas to kingdom come!"

Sara caught the motion of her secretary waving from the doorway. "Ms. Hughes?" June interrupted. Sara saw the worried expression on June's face, and knew something was wrong.

"What is it, June?"

"It's Cody, he's been hurt! They have him in the hospital in San Marcos. It sounds bad."

Sara stood and went behind her desk to get her purse and keys. She looked desperately at Pokey as she walked to the door. "Pokey? Can you take this from here? I've got to go." She said badly shaken. "Cody's been hurt!"

"Of course. Fellas please come with me to my office. Sara, if you need anything call me at once."

Sara was already gone.

The piece of hide was as thick as a pig's skin. It measured roughly eight-foot by five. From the markings on the skin, it appeared to be alligator or crocodile. You could make a great pair of boots out of this, Tom thought. Along one edge, the color changed from a darker thicker skin, to softer and lighter. He decided from the change in texture it was a strip of hide along the side, between the upper and lower body, probably right behind the rear leg in the forepart of the tail. He went around the hide several times, and decided it was from the right side. It looked as if it had been scraped or cut off somehow. From the size of the fragment, it would have to have been an enormous creature. Using a toy alligator, he made some rough calculations. He looked up from his figures in disbelief. To be sure, he performed the measurements again and got the same result. Incredulously, if his figures were correct, this animal would have to be forty feet long, and weigh in the neighborhood of four or five thousand pounds. No alligator could possibly be that large! Was this a student prank? To Tom's knowledge, no crocodile had been so huge.

Tom was supposed to leave for Florida that afternoon, but he decided he wanted to study this skin in more detail. A couple of more hours would not matter since he was driving straight through anyway. Tom brought his laptop to the garage and booted up. He signed on, and went to academia's finest and most often utilized research tool – Google. He entered a google search for 'huge alligator', and read.

He read the first hit he saw. *Carnufex carolinensus*. A pre-historic crocodile recently discovered in North Carolina, dated March 2015. *Carnufex* is one of the most recent "crocodylomorphs" ever found in North America. Like most early crocodiles, *Carnufex* walked on its two hind legs. *Carnufex* was one of the earliest and largest classes of creatures that include modern and extinct crocodiles. The creature was an apex predator, measuring some nine feet long, and preying on early reptiles and mammals. Found in Chatham County, North Carolina in the Upper Triassic Pekin Formation, they called it the Carolina Butcher!

The teeth of an alligator or crocodile are designed to grip, but they cannot rip or chew flesh. The teeth can crush through a turtle shell or a mammal bone with no problem. All alligators and crocodiles have extensive modification of the shoulder, pelvis, and spine, which enables them to walk on land and swim in water. They propel themselves through the water by moving their tail from side to side. The tail is extremely muscular, and is controlled at will by the animal. Many animals use the tail as a club to knock prey off its feet. Their feet are partially webbed which also helps with mobility through water, and sharply clawed. They can run incredibly fast on land, but only for short distances.

Tom decided *Carnufex* was smaller, but could be a possibility. He examined several others, and eliminated them of various reasons. *Angistorhinus* (narrow snout) of the late Triassic period was about the right size, and from the swamps of North America. A possibility. *Araripesuchus* was only as close as South America and way too small. Probably not. He went through descriptions of a dozen or more crocodile-like lizards without success before he found something interesting.

Dakosaurus (tearing lizard) lived in the shallow seas of North and South America during the late Jurassic and early Cretaceous periods. This creature was fifteen feet long and weighed over a ton. Now we are talking. He remembered that Texas and most of the central part of the Americas was once a large, shallow, inland tropical sea.

Then he found *Deinosuchus* (terrible crocodile). It habited the rivers of North America in the late Cretaceous age, and was thirty-five feet long and weighed five to ten tons! Bingo! A definite possibility. This crocodile was so huge it ate other dinosaurs! North American tyrannosaur fossils have been found with evidence of *Deinosuchus* bite marks! *Deinosuchus* was remarkably similar to modern crocodiles.

Sarcosuchus? Now we're talking. Sarcosuchus is closely related to a North American genus called *Terminonaris*. Tom clicked on the link for *Terminonaris*. This animal lived in the late Cretaceous period. This giant crocodile was some 25 feet long. It was first described by Osborn in 1904. Remains have been found from Canada to Texas. Tom looked at the skin laid out on his makeshift table. *Terminonaris* lived here in Texas! The terminator!

Sarcosuchus imperator was also a giant relative of modern crocodiles. Fully-grown animals have been estimated at 40 feet long. The snout comprised approximately 75% of its head, with thirty-five sharp teeth in each side of the upper jaw, and 31 on each side of the lower. At the end of its snout, was an organ, called a bulla. Opinions on the purpose of this bulla range from being an olfactory enhancer, to a vocalization device. Crocodilians are known to be the most vocal of all reptiles and have a variety of different calls depending on the age, size, and gender of the animal. Male alligators use infrasound during some calls. Infrasonic waves from a bellowing male alligator can cause the water to "dance" around the animal. Imperator was the largest of the crocodiles and crocodile-like reptiles, and are estimated to have weighed eight tons. The king of them all was *Sarcosuchus*, which was a "SuperCroc" some forty feet long and nearly ten tons. He looked at a picture someone had posted that showed *Sarcosuchus* laying on a river bank next to a six foot tall man – it's snout opened, and could easily have swallowed the man whole!

These crocs had been extinct for thousands of years. Tom continued to read that the one way in which prehistoric crocodiles were more impressive than their terrestrial dinosaur relatives was their ability, as a group, to survive the massive extinction event that wiped out most of the planet's dinosaurs, called the K/T Extinction Event, or the Cretaceous-Tertiary Extinction Event. In 1980, Cuban born physicist Luis Alverez and his son Albert put forth a startling hypothesis. By investigating ocean sediments laid down thousands of years ago, they discovered iridium-rich sediments scattered all over the globe. Only a meteorite or a comet could have delivered this load which blotted out the sun, killed off vegetation, and slowly starved the dinosaurs to death. This was closely followed by an extended period of volcanic activity. What he read next caused his eyes to open wide. Some crocodilians, **by seeking shelter in deep caves**, escaped this extinction event. That is why alligators and crocodiles are still here, virtually unchanged from prehistoric times.

Tom went over to the hide stretched across the sawhorses. He rubbed his hand along the rough skin. "What are you big boy?" He thought for a while, and decided Florida would have to wait. He reached for his phone and dialed Jesse's number.

"Jesse, I need you and Jake to come back to my office as soon as you can get here."

"What's up, Doc?" Jesse joked.

"I think I've identified your skin. I think we're dealing with a crocodile that lived thousands of years ago called *Sarcosuchus*. It was a croc so big it ate dinosaurs for lunch!"

"An extinct crocodile?"

"That's right – except for one thing," Tom said as he bent over the hide.

"Yes, sir? What's that?"

Tom looked up as the realization spread across his face. His eyes widened with awareness and fear, he said, "It's not extinct anymore!"

Chapter 8

Hootie took off his cowboy hat and wiped his brow with a handkerchief. "It may be spring," wiping the sweatband of his hat, "but summer ain't getting cheated!" He looked up at the blazing sun, and calculated the heat. "Gotta be a hundred at least!" he announced to no one in particular.

Hugh pulled out his cell phone and reported, "Weather bug says only 97."

Hootie laughed, "You gonna believe me or your lyin' phone?"

Hugh checked the time. "Phone says it's four o'clock. Why don't we knock off and adjourn to the Pump House Tavern for a cold beer?" Hootie did not argue with that. They slid into the truck seats and bounced through the open gate onto the highway. Hootie closed and locked the gate while Hugh waited. The heat waves rose from the black tarmac surface as they drove back into town. Mirages in the distance made the highway look wet, even though it had not rained.

The Pump House was not well air-conditioned, but it was better than being out in the hot sun. The ice-cold beer did not hurt either. Clint was due to land at the La Salle County Airport in Cotulla soon. Clint was sure to see Hugh's truck in the lot when he passed and would stop in to share a beer and talk.

"Crews come back first thing tomorrow," Hootie said making conversation. "Work order says to pull the bit. What do you make of that?"

Hugh shrugged, "Pull the bit. Vac out the hole, cap it off, like he said."

"What do you think Gunderson is going to do?" Hootie asked.

"I don't know." Hugh scratched his head. "Maybe nothing. He don't usually pop off unless he means it. But like Clint said, it ain't his rodeo anymore – we're not drilling or fracking. Technically, he can't do a thing."

Hootie hesitated, and then asked, "Do you know what Clint is up to?"

Hugh looked him straight in the eyes. "Do you really want to go there with me?"

Hootie looked away, "I guess not."

Hugh's voice softened as he quietly confided, "He hasn't told me anything directly either. But I agree, he's up to something. It worries me. I guess he thinks the less I know, maybe the less I can say if it ever comes up. And the less I tell you, the more you can claim you don't know."

"My name is on that manifest. Am I in trouble – if all hell breaks loose?"

"I don't know. Damn Clint for not handling his own dirty work! I've been with Clint a long time. Maybe it's time for me to move on; I don't know. Who knew that box would come in a day early? You get your story straight, and stick to it. You didn't order it! You didn't inspect it! You didn't even notice what was in it! You only signed for it. Nothing else. You don't even remember signing for it!"

Hector came over with two more Bud Lights, so Hootie waited until he returned to the bar out of earshot. Leaning closer to Hugh he confided, "I took it to Cotulla."

Hugh looked around to make sure no one could overhear, "No one knows that but me and you and Clint and the fence post. Keep it like that!"

Hootie started to ask what Hugh thought was in the box, when strangely colored flickering lights began reflecting on the walls of the tavern. The sudden movement distracted them. Something big was going on outside. Hugh whipped off his sunglasses and peered outside, "What the hell is that?" Their chairs scraped over the rough wood floor as they rushed to the window.

A line of black SUVs, with their headlights on, streamed past the Pump House, followed by nearly as many local yokels with flashing blue and red lights. Hootie looked at Hugh who already headed for the door. "Get to the truck! We need to go!"

When they drove up to the gate, the officers had parked their police cars all along the bar ditch down the side of the road. A group of men in white shirts and Stetson hats were near the gate, surrounded by a crowd of plain clothes and uniformed officers. A line of Sheriff's deputies with long guns was standing along the road near the vehicles. One officer stood near the gate with bolt cutters.

Hugh roared past the deputy trying to direct traffic, pulled up as close as possible, and jumped out. "Hey! You don't have to cut the lock! I'm here!"

You can spot a Texas Ranger a mile away. Starched white shirt, starched blue jeans with creases down the legs, black cowboy boots, and a silver-belly hat. Pure Texas – George Strait with a badge. The closest Ranger walked over to Hugh and asked, "Who are you, sir?"

Hugh identified himself as the site foreman, and Hootie as the shift supervisor. "What do you guys want?"

The Ranger's badge on his chest reflected the dancing lights from the patrol cars. His eyes were shadowed beneath the brim of his hat. "Will you please open the gate? We'll go in and talk," he motioned with his head. "We need to get everyone off this road." It was more a directive than a request, Hugh realized.

Hugh opened the lock. Hootie swung the gate open and held it as several vehicles entered the property. Most of the Sheriff's cars and deputies stayed outside on the road, lights still flashing. Turning to walk back to the office trailer, Hootie noticed the officers had put the rifles away. The lead Ranger spoke again. "Sir, are you in charge here?"

"No sir," Hugh answered. "That would be Clint Marshall the Field Manager. He's the lead operator." Hootie noticed one Ranger writing everything anyone said.

"Is Mr. Marshall here at this time?"

"He should be here any minute. What can I help you with?"

"Mr. Shipmann, my name is Captain Robert Layton Cobb, with the Texas Rangers, representing the Texas Department of Public Safety. I am accompanied by an officer of the United States District Court in Austin, Mr. Dollarhide." He nodded toward one of the suits standing nearby, who nodded back. "These other gentlemen are officers with the La Salle County Sheriff's Department."

An officer stepped forward and introduced himself as Sheriff Acosta. The Ranger continued, "I have important documents to deliver to Mr. Marshall when he arrives. When do you expect him?"

"He should be here within the hour."

"Do you have any weapons on site?"

"I have a CHL, and a .45 caliber handgun in my truck," admitted Hugh.

"May I see that CHL please?" While Hugh took his permit from his wallet, the Ranger looked at Hootie. "What about you?"

"No, sir."

The Ranger examined Hugh's concealed handgun permit and asked, "Sir, would you temporarily surrender your weapon to the Deputy here?" pointing at a nearby officer.

"Sure." Hugh turned back toward the truck, but the Ranger stopped him.

"IF – you will give the deputy permission to enter your truck, and tell him where the weapon is located, he will secure it for you – if you don't mind. You'll get it back."

"Ok, sure. It's in the compartment between the seats."

While the deputy retrieved the pistol, the Ranger asked, "Are there any other weapons on the site?"

"Not any I know about."

"None in the office?"

"No, Sir. Here's Mr. Marshall now!" Hugh pointed as Clint drove through the gate.

The Ranger went through the exact same list of questions with Clint. The only difference was Clint refused to surrender his handgun, so the Ranger asked him to stay away from his truck for the time being. Clint agreed.

The Ranger nodded at another man, and Mr. Dollarhide stepped forward with a sheaf of papers. "Mr. Marshall, I am a deputy clerk of the U.S. District Court. In the presence of these witnesses, I am serving you with an injunction of the court, duly signed by Judge Solomon Isaac. This injunction suspends your permit for the operation of this drilling site until the Judge rules, or the expiration of ninety days – whichever comes first. Do you have any questions?"

"I understand. You need to know, that we are in the process of abandoning and capping this well tomorrow, when my crew comes back. My foreman has a work order to pull the drill bit. In my opinion, it would be a risk to public safety not to take action to close this well."

"The court agrees," Mr. Dollarhide nodded. "Provisions have been made within the order to safely shut down the well. You may proceed with pulling the bit and capping the well in accordance with state laws, environmental regulations, and public safety. Law enforcement officers will remain on site until you cap and render the well inoperable. Then they will tape-off and post signs. No one will be allowed to enter after that. You will be given time to remove all of your personal property, tools, and equipment. Do you have any other questions?"

"HNH has several on-going operations across the state. Does this injunction stop any other company operations in progress now or in the future?"

"Mr. Marshall, this injunction applies to HNH Oil Company Texas permit number 45982074, for Dilley Chalk Number Two. This order does not affect any other operation. Once you sign acceptance and acknowledgement today, a copy of the injunction will be delivered to your corporate legal department in Houston. A hearing has been set for Tuesday, May 5th in the Judge's chambers. Directions are included in the paperwork I just gave you, and is in the legal notice mailed to your corporate offices. Is there anything else you need to ask?"

"Not at this time. What if I don't sign?" Clint smiled jokingly.

Mr. Dollarhide did not smile. "Then the officers here will take control of, and secure this site. Officers will escort you and your crew from the property immediately, and an appointed crew will come in to shut this well down. Do you have any further questions?"

"Where do I sign?"

Sara could hardly believe the helpless body in the hospital bed was her son. He was almost unrecognizable; his face was so swollen and bruised. Tubes and wires ran from his body to the machines stacked on a rolling pole beside the bed. A monitor beeped with regular precision as she watched the blue line rise and fall with each beat. She counted each precious beat a blessing. His breaths were shallow, but regular. Every breath was a gift from God.

Cody did not speak or open his eyes. He gave no indication he knew Sara was even in the room. She went to his side, and untangled his blond hair. He would not like his hair mussed like that. Have to maintain the skater image – what did he say? Rad? What had happened? What had gone wrong to injure him so badly? Had he crashed on the half-pipe? Was it a car wreck? Did a car hit him? She tried to remember what he had told her about his next adventure. It was always something. She remembered something about a cave somewhere. Where was it? Then she recalled him talking about going with some friends to a cave near San Antonio. Did something happen there? How relieved she had felt, knowing that he would not be with the rowdy kids down on South Padre, where there were fights and drunken escapades. He would be safe in a cavern. What could have happened in a cave to injure him so? Maybe he fell in a deep, dark hole.

She tried to remember the caves she had explored. Natural Bridge, near San Antonio – with lighted, paved passages. It was a little dim, but pretty safe. Wonder Cave in San Marcos was smaller, but a little rougher and narrower, but well lit. If you paid attention, the walk was not too strenuous. Then there was … she could not remember the name. However, like all the others, nothing that seemed threatening or dangerous about any of them. She always feared the ceiling would cave in on her, but that never happened. About the worst thing that might happen is you might bump your head on the low ceiling. Thousands of people a day go through Texas caves without incident. It was a

lot safer than cavorting around on a beach with a bunch
of drunk kids.

Her thoughts were interrupted as a doctor entered
the room. Accompanied by a nurse, he nodded at Sara
and walked to Cody's bedside. He opened and read
Cody's chart. He flashed a small light into Cody's eyes.
While the nurse recorded readings from the machine, the
doctor turned to Sara. "Are you the mother?"

The coldness of his question was like a slap in
Sara's face. "I'm his mother," she snapped. "I'm Sara
Hughes. This is my son, Cody."

"I'm Doctor Bryan, Miss Hughes. Your son
Cody is in very serious condition. He is breathing on his
own, but the swelling is not going down. We're
watching him closely to see if surgery is going to be
required."

"Do you know what happened?"

Dr. Bryan looked at her over the top of his
glasses, "He was brought here early yesterday morning
by a friend named Jesse Perrine."

"Jesse? His friend at school." Sara remember the
handsome young skateboarder with the long black hair.

"Mr. Perrine reported they were in a cave, and
Cody fell face first into a rock wall. The injuries appear
to support the story. We pulled several rock fragments
from his face and head. We don't suspect any foul play."

"Jesse wouldn't hurt Cody. Is he going to be
ok?"

"If we can control the swelling, it looks
promising. With head trauma, it is hard to predict. We
are watching closely. We will keep you advised as we

go along. We have several authorizations for you to sign; our unit clerk will help you with that. You'll need to go to the admitting office to get the insurance paperwork processed."

Noting the expression on Sara's face, he added, "Look. Cody is in serious condition, but he's not critical right now. He has had a severe traumatic head injury, and we cannot determine yet if there is any permanent impairment. The first few hours are critical, but we are nearing the end of the most dangerous period. That is promising. He is unconscious, and that can be good or bad. Good because there is no awareness of pain, but bad because it hinders our evaluation of mental capacity. Brain wave patterns seem encouraging, and he has not experienced any convulsions, which gives us hope. His pupils are dilated, which indicates a concussion at the very least. Once he is awake, we can determine if there is any permanent damage. Until then, all we can do is maintain, keep his vital signs in check, and hope for the best. We will keep him here in ICU until we are sure he is stabilized. It could be a few more hours, or several days."

"Can he hear me?"

"We aren't sure. Research indicates that he may have some awareness. He is in what we call a diminished state of consciousness, meaning he can't respond in ways we would expect. Watch for signs. He may blink, or wiggle fingers or toes, or he may make some other sign to try to communicate. If you see any of those, make sure we know about them. Meanwhile, any stimulation you can give him will be good. You could massage his legs and move them around. That will improve the circulation. Read or talk to him as if he were awake. Keep everything positive and light, no stress, nothing that might upset him. Keep visitors to a minimum, but some visitors may be good."

Sara watched as Dr. Bryan gave the chart back to his nurse. He would check again later in the evening. He would be on call all night if Sara needed anything. Sara turned back toward her son. The sunlight streamed through the window casting shadows along the wall. Outside, the world continued to turn as if everything were normal.

Tom paced his office as he talked. Jesse and Jake sat in uncomfortable chairs, listening to what felt like a lecture. "So Texas was covered by this huge, shallow, tropical sea. Right? Called the Cretaceous Seaway, or the great North American Inland Sea; it went all the way into Canada. The water was shallow, and dinosaurs of several types roamed through it – you can still see their tracks lots of places in the hill country, and up by Glen Rose. As the Laramie Formation pushed the Rockies upwards, the plates tilted and the water drained off into what is now the Gulf of Mexico. The bottom of this sea teemed with life; plants, fish, and huge clams. Many predators were attracted by the easy pickings along this warm water lagoon."

"One predator in particular. Have you ever heard of Sarcosuchus?" Jesse and Jake shook their heads no. "Sarcosuchus was a huge, crocodile-like meat-eater. He was forty feet long and five to six tons. This monster was so massive it could, and did eat dinosaurs!" Tom showed them a drawing from the internet picturing Sarcosuchus bursting from the water to grab a Tyrannosaurus Rex.

"The sea dried up around the same time something happened to cause the dinosaurs to go extinct. No one knows for sure what this extinction event was, but general belief is a comet nearly a mile wide crashed into the earth, and blotted out the sun for decades. Plants and the entire food chain died out. This K/T Extinction Event, or the Cretaceous-Tertiary event, coupled with the geological uplift destroyed the habitat of these huge creatures living in and around this great sea. They all died. Except a few survived – some lizards, and alligators and crocodiles mostly."

"Prehistoric crocodilians were of various sizes, but many of them were huge! Like the recently discovered fossil of *Carnufex Carolinensi*."

"Carnufex?" Jesse repeated.

"The Carolina Butcher! Big enough to eat a man – if men had been around. In fact, crocodiles kill over 200 people a year – even now. Did you know that? Anyway, based on the behavior of those Malaysian crocodiles I mentioned earlier, I think these guys swam into some of those underground cave systems, and somehow survived the extinction event. The erosion of silt from the geological uplift that created the Rocky Mountains covered them up. The sea floor dried, leaving the hardened mud, which became limestone. They were trapped in their own little habitat, underground, for all those years. No one knew they were there, until you found that piece of skin. They slowly evolved to be able to subsist on whatever prey they could find in the wet, semi-submerged caves. They are trapped down there and cannot get out because of their size. They have lived undetected for thousands of years, right under our noses. They are down there now!"

"You mean huge, dinosaur-like crocodiles live in the Texas aquifer?"

"That's what I'm thinking. We have to go back to see."

"Go back? No way! I'm not going back in that cave." Jake shook his head.

"We need proof! We need pictures. Don't you know what this means? Prehistoric, super-crocs exist in the modern age! This discovery is unprecedented – it is amazing! We need photographic evidence – no one is going to believe us!"

"If you want pictures, we have some…" Jake offered.

"What?" Tom was stunned. "You have pictures?" Tom placed his hands flat on the desk and looked at them.

"First time I'm hearing about this," Jessie looked at Jake unbelieving.

"Sure, remember when we sent the sub over to the other side? The camera was running, and I recorded it on my tablet."

Tom's mouth hung open in amazement. "Show me!"

While Jake retrieved his tablet from the jeep, Jesse asked, "How did it live for all this time? How did it stay warm enough? What did it eat?"

Tom scratched his head, "I don't know, except large animals can sometimes live on extremely small food sources. Whales for instance feed off tiny plankton and algae. Look how big they get. Some plant-eating dinosaurs were fifteen feet tall. Alligators only eat once a week or so anyway. They may eat each other. To answer those questions, we have to go back in the cave to find out."

Jake returned and plugged in his tablet and booted it up. He found the file and hit the play button. They crowded around the little screen. Soon they could see Jesse and Cody sitting on a rock at the edge of the water, as the camera panned around in circles. "Where was I?" asked Jake.

"The boat was swimming around you, ditz!" laughed Jesse.

"Oh, yeah…" admitted an embarrassed Jake. Soon the scene changed as the camera went underwater. "She's going through the tunnel now, to the other side." As they watched, the sub maneuvered along a jagged cave tunnel. Soon the camera surfaced again on the other side. It was inky dark, except where the subs little light shot into the blackness over the water.

"Have you got sound on this thing?" Tom asked.

"Yeah, but I didn't turn the mic on. I didn't think we'd need it."

The sub swam around in a great arc and then finally came to a stop. Suddenly the picture fragmented and disappeared. "Back it up to where it stopped," Morrison requested. Jake rewound the clip to that point. "There! Stop! What is that?" asked Tom.

"What? Those two red dots? Reflections maybe." Jake suggested.

"Look closer," Tom suggested. Now Jesse could see four little, red dots. Two large ones glowing like red-hot coals, and two smaller ones directly beneath the larger two. "What is that? Jesse wondered. "Play the clip forward in slow motion if you can," urged Tom.

"The dots are getting little larger," Jake noticed.

"They aren't getting larger, they are getting closer. Stop!" Tom said and Jake pushed the pause button.

Tom looked at the two students. "Have you guys ever been to the Everglades?" They shook their heads no. "Well, I have. And I've been out there at night. A boardwalk juts out over a pond on the Anhinga Trail. Alligators are everywhere. I went out there during college every year; working at the park. A bunch of us would go out there at night to hang out and drink beer. We'd take flashlights to shine the night critters, including the alligators. You know what? Their eyes glow like red coals of fire. Just – like - these!" He tapped the screen three times with his index finger.

"There are two of them!" Jake asked.

"No, I don't think so." Tom said. "Their eyes glow so bright in a strong light, they reflect on the water. If one is looking at you, an alligator's eyes look just like four red dots! Just like this!" His fingers tapped again in rhythm with his words. "That, my young friends is an alligator! Play it forward slowly – frame by frame if you can!"

Jake advanced the movie a slowly as he could. As the scene blinked out, a huge splash of water rose from the surface blocking the picture, and for an instant, the light flashed on sharp white teeth. Tom looked at Jake. "And he just ate your boat!"

Chapter 9

Everyone on both crews had heard the rumors; a shutdown was imminent. They were going to be out of work again. Tuesday morning, they called a meeting of both crews, and Hootie and Kline met with the assembled roughnecks, while Hugh and Clint watched from the porch of the portable office.

"Alright, guys! Listen up." Hootie yelled. "Ok, here's the deal. We are splitting into two crews, but both crews are going to day shift. For the next couple of weeks, we don't have any lay-offs planned, but you should be aware that this job is coming to a close. For whatever reason, we can't reach the oil. I have orders here, signed by Mr. Marshall, to pull the bit on this well. That should take a couple days. I want the night crew to work on that today and tomorrow, and have this well capped by tomorrow evening. The boss has authorized standby pay for your crew for two weeks with a 24-hour callback. I'm sorry men, but this well just ain't producing."

"What about after two weeks?" someone yelled.

"If you can find a slot on another crew somewhere, take it. There is no guarantee HNH will be able to start a new well in two weeks. I think some time in the future, we will, but a date or the probability of that has not been determined yet. I'll be happy to give you all excellent references, and I'll make any calls you need me to make to help you find another berth somewhere. If the situation changes, you'll be the first ones we call back – if that ever happens."

"What about the day crew?" another roughneck called out.

"We want you guys to report over to Dilly Chalk #1 this afternoon – as soon as you can get over there actually. As soon as this briefing is over, go pack your gear and move your lodging to Cotulla unless you want to commute."

"We're gonna re-open Dilly Chalk #1?" from the crowd.

"No. Not yet, anyway. We'll be keeping you guys on standby, until we can determine what to do. We've got a few tasks for you over there; that might take a day or so – then you'll go on four-hour standby for at least two-weeks – with standby pay. We need you available for a call within four hours." Hootie emphasized. "If we call, we want you on-site, sober, within four hours of the call. Anymore questions?"

"Are there any plans to start a new site – Dilly Chalk # 3?" The men laughed.

Hootie looked over at Clint who shook his head no. Hootie turned back to the men, "None we know of right now, but it don't look good. I'm sure they are looking at all the options. We'll tell you more as it becomes known. Make sure we have your latest contact information, address, and cell number."

"What are we going to do over at #1?"

"You'll find that out when you get there. Right now, I have an announcement." Hootie paused waiting for the murmuring to die. "All of you know our foreman Hugh Shipmann. Hugh is moving to Oklahoma to take over another HNH drilling operation up there. Go by and tell him so long before you leave, and if you are interested in working in Oklahoma, let him know. Any more questions?"

Not hearing any, Hootie dismissed the men. Several of them milled around and talked among themselves, and several went over to shake Hugh's hand. Several men indicated they would like to go to Oklahoma, if Hugh could take them on. Most of them were staying in Texas where their families were. It was hard to pack all your belongings and move so often, but it is the life of a roughneck. Divorce and alcoholism is rampant among the hard men who work the oil fields. Even Hugh joked he had been married twice and divorced three times. Funny as it sounded, it was a fact; depression and worry were frequent companions for the men who worked away from home, and lived in small trailers in man camps scattered around the oil fields. Fights and feuds were frequent, and they sometimes turned violent. Probably not a week went by, when the local sheriff did not pick up one of their men for something. Usually for being drunk, bored and rowdy. It came with the job.

Kline told his crew to be back after noon to start putting the well to bed. Everyone gradually drifted away. Hootie and Kline shook hands with Hugh and wished him luck on his new job. Finally, Hugh waved and drove his truck and fifth wheel through the gate onto the highway. Hootie watched him drive away, "There goes a good man. I'm sorry to see him go." Kline sadly agreed. After a few minutes, Kline also got in his truck and left, leaving only Hootie and Clint on the well site. Clint had gone back into the office. Clint had said he wanted to talk to Hootie after everyone was gone. Hootie climbed the wooden stairs to the office and sat at his desk – waiting. While Clint went through papers and signed documents, Hootie wondered if Clint was going to let him go now or later. Clint had been loyal and had always taken Hootie with him to whatever site he was working on. With this second failure, maybe Clint was out too. He waited quietly. Whatever was going to happen was going to happen.

After a while Clint looked up and asked, "They all gone?"

"Yep."

"You got any questions you want to ask?"

"Nope."

"You aren't happy with me, are you?"

"Not really – but I guess you got your reasons."

"Hootie," Clint paused. "If we can't talk, then we can't work together. What's on your mind?"

"Ok. Why did we quit now? I've never known you to quit early on anything. We still had most of two weeks left. Now, I'm having to send people home."

"Because I don't think we are going to get through – and I don't have two weeks to keep trying. Something has to happen sooner than that."

"Why sooner?"

"I can't say – except to tell you Wilson Howlett is dying – maybe real soon."

"Wilson?" Hootie was surprised. "I knew he was old and sick. But dying?"

"Yeah. He's been sick a long time – totally out of it. There's a problem with Nobles, and TJ needs a well to produce as soon as possible. I've got to do what I can to make it happen."

"Why, boss? How is quitting this job going to help that? Besides, look, it's not your problem. Even if Wilson dies, TJ will inherit the company. He's been running the damned thing for the past year. I don't see no difference."

"I can't tell you things I was told in confidence, Hootie, but, there is a difference – or will be. We got shut down by the Rangers, so we don't have any options here. We've got to cap this well or go to jail. So if we're going to find oil, it's got to be Dilley #1. That's all we've got left."

"Is that where the stuff in the box comes in?"

"Yeah." Clint told a little about Elmer Pawson's plan, and the dangers associated with it. "I'm gonna use it on #1 this week."

"Why are you doing this boss? That's a huge risk. Is it for the money?"

"Money?" Clint was disappointed Hootie would even ask. It must look that way. "Money?" he spat the word out as if it had a bad taste. Neither man said anything for what seemed like minutes. 'Hell, he told me to say what was on my mind,' Hootie thought. They sat in silence. When Clint spoke, it was in a calm, even voice. "I guess it seems like that to you. But, no. It's not for the money." He paused and gathered his thoughts. "Hootie, when I was around your age, I was a lot like you. You remind me of me back then. I was a hard worker. I could get men to work, and be happy about it. I was even funny once – like you are. You're a good man, Hootie. Better'n me in some ways." Clint's eyes turned as he gazed out the window. "But way back before that, before I became a lead, when I first started out, I didn't have nothin'. I didn't have a pot to piss in. I was seventeen years old. I was a go-nowhere, know-nothing roughneck, full of piss and vinegar! I was in it for the money then, and the women, AND the booze. I got fired off more jobs than I can remember. Gambling, fighting, drinking – you name it – I did it. It got to where no one wanted to hire me, and if they did, no one wanted to work with me. I'd knock you on your ass for no reason at all. It wasn't pretty. I was angry all the time. I went through women like they were Crown Royal – and I went through a bottle of that every day."

"Then I met TJ." Clint seemed so far away in his thoughts, Hootie was not sure he was still talking to him or rambling to himself. "Old TJ." Another hesitation lasted for several seconds, "You know, TJ don't have any sons. And I didn't have a dad to speak of – he left when I was just a kid. I heard he got killed in a roll-over out in some oil field somewhere. Mom died soon after that. Grandma did the best she could. I came up hard, and didn't even finish high school. When TJ came along, he saw something in me – I don't know what. Whatever it was, he talked to me about stuff. I don't know. Stuff I can't even remember. Like, how a man ought to live, and treat his friends. He didn't preach, he just kept talking about things like responsibility and getting the job done right. He used the word 'pride' a lot. He put up with all my crap, and cleaned up all the things I messed up. But somehow, somewhere along the line – I didn't even realize it at the time – he taught me how to act. How I ought to be. I didn't have to be the roughest neck on the job. He told me I had a brain, and he wanted me to use it. Use it to figure out problems and come up with solutions, not excuses. He sent me to school – paid for it himself and gave me time off to do

it. He didn't want me to just bust my way through like I
had been doing. He taught me to value people, because
unless I was going to get out and hump it myself, I was
going to need other people to do the heavy work. I
hadn't ever thought of it that way before. But, it made
sense. Things like that. I don't know why, but he had
confidence in me – and he kept putting me in charge of
crews and jobs. He never let me down. Not even once.
Even when I was wrong, and messed up. Which I did a
lot! He showed me how to do it right the next time."

Clint looked at Hootie again. "Finally, I became
a shift lead. Like you. Then after a few years, I became a
foreman. Now I'm a project manager for a big oil
company. Project Manager. They pay me plenty – I
can't even spend it all. No. It's not about the money. It's
for … him, I guess. He's the only person on this planet
who ever showed any interest in me, or ever gave me a
chance in this life. I'd wade a river of crap for that man
– and he knows it – damn him! So you go on over to
Dilley Chalk # 1, and do what I told you to do. Don't
ask why. This ain't the time. Just do it … do it for me.
Ok?"

Hootie realized that he was to Clint what Clint
was to TJ. It pleased him somehow. "Sure. Whatever
you say, boss." Hootie rose from his chair.

Clint smiled. "I knew I could count on you.
That's why, when we get a new well, I'm making you
my foreman."

"Thanks! I appreciate that, Clint." Hootie smiled
and reached for the handle of the door.

"Hootie?" Hootie turned back toward the desk.
Clint's whole demeanor had changed, and Clint was
back to being Clint again. The soap opera was over.

"You don't work for HNH anymore."

"You're firing me, Clint?"

"No! You just don't work for HNH anymore – you work for Rio Frio now."

Hootie showed his surprise. "What? I do? I thought they were washed up. Who owns Rio Frio?"

Clint slowly nodded his head, "I do."

Sara sat in the hospital room, as near Cody's bed as possible. She was determined to be close by when he awoke. Cody had spent a peaceful night, and although he was not conscious, Sara was grateful he did not seem to be in pain. As the morning sun streamed through the window, Sara realized she had not eaten since the day before. The nurse told her she might as well eat Cody's breakfast, since they were going to bring a tray anyway. Sara picked at the tasteless scrambled eggs, and wrapped the bacon in toast. It was turkey bacon.

Around ten, Dr. Bryan stopped by and checked on Cody's condition. Sara had some questions. "Is my son going to be ok?"

Dr. Bryan sat beside her in a visitor's chair. The doctor reached out and gently placed his hand over hers. Sara tried to hide the odd tingle she felt. "Ms. Hughes. I'd love to be able to give you some assurance – I truly would. But we just don't know. The fact Cody has remained unconscious for so long is not a good sign. However, his brain waves are in the normal range. We don't think there has been any permanent brain damage, but no one can say for sure what the effects will be once he regains consciousness. Personally, I think he has a good chance, but I can't make any promises. There is just so much we don't know about these kinds of injuries."

"What can we do? Do we have any options?"

Dr. Bryan let go of her hand and stood, "I think the best option is what we have been doing. Waiting for Cody. The body is amazing, Ms. Hughes. It has this unbelievable capacity to heal itself sometimes."

"You can call me Sara."

"Thank you, Sara. You can call me Dr. Bryan." His smile was charming.

They laughed together at the joke. It broke the tension and made Sara feel better. "Shall I call you, Representative Hughes?" he asked.

"No. That's not necessary. Sara will be fine."

"Thank you" a sly grin crept across his face. "You still have to call me Dr. Bryan." They laughed again, a little harder this time. "Just kidding. I'm Colton," he grinned and stretched out his hand again. With trembling fingers, Sara took it. She could not help but think he was cute. She noted there was no wedding ring on his left hand. For the first time since Frank died, Sara felt comfortable with a man not named Pokey. She felt that if anyone could help Cody it would be Dr. Bryan. "Sara, as I said, I think Cody is going to be ok. Meanwhile, we just keep watching. If he shows any sign of breathing problems, or goes into any convulsions, get on that buzzer and ring for help quickly."

"I will. I'll be right here all the time," she said.

"I know you will." Dr. Bryan walked to the door and looked back. "If you need anything, I'm on call again tonight. If you have any questions, ask them to call me – anytime. I'm anxious for Cody too. We all want to help him."

After the doctor left, Sara felt better. She felt like Dr. Bryan really cared for Cody. She read all the literature found around the lobby about head injury and recovery. She read some patients in a coma could hear and understand, but they cannot respond. They called it a state of diminished consciousness instead of a coma. Sometimes caregivers used the term 'Locked-in Syndrome'. It meant the patient was 'locked in' himself, and could not respond, even though he may be aware of some things going on around him. She learned it is good to read to an unconscious patient. Talking, praying, singing – anything to stimulate them was good.

Before lunch, a hospital person came into the room, and announced herself as Cody's case manager. She asked many questions, and Sara wondered if this woman had even read Cody's charts; but she responded with the information she requested. She was a middle-aged woman, but she was not dressed in hospital attire – she wore a dress and had on nice shoes. She was professional, but not warm and friendly at all. Finally, the woman asked, "Does he have DNR orders?"

"I don't know. What are DNR orders?"

"Patient orders tell us what the patient's wishes are. Since he can't tell us, we need his parent or guardian to fill out the order. I'll leave them here for you to read, and sign if you want."

"What's DNR stand for?"

"Do Not Resuscitate. That tells us that the patient does not wish us to take any extreme measures to resuscitate him if it becomes necessary. No breathing machines, feeding tubes, or artificial life support. Sometimes patients can stay on life support for a very long time, and continue to suffer. Some patients do not want to live like that. If they cannot have a quality of life, some families prefer to just – let them go. Is that your wish?"

"Absolutely not!" Sara declared. "If you can save his life, you do it for as long as it is possible to do so. That is my son lying here! He has a name – it's Cody." Sara could hear her voice rising despite her effort to control the volume. "I don't care what you do – pray for a miracle from the Almighty, or deal with the devil; but you keep him alive any way you can – for as long as you can!"

The case manager left the room as Sara ranted on, "And, he can hear you!" she shouted. "Don't come back in this room with an attitude like that!" She sank into a chair and cried.

"We have to go back into the cave," Tom insisted.

"What do you mean, we have to?" Jesse said. "You want us to go back in a cave with a prehistoric monster in there?"

"I'm going too! I'm going with you." Tom urged.

"No way man!" Jake barked. "Have you ever been in a cave? Do you have any experience? Do you have any idea what to do in a cave?"

"No, but I'm fit and able. We have to go back in to find more evidence. Guys! This is the discovery of the century. Imagine. An extinct crocodile alive after all these years! You guys found it – you'll be famous."

Jake tried reason. "Professor Morrison, with all due respect, a cave is a dangerous place. We've already got one person laid up in the hospital. We don't need another. It's dark and cold and wet. You have to swim underwater just to get inside that cave. Then you have to wade through cold waist-deep water, and swim nearly a mile before you climb out on a dry surface."

Jesse paced the room as the discussion went back and forth. It was Jake's decision. As the senior caver with the most experience, Jake would be responsible if anything happened to Tom. Jesse looked around and read the diplomas and pictures on Tom's bookcase, as Tom made his case.

"I know I seem old to you guys. But I'm in great shape. I ride 15 miles a day on my bike. I run marathons. I'm only ten years older than you guys anyway. And I can swim; really well."

"It's more than that," Jake countered. "There are ropes, deep pits, and tall rocks you have to climb. Narrow places you have to squeeze through. Claustrophobic places. Spiders and centipedes, and stuff to make your skin crawl. And, there's the dark. It is so dark you can't see two feet sometimes. The passageways twist and turn, and you get confused about which way you came, and which way is out. The physical requirements are demanding, even if you are in shape."

Jesse picked a framed photograph from Tom's bookcase. Then another one. Jesse's mouth fell open. "Jake," he interrupted. "I think he can handle it."

Jake turned to Jesse with an exasperated look. "What?" he demanded.

Jesse passed the frames over to Jake. Jake looked at them, and shrugged. "Ok. You are on your own, man! If you get hurt, I'm not responsible. If you get crazy in there, we're calling it quits! If that thing tries to eat us, we quit and come out! Understand?"

"You're the boss," Tom agreed. "Just show me where the croc is. I'll take care of the rest."

Jake laid the picture frames side by side on Tom's desk. He studied the pictures again. One picture showed Professor Morrison with the Florida State University swim team. The other showed a picture of a shirtless Tom, wrestling a fifteen-foot alligator!

Chapter 10

"Just look at my nails!" Katie wailed.

Rita laughed, "What nails?" holding up her hands. "It's the price of climbing. If you want to do girly stuff, you can keep your nails and your fluffy hair, but" she paused, "you won't get this great view!" The girls looked off into the colorfully painted rises and valleys, which give the Hill Country its name. It is gorgeous in the springtime above Echo Canyon.

"That's not all you have to give up!" Katie moaned. "I haven't had a date in weeks."

"Go into town tonight and get hooked up, if that's what you want!" Rita snapped. "Bob," stretching out the name, "is probably still on the RoofTop down on 6th Street," she laughed.

"No one, NO ONE, would pick me up with hands like these!" Katie inspected her fingers.

Rita ignored the complaints, knowing if Katie's foot ever slipped while her fingertips were crammed into a dime crack, it would jerk her nails off to the quick. Rita knew from experience it was a bloody mess. If you yank a nail off, you don't climb for a couple of days. Katie was better off not having nails. "Now look. This is Orange Peel. If you are going to climb Morning Glory in Colorado with us, you have to get past this level. It's rated 9.5, but most of us feel it is at least a 10.1. Either way, you must have several 10s under your belt to be able to climb Colorado with us. This is not an easy climb. It's rugged – but you can do it. I've seen you work; all you need is confidence. We didn't make it yesterday, but you learned a lot, so we're going to give it a go again. I'll be right here with you."

"You can get up this thing every time?"

"Free solo," Rita bragged. "But, that's me. I've been doing this a long time. If we can get you up a couple of times this afternoon, we'll take off the top rope, and you can try a free climb this evening if you want to. Then, you'll be ready to ascend False Determination tomorrow afternoon. A day early! But don't get ahead of yourself. Stay in your head. Work this cliff, not the next one."

Orange Peel got its name from the noticeably orange colored surface, probably from the iron impurities inside the mainly granite rock. Two routes, each bolted, lead toward the summit. After mounting a couple of large boulders at the base, a climber faces a long line of shallow finger cracks. Once you get half way up, you can find some flakes with some good handholds, giving your aching fingers some relief. Above that, you will reach the anchors where it is smooth sailing the rest of the way. The way Katie was climbing, with a top rope, the climb was less than a nine, but for a beginner the feel was amazing. If she did not use the anchor rope, Katie would be ready to try a free climb. Then her confidence might encourage her to try it solo, but Rita wanted Katie to have a few more assents before trying a solo attempt.

"Jam those beautiful fingernails into that crack up there!" Rita instructed like drill sergeant, smiling from below.

Sara finished the first section of "Paper Towns" and laid the book on the table next to her chair. It was a good read, but she sincerely hoped her son and his friends were not participating in the type of dirty, revenge behavior depicted in the book. Convinced her son could hear, Sara had been reading aloud. She thought he might like this book since it was popular with young adults, and it was soon to be a movie. It was not her type of reading though. At least she knew what a paper town was now. She made a mental note to ask her assistant to bring her laptop down from Austin. It looked like it was going to take longer for Cody to recover than she had thought. Looking at the hospital room, she tried to figure out how she could arrange it to do some work while waiting. Was there a Wi-Fi available?

One hundred and sixty-five miles away, in a similar room, Wilson Howlett was nearing the end of his long journey. TJ sat nearby watching his father sleeping. It seemed like he slept all the time now. Of all the people Wilson had known over the years, he now only recognized his wife and TJ. Wilson had a daughter, but she was so distant, and rarely visited. Before the disease stole his mind, Wilson's ability to recall names had been phenomenal. He knew the names of people he had not seen in years. He knew the first names of everyone who worked at HNH, and most of their spouses. Now, he could not tell you what he had eaten for breakfast. He was a smart old man, though. He had figured out a long time ago what was happening to him, so he managed to hide the memory loss as long as possible. He rarely used names, and everyone he saw was a friend. Up until last week, if anyone came into his room, Wilson would rise up and shake their hand, and say something like how

great it was to see them again. It worked mostly, except
when the visitor was someone new he had never met
before. The fake only went so far.

Wilson was not eating much. He seemed to be
having difficulty swallowing. The weight loss showed
on his small frame, reducing him to skin and bones. His
angular jaw jutted out even more than normal. He had
fine teeth, and they still flashed a brilliant, friendly smile
from time to time. Lately, Wilson had not been smiling
much. The doctor said if he did not eat, they might have
to consider installing a feeding tube. A few years earlier,
Wilson had forced TJ to promise he would never do that
to him. Now TJ would have to decide if he was going to
hold to his promise. After all, Wilson had coerced him,
hadn't he? Should you be held to a promise made under
duress?

Before he lost his ability to make informed
decisions, Wilson had signed the DNR order himself,
making it plainly clear he wanted to be as pain free as
possible in the final stages, but he did not want to be
"hooked up to those damned machines." He wanted to
die as he had lived – with dignity. TJ had not imagined
at the time how hard it would be to keep those promises.
His mother, Wilson's wife, Imogene, was a complete
basket case. TJ tried to keep her away as much as
possible because all she did was cry and wring her
hands. However, she had to visit sometimes, and when
she did, Wilson always seemed to perk up a little. It was
if he were trying to comfort her, instead of the other way
around. It was painful to watch. Wilson married
Imogene right out of high school, and she worked as a
waitress putting Wilson through engineering school.
Imogene never went back to school herself, electing to
stay home and raise TJ and his sister Anne. Despite
owning a huge oil business, and the long hours it

required, his wife was the highest priority in Wilson's life. He did not tell her everything because she worried so much, but he always told her the good things. Everything Wilson ever accomplished in his life, he attributed to his wife. He always claimed to have "married up." It was not true – her parents were low-life alcoholics. Nevertheless, Wilson always made her feel like she had enriched his life, and was the source of all of his success. It was mostly true.

After they had 'made it', life was easier for the whole family. Big houses, fancy cars, the best schools, and the highest of Houston society. Everyone liked Wilson. He was the epitome of a self-made Texas oilman. He was loyal to his life-long friend and partner, Phillip Nobles, and never once tried to cut him short. Their partnership had lasted sixty years – longer than some people's lives, and way longer than most marriages. The only thing Wilson had kept from Phillip was the advancing disease that was erasing his memory. To Wilson, not changing his will was not the mistake TJ thought it was. Not changing the will was simply how a partner behaves. Had Phillip gone first, Wilson had no doubts in his mind that Nobles would have done the same. They had lived all their lives on the faith of that friendship, and Wilson was not going to break that trust here at the end. The way Wilson figured it, half of everything he owned was Phillip's, and vice versa. So his Last Will and Testament provided half of HNH would go to his partner Phillip Nobles, and the other half to his wife and son. TJ had tried to change his father's mind many times – always without success. No matter how many times Wilson had tried to explain it to his son, TJ could not understand it, which made the old man saddest above anything else he had known. It did not matter now. Wilson was way past caring about such things.

TJ went into the hall and dialed Clint's number. "How is it looking out there?"

"Well, you know, the Rangers shut down number two. We're pulling the bit and capping it off. Hugh left for Oklahoma. All crews are on standby."

"Standby for what?"

"Number one." Clint lowered his voice. "The permit hasn't run out on number one yet."

"You are going back to number one?"

"I don't see what choice we have, TJ. It's all we've got. How's Wilson?"

"Worse. I think he's only got a few weeks. He's near the end."

"I'm so sorry, TJ. He's a good man. How's your mom?"

"You know Imogene." TJ sighed. "She can barely look at him without crying. He still remembers her – and me. If it gets so bad he can't remember her, it will break her heart. I'm not sure about Anne; she isn't here much. He's rarely awake these days. He's shutting down, Clint. What's your plan?"

Clint chose his words carefully, "I'll do it tomorrow morning."

After ringing off, TJ placed his phone in his pocket, and re-entered the room. Wilson was awake. He carefully took his father's wrinkled hand and kissed it as he whispered, "Hang in there, Dad. It's going to be ok in a few days – you'll see."

Tom had not imagined how hard it would be to get into Honey Creek Cave. They had said it was an effort, but Tom had imagined it would be simpler to get inside than it was. The dive and short swim were no problem but he had underrated the dark and cold. He wondered what else he had misjudged. Jesse and Jake were already in by the time he burst out of the water.

As they waded along the tunnel to the first ledge where they could crawl onto dry rock, Tom decided this was a good time for an alligator primer. "Let's go over some information on crocodiles and alligators, guys. First, this is no longer a cave exploration. We are looking for the croc – a big one! If we find it, you need to know some things."

"Stay well away from the tail. It is extremely heavy and the croc can move it like a feather. If he can club you with that tail, it'll try. It's extremely tough and muscular. That tail can break your arm or legs with one swipe. It has more than a ninety-degree swing to either side. So stay at least a tail's length away from its side."

"How are we going to find it?" Jake wondered aloud.

"It'll find us. Crocs hunt by lying in wait for its prey. We can spot it with a strong light. Do you remember that video clip on your iPad? Some animal eyes have a layer, called *tapetum lucidum* behind the retina, which contains crystals that reflect light. It helps their night vision. A lot of other animals have it – deer, cats, dogs, and the like. Not all do. Humans don't, and neither do horses or pigs. Sometimes human's do get red eye in photos, but it is not the same. If you notice in human red-eye photos, only the pupils are red. When you shine a light, a crocodile's eyes glow like little red coals from a fire. If you only see one red dot, the alligator is not facing you. If you see two, it's looking right at you. If you see four, two-on-top-of-two, then it's probably a reflection off the water. If they are lying side-by-side, it can look like eight pairs! If the light is off to one side or the other, or it isn't looking your direction, you won't see the glow at all."

"Its eyes, nose and ears are high on the snout. They can swim nearly submerged, yet they can still hear, see, and breathe. Modern gators are the world's largest reptilian predators. This one is gargantuan – three or four times larger than the largest ones around these days. A normal croc can swim nearly twenty-five miles an hour. When it submerges, a clear membrane slides over the eyes – like swimming goggles."

"When a croc attacks, it explodes out of the water, propelled by a powerful tail and their hind legs. While you are stunned, they grab you and try to drag you into the water so they can drown you. Once they have you beneath the water, they may go into their death roll. These are dangerous killers. Just ask the two hundred people they kill every year! They don't necessarily go after humans, but they will eat anything if given the opportunity."

"They are known to be fiercely territorial. They are the king of their habitat, and they will attack if they feel threatened – especially during mating season. They even eat cattle. Those in Africa attack and kill hundreds of migrating wildebeests every season. They have no natural enemies except man."

Jesse had a sudden thought, "Mating season? You mean there may be more than one of these things down here?"

Tom smiled, "Maybe."

"Oh, hell no!" barked Jake.

"Well, I don't think this one is over a million years old. Do you?" Tom reasoned. "Who knows? They reproduce somehow. Science has recently discovered Komodo dragons and Monitor lizards can self-reproduce. Parthenogenesis is possible in reptiles; and this gator is a reptile." Tom looked around in the dim light. "Do we ever get out of this water?"

"We're almost to the place where we can climb out," Jesse answered. "They can have babies without mating? How does that even happen?"

"Plenty of species do. It's fairly common. The list is pretty long; whiptail lizards, aphids, gall wasps, all kinds of crustaceans, worms, and many reptiles and snakes – even some birds, and honey bees!"

"Honey bees?" Jake chortled. "You mean the birds and the bees talk isn't true?"

"Honey bees do not have sex." Tom chuckled.

"What else do we need to know?"

"If it comes at you – run! Do not run in a zigzag pattern like you may have heard. Run as straight and fast and as far as you can. They have powerful legs and are surprisingly fast. But they won't pursue you far. Just don't run toward water. You are no match for the animal in water."

"If you get grabbed in the water, or if it pulls you in there, you can do some things to improve your chances. If you're not already dead, then it is going to try to drag you into deeper water to drown you. If you can keep your head and think, you may be able to survive. Don't fight to try to open the mouth – you probably couldn't do it with a car jack. The jaw closes with a force of thirteen tons per square inch. Jaws of Life probably couldn't get you out. So don't waste your energy. His skin is so thick you're not going to pierce it, and the head is a solid mass of bone. Crocs only have a couple of weak spots."

"His teeth are mostly blunt, and used more for crushing than chewing. They can slice edgewise, or gnaw through skin and bone, but their preferred method is to rip. Once he gets you deep enough in the water to maneuver, it will probably start to roll. This is called the death roll." Tom paused for effect. "He will wrench you around trying to tear you against the force of your own weight, or against a rock or something. Do not resist, go with the roll as long as you can. You'll be underwater; you'll probably drown before he eats you."

"There's nothing you can do?" Jesse asked.

"Very little. Keep your head, and be aware of what is happening. Be ready to act fast. Sometimes, it may let go for a moment. Get as far away as quickly as possible. If you do what I told you, there is a good chance he will open his jaws for a few seconds. Maybe to get a better grip. Get out and get something between you and it if you can. Find somewhere small to crawl into – small enough it can't reach you. That roll takes a lot out of them. It uses a lot of energy and stamina, and they'll lay back a little while to regain strength. If you move fast enough you might escape."

"All the while you are in his grip, keep wailing on his head and snout as hard and as often as you can. Use anything you have, your fists, poles, a knife, or a rock – anything you can lay your hands on. Concentrate your attack on the head and eyes. On top of the snout are his nostrils; called a bulla. It's pretty tough and gators don't like you to mess with it. That's why they spend so much time with their eyes and snout above the water. They like to keep it dry. The bulla cavity is part of the olfactory system, which we believe they use to emit vibrations and noises. Some scientists think they also use it to detect minute vibrations in the air and water around them, giving them the ability to detect if other creatures are nearby. Get your fingers, hand, or anything sharp inside the area around the bulla. Rip it or tear it, if you can. If you have a knife, go to town on it and the eyes. No knife, then use your hands, a stick, anything handy. If you can get your finger in his eye socket, and make him uncomfortable enough, he will let go and back off. Use the time to get away. Gators will sometimes lose interest if you are too much work."

"If you have an arm inside his gullet, you have an excellent chance of getting away. Crocs have a flap of tissue behind the tongue covering their throat. The flap closes when they dive, and keeps the throat clear of water. If you can, reach inside and push the flap in. Water will flood into the gator's lungs, and the mouth will open long enough for you to reach the surface. Pushing in that flap may be your only and last chance to get away. Be ready to swim in the opposite direction when you can, because he will be back. Especially if he is hungry. They only eat once a week or so.

"Is this a croc or an alligator? You keep using both words." Jesse asked.

"I won't know until I see it up close. Alligators have a u-shaped snout, and crocs are more pointed. You can see a croc's teeth from the side, not usually so with a gator. Anyway, it doesn't matter much – either one can kill you. If you don't fight back – you're dead!"

Chapter 11

Clint rolled into Dilly Chalk #1 early, as the sky was turning pink. Pre-dawn fog draped the dew-laden fields. Little yellow halos encircled the rig lights. No one was around. He pulled an unmarked cardboard box from his back seat and carried it into the corrugated steel maintenance shed. He slid closed the dead bolt, locking the door from the inside. Even in the cool morning, it was hot and stale inside the shed. It smelled of pump oil and earth. He jerked a string dangling from a bare lightbulb hanging from the ceiling on an electric wire wrapped with many layers of black electrical tape. The light was dim, but he could see Chango's wooden box resting on a table in the center of the room. Strange shadows danced across the room, as the naked bulb wobbled back and forth. He levered up the cover of the box with a screwdriver. Inside was a square aluminum briefcase with rolling combination locks. He placed the case on the table, and put the wooden box on the floor at his feet. The combination was the last four numbers of his cell phone; the locks snapped open when he pushed the button.

Inside were two, canister-like tubes, about 10-inches long. They were about 8-inches in diameter with flat bottoms and tightly fitted tops. He pried open another wooden box and inside he found two square, metal tubs. The tubs were army olive drab green, with lids on top to be pried open like cocoa cans. Clint gathered other materials from various shelves and boxes, and lined everything up on the table. He mentally inventoried the supplies, and went over in his mind the sequence he would follow over the next few minutes. There was no margin for error. When everything was in place, Clint pulled open the canister tops. They made a satisfying "whomp" as he pulled each lid free. The tubes were empty and clean inside.

Clint stood the canisters upright on their flat bottoms. He wrapped long, sand socks around the bases, so they would not tip over. With a red magic marker, he marked one tube with a number one and marked the other with a two. He placed a plastic funnel into the open mouth of canister number one. He read the black, stenciled label of one green tub, and placed it back on the table. Taking the other tub, he read the label, and carefully cracked open the lid with the screwdriver. He poured about half of the contents into canister number one. He emptied the remainder of the granular grey substance into canister number two.

Clint's cell phone suddenly buzzed and vibrated. Clint nearly climbed out of his skin! He had forgotten to turn his phone off! He stumbled to the farthest corner of the shed, tripping over the wooden box as he retreated from the table. Hootie's grinning face appeared on his phone screen. With cold sweat on his brow, he answered the phone before it could ring again. "Hootie! Damn it!"

"Bad timing, boss?"

"Sort of!" Clint wiped his brow with the back of his wrist. He felt like he was having a heart attack. "Phone scared the hell out of me, that's all! Everything in place?" he huffed.

"Yep." Hootie ticked off the steps. "Finished the work order yesterday afternoon; well head and injection port installed, bit reinserted and in place. Pumps primed, fire suppression unit charged, and air tanks full. You have a clean, dry hole. Crew's on standby in the area until further notice."

"Good. Now … I want you here in thirty minutes. I've got some work for you to do. Come alone," Clint repeated. "Alone. After you finish, I want you to make yourself scarce for the rest of the morning. Be ready to get the crew together this afternoon if I call. I'll need everyone to get out here as quickly as possible and start pumping oil. If I don't call, don't do anything. Got it?"

"Got it."

"And whatever you do, don't call me back for the next few minutes! If you need anything, save it 'til you get here!" Clint switched his phone off, and put it in airplane mode before returning to the table.

He opened a zip-lock bag of white powder, and read the label. He carefully poured half the baggie into each tube. Then, with a screwdriver, he pried open the remaining green, metal tub. Using a small scoop, with shaking hands, he carefully and deliberately scooped out the dark, granular substance, and placed it gently into the mouth of each canister. Clint worked slowly and methodically, taking care not to bump anything. When the tub was empty, he put the lid back on it and placed both tubs back into the wooden box. His shirt was soaked in sweat. He suddenly remembered something he had forgotten. He carefully inspected the outside of the wooden box, looking for writing or numbers on the outside. He used black spray paint to cover any identifying marks he found.

He removed a tubular Styrofoam florist block from a paper bag. The green foam was slightly larger than the diameter of the canisters. He sliced off two, 2-

inch discs from one end of the foam tube. With an awl punch, he bored a small hole through the center of each disc, and threaded a string fuse through each. He carefully inserted the threaded discs into each nearly full aluminum tube. He looked inside each tube. There was about three inches left in the top of each canister. He pushed the Styrofoam discs firmly inside, hearing them squeak against the aluminum sides. He inserted a spring lock in each to keep anything from moving.

He fished two key fobs with buttons from the cardboard box, along with two ignition devices commonly used to ignite gas bar-b-que grills. He unlocked the shed door, walked over to his truck, and lowered the tailgate. Placing the ignition switches on the tailgate, he clicked the red button on one of the key fobs. One ignition switch clicked and emitted a white spark. He made a red X with the magic marker on the matching switch, and on the correct key fob. Finally, he tested the other key fob to make sure it activated the other switch.

Satisfied that he had identified the correct switches and fobs, he placed the marked key fob into the glove compartment of his truck and locked the door. Then he carried everything else back into the shed. He placed the unmarked key fob into a hard, square plastic package, and placed it inside the fitted aluminum briefcase. Then he screwed the marked switch to the spring clip in canister number one, and threaded the fuse. He attached the unmarked switch and fuse into tube number two. Finally, he packed any remaining space in each canister with dry kitty litter. He filled each to the brim, and carefully slid the fitted lids back on. He placed canister number two into its nest inside the aluminum briefcase with the unmarked key fob. He closed and locked the case. He placed tube number one on its side on a shelf along the shed wall, and blocked it so it would not roll. He gathered the empty packages, bags and containers, and placed everything into the wooden box. After nailing the lid shut, he placed it on his tailgate outside along with the locked aluminum case.

When Hootie arrived, Clint went over the instructions. "That wooden box should never be found again," he said pointedly. "Don't burn it, and don't throw it into any water. Get rid of it, and don't tell me where. Best way would be to bury it deep; somewhere out in the brush." Hootie nodded. "And that locking aluminum case? I want you to hide it too – somewhere closer. Somewhere you can put your hands on it really fast, if I need it. Wrap it in a garbage bag and bury it in a different location from where you got rid of the box. Make sure no one will be able to find it and dig it up. Remember where you buried it. If I need it, I'll ask you to go get it for me. So hide it somewhere you won't forget. DO NOT keep it in your truck – bury it! Understand?"

Hootie nodded. "What's in there?"

"Damn it, Hootie! Sometimes you ask too many questions. All right … What is in there? You want to know? Follow me." Clint turned and led Hottie back into the shed. Clint shined his flashlight on the smooth, aluminum cylinder lying on the shelf. "What's in the briefcase is another one exactly like this one," Clint said. "That and a remote control key fob, with a red button on it. It looks like the key fob you use to unlock your truck. Combination on the case is the same as the last four numbers of my cell phone. Whatever you do, whatever happens; do not push the red button within a hundred yards of that cylinder! You understand?"

"It'll blow up, huh?"

"No," Clint slowly shook his head. "It won't blow up. It'll get real hot, though – hotter than anything you've ever seen. Ten times hotter than a blowtorch or a welding rod. It will burn right through the steel floorboard of your truck, and then make glass out of the sand underneath. It'll keep burning until your gas tank blows! If you are too close when it goes off, it'll incinerate your clothes, boil the flesh right off your body, and set your bones on fire. Do not push the red button!"

"This is where Cody was hurt!" Jesse pointed toward the black pool edged against the rough cavern wall.

Tom peered into the murky pool. He could not see the bottom. "How deep is it?"

Not too deep right here," Jake assured him. "It comes to about the middle of your chest.

"There is an underwater tunnel down there that leads to the other side of the wall?" Tom asked.

"Yes. That's where we sent the boat and where we found the hide."

Tom splashed into the cold water holding the edge of the rock. "Feel around with your feet over against the wall, and you'll find the passage," Jake urged. Tom groped around under the surface with his feet until he found the depression. He dove to look at the opening, and felt along rough rock with his hands until he had to surface for air. He slung his head around to shake water from his face and hair and asked, "How far to the other side?"

"About fifteen feet."

Tom pulled himself from the water and sat next to Jesse. "Ok. I want to go over. Pull out one of those GoPro cameras and rig it to the tablet. Be sure to turn on the microphone this time."

Jake recommended, "I think we need to keep one of us on this side to pull us back through if we get in trouble. Jesse, you stay here and monitor the tablet. Tom and I will go over. If you have to pull us through, do it from here; be careful not to get pulled into the wall."

Tom rigged the camera and strapped on a headlight. They tied a safety line around their waists. They waited until Jesse had secured the free ends of their ropes to a rock across from the pool. Tom packed two more cameras in a waterproof bag, and he and Jake dove beneath the surface and swam to the other side. Jesse watched as the scene unfolded on the flickering tablet screen. At first, he could see nothing, but eventually he saw their lights slice through the darkness on the screen. They were on the other side. Jesse waited. The sound was on, and he could hear their conversation. The sound of splashing and their voices echoed from the walls.

They moved around the edge to measure the size of the pool. They stayed together, and moved slowly. They stopped at a place where the water disappeared into a large tunnel nearly twenty feet wide. Crossing the inlet, they continued their circuit. Several feet further, they came to another lead nearly as wide, but this one dry. Taking note of it, they completed their lap around the room, arriving at their starting place.

"Jesse! Can you hear me?" No response. They called several times until Tom realized even though

Jesse could probably hear them through the recorder, he had no way to respond. Tom told Jesse, "If you can hear me pull twice on my rope." After receiving two tugs, Tom said, "OK. Jesse, leave the ropes tied to that rock, and swim over to this side. Bring your gear." Jesse placed the tablet into a dry bag, and after securing a safety line to himself, swam through the tunnel. He drug his equipment bag behind him.

Reaching the other side, he surfaced within a few feet of the others. They untied their lines from their belts and tied them to an extending rock near the underwater tunnel. Then Jake stopped the recording, and saved the file. He immediately started recording a new video. "We are going to check the water tunnel first," Tom decided. They attached new safety lines, and moved into the entrance of the large wet tunnel, disappearing into the darkness. Tom looked at Jake. "Have you been in here before?" Receiving a negative response, Tom made a plan. "We'll leave Jesse here again with the ends of our ropes. If we have to come out fast through the water, he can pull us along. If the croc is behind us, we'll need to head for the small tunnel back to the other side and safety. The croc obviously can't fit through that narrow opening." Jesse stood with cold water up to his hips in the dark, holding the safety ropes as the two disappeared into the gloomy, dark passageway.

Jesse yawned as he watched the small tablet screen, as it recorded their journey through the large, watery passage. At some point along the way, the two climbed out of the water onto a dry floor. It was faster going then, and the camera moved through the dark chamber's twists and turns. Jesse flashed his light along the cave walls, and noted a small ledge jutting out from the wall, some ten feet above the water. Jesse tied the lead lines to a heavy rock, and climbed the face of the cavern wall to the ledge. It was dry up there, and large enough for Jesse to lie down.

Jake and Tom moved as quickly as they could through the main tunnel. Other leads of varying sizes went off in all directions along the way, but they ignored the side tunnels. They soon came to a rock wall at the end of the tunnel. "End of the line," Jake noted. "It happens like this sometimes. You find a promising lead, and then it just peters out."

"What about those side tunnels?"

"None of them charted," Jake shook his head. "No telling where they go. They might go for miles, or they might end in a couple of feet. There is no way of telling without going in. Most of them looked pretty tame. You have to be careful in these unknowns. It's easy to stumble into a fifty-foot drop-off in the dark. Even a pothole can break your leg. First time in, you have to go slow – like we did on this one. What now?"

"Mark the location of those side leads on the way out so we can look at them later. For now, let's go back and try the dry passage." They turned around and made their way back along the dark tunnel. A couple of times they stopped and lit the inside of a promising passage, but did not go inside any. Jake made notes of each one as they passed. Rounding a corner in the gloom, they found their passage blocked. A wet, glimmering wall of rock filled the entire passage, and kept them from going any farther.

Tom was confused. "Did we take a wrong turn?"

"No way!" Jake assured him eying the wall. "This is the way we came. We didn't pass any lead larger than this one." He scratched his head. "I don't get it. This has to be the way we came in. Why is it wet?"

"Maybe something fell and blocked the path while we were at the other end? A cave-in?"

"No. We would have heard that."

"Then what?"

"I don't know. I've never had anything like this happen before," Jake laughed.

Suddenly, the glistening wall swelled and slowly slid right a few inches! Their eyes widened in fear and shock as they became aware of what they were seeing. The wall was alive! Tom grabbed Jake's arm as he croaked in a raspy whisper, "Quiet! That's it! We found the croc!"

They watched in disbelief and horror as the crock slowly oozed to their right. As it moved, it made a scraping, dragging sound. Tom snapped pictures. The sudden flash of light in the dark cave blinded them both.

"Stop! You'll ruin our night vision!" Jake whispered.

Tom ignored him and kept taking pictures as the tail drug past. The croc slid by until only the middle part of its tail remained in the passageway. Even then, it was about four feet high. Realizing their chance, they unhooked their safety lines and scrambled over the fleshy wall. "It doesn't have room to bat us with it!" Tom yelled to Jake. They ran as fast as they could through the corridor, knowing the tunnel was too narrow for the croc to turn around. Jake knew the croc might come back in ahead of them if it found a loop. After a few yards, Tom turned and snapped more pictures. Jake ran on. Not wanting to be alone in the tunnel, Tom hurried to catch up with the fleeing youth.

High on the ledge, Jesse watched the two explore the cave on the tiny screen. He saw them reach the end, and turn around. He watched as they checked out a few side leads. His mind drifted to Rita. He thought over the good and bad of transferring to UTSA. Why couldn't she transfer to Texas State? Sudden yelling drew his attention back to the iPod screen. He could not believe his eyes when he saw a solid wall of rock moving. What the heck was that? He saw bright flashes as the camera popped off inside the tunnel, and heard the sounds of running. They must have found the croc! The sounds of their running were getting closer. Almost immediately, a shrieking Jake erupted from the tunnel in a panic, and dove into the water, swimming for the safety of the other side. Where was Tom? Jesse looked at the screen, which had now turned blank. He started to jump from the ledge into the water, when Tom suddenly emerged from the tunnel. He was not yelling, but he was obviously in a hurry. Tom quickly jumped into the water and swam for the other side. Not knowing if the croc was close behind them, Jesse decided to stay where he was for a moment. The crock could burst through the tunnel any second. Jake and Tom had escaped through the narrow underwater tunnel.

After several minutes, the monster did not appear, and no further sounds came from the dark tunnel. Jesse decided he should try to join the others, who were probably wondering what had happened to him. He slowly climbed from the wall, and gingerly entered the water. His body had to adjust to the cold all over again. Then he waded with heavy, plodding steps through the chest-deep water. He had almost reached the underwater passage, when the water behind him began to behave strangely. It wasn't bubbles, exactly. Jesse turned to look, and was mesmerized by the sight. It was amazing and beautiful. It looked like little balls of water bouncing off the surface – bouncing like popcorn. Was it an underground heat vent, boiling the water? He reached out to see if the water was hot. It was not. Where had he had seen this before – where? On television – National Geographic! The realization suddenly struck him like a slap in the face. Alligators can make the water dance! Fear gripped him like a vice and his blood turned cold. The croc was in the water with him! Slowly and carefully, he moved closer to the escape tunnel. Taking care not to splash, he moved as slowly as he could. He peered into the blackness looking for the safety ropes. He felt a sudden strong current sweep against his feet. Something huge moved beneath the water nearby. Calculating where he thought the tunnel was, he suddenly dove and swam as hard as he could for the tunnel. He missed the opening, and bumped his head hard on the rock wall, nearly knocking himself out. Shaking off the impact, he surfaced. He shook his head to clear his vision, and saw the safety rope nearby. Quickly untying it, he hooked it to his belt, gave the line two large yanks, and blacked out.

Chapter 12

Katie was on the last leg of the False Determination ascent when she felt herself begin to slide off the mountain. She knew she had to break the slide or she would be in big trouble. She knew an anchored safety line ran next to her, but if she touched it – if Rita even saw her look at it – she would have to start the climb all over again. The entire morning would have been lost. Remembering her training, she hugged the mountain and spread her arms and legs as wide as possible, flaring out, searching for some purchase on the rock face. She knew Rita, fifteen feet below her on the sheer face, would not miss the fact she was slipping. Katie believed she could recover without hooking her caribiner to the safety line. She did not want to let go of her tenuous hold on the cliff to find her descender line, still thinking she could recover. Her foot caught briefly, then slipped from a flake; it barely slowed her descent. She tried edging her shoes, but they slipped on the smooth rock. Katie realized she was in trouble. She grabbed for a safety nut as she went sliding by, but her hand slipped off the metal protection. She searched desperately for a hold, and found none. She was sliding off the mountain, and gaining momentum.

Below and to Katie's left, gravel and flakes of dirt from above pelted Rita. She heard the unmistakable rubbing sound, and immediately realized Katie was in an uncontrolled descent. She looked up and believed Katie had a good chance to recover. There were at least three safeties between them. Rita looked down and realized a fail from where they were located on the cliff would be

fatal. There was nothing below to catch or break her fall.
They were on a small bubble on the side of Enchanted
Rock. Beyond the hump, the cliff curved sharply back
under a few degrees. Small pieces of rock bounced off
Rita's shaded glasses. Still, if Katie were able to get out
of this difficulty, it would be good training.
Automatically Rita called out the locations of the three
safeties. More and more gravel fell on her helmet.
Instinctively, Rita moved to her right to be close enough
to assist Katie if she slid past her position. She braced
herself on the wall near a climbing nut, and hooked her
caribiner to the safety line. Rita had her left foot on a
small ledge that felt solid enough as long as it did not
flake off. Rita located a purple hex inserted into a small
crack to her left and cranked on it as hard as she could.
It held. When she looked again, Katie was trying to
smear, but the momentum of the slide was overcoming
the friction. This was going to be an epic fail; Rita
realized Katie was sliding too fast now to recover; she
would have to use a safety.

"Grab the safety," she yelled as loudly as she
could. She saw Katie grab for the safety line with her
bare hand, and miss catching hold. "Hook on! Grab your
descender!" Rita desperately screamed. She saw Katie
finally grab the line with her left hand. Rita could see
the safety line feeding through Katie's fist, coming out
bloody as the rope slid through her palm. "Descender!
Get your 8 on it!" she shrieked. Katie panicked, and
scrambled to grab on to anything she could reach.
Because of momentum, Katie could not get her free
hand over to the safety rope. She picked up speed as she
slid farther down the rock. It was happening so fast.
Everything was in slow motion; like a sports channel
replay.

In a reflex to the white-hot pain in her palm, Katie made an epic mistake and let go of the safety rope. Big mistake. Blood was dripping from her hand. The rope had cut through her taped palms, and blood was running down her arm onto her shoulder. Katie reached for the safety line again, but now her hand was so slick with blood she could not possibly hold on. She fumbled for the descender hanging from her equipment belt.

Katie's feet were already at Rita's head, when Rita checked her safety once more. Rita jammed her right foot as far into a crack as possible. She installed a figure 8 below her knees, and attached a caribiner. If she were quick enough, she could latch the caribiner to Katie's harness as she slid by. Not having time to clip on to the purple hex, Rita stuck her left hand through the steel cable loop. With her right hand, she reached for Katie's equipment belt as she skidded by. Missed. Rita grabbed for Katie's shirtsleeve, but she was out of reach. Rita missed Katie's hand. Rita could see the look of fear in Katie's eyes as she slid past. Katie was seconds from death. In a last desperate attempt, Rita lunged out as far as she could reach and grabbed anything she could grab. At the last moment, Rita felt her fist close on Katie's hair. Katie's helmet went flying into the deep canyon. Rita held on as hard as she could. The wire loop on the hex cut into Rita's wrist, but the purple nut was holding. Rita looked down her extended, aching arm. Katie was swinging by her ponytail, like a circus act, two hundred feet above the canyon floor.

Jake burst to the surface on the safe side of the wall. He spat water and wiped his face, and leaned against the rocks to rest. He pulled himself out of the water and tried to calm down as his chest heaved. His legs shook uncontrollably as he sat on the cold rock. Tom surfaced nearby, and tossed his head to clear the water from his hair and face, as if he were an Olympic diver on TV. Jake imagined Tom had practiced a long time on that move to get it right. Image; even in the face of death!

Tom pulled himself out of the water with his forearms bulging. He twisted around, and sat on the edge of the rim. He coughed and looked around the dimly lit chamber. "Where's Jesse?" Jake looked around the room. Jesse was not anywhere in sight. The realization struck simultaneously. "He must still be on the other side!"

Jake moved quickly to the ropes, and snatched one to check for tension on the line. "Check the other ones," he yelled at Tom.

Tom tugged on the other ropes. Suddenly one of the ropes jerked twice. 'Hey!" he called, "I just got two tugs on this one."

"It's Jesse! Pull hard. Pull him through the hole!" Jake yelled, as he scuttled over to help. Something heavy was on the end of the line. "Keep pulling!"

Lengths of wet line slid from the water and looped in limp, tangled coils on the ledge. Once or twice, the rope hung on something, and they pulled hard to free it. After several seconds, Jesse's body emerged from the hole. Jesse's body was limp and motionless. He sank immediately as they stopped pulling. Jake jumped into the pool, and pulled Jesse to the surface. They heaved him out of the water onto the flat, rock floor of the cave. Jesse's lips were dark purple, and his skin had a bluish cast. He was not conscious, and he was not breathing. Blood seeped across his face from a deep gash on the crown of his head. "He's shut down!" Tom yelled. "His airway has closed by drowning reflex. Maybe he didn't breathe too much water." Tom moved to Jesse's head and placed his lips on Jesse's mouth. He blew hard five times. "You have to blow hard to open the larynx," he explained. Tom turned Jesse's head to the side after each breath. Huge amounts of water gushed out. Chest compressions came next, and water spurted from Jesse's mouth with every deep thrust. Tom blew into Jesse's mouth a few more times, and went back to the compressions again. The water coming out of Jesse became less and less. What came up now was vomit mixed with a frothy pink stuff like a melted strawberry smoothie.

Despite the vomit and the sticky mess on Jesse's face, Tom did not hesitate to put his mouth back to Jesse's lips. Jake noticed the breaths were quick, powerful, and compact. They were much faster than he thought they should be. None of this was as Jake thought it would be when he took first aid training. The whole thing was far more tense than he had ever imagined, and a lot messier. He blanched as the sight and smell of the vomit made him queasy. Tom was placing a lot of weight on Jesse's chest and abdomen, Jake could see his rib cage deflect under the pressure. Then, five more breaths.

After a few seconds, a moan bubbled out of Jesse's mouth, and his body convulsed and tensed. His legs kicked out spasmodically. Jesse coughed and spat more puke mixed with water. Tom stopped the CPR. "Let him cough it up." Jesse's eyes opened. He had the dry heaves. His arms flopped up and down, and his legs looked like he was trying to run. He was coughing and frothing at the mouth, but he was breathing on his own.

They wiped his face, and rolled him over on his chest, his arm cradling his head so he would not choke on his own vomitus. Now that Tom was finished, Jake moved around and worked on Jesse's scalp wound. Tom examined Jesse's eyes with a pin light. "What happened?" Jesse asked his voice weak and hoarse.

"You almost drowned. How do you feel?" Tom checked his pulse and measured the beats with his wristwatch.

"I think I'm ok. My chest hurts, and I have a sore throat. It hurts to breathe, but I think I'm all right." It did not sound like Jesse's voice at all.

"Just lie still for a few minutes. You're ok." Tom assured him. Tom jumped into the pool and washed his own face and hair. He sucked some water into his mouth and spat it out.

Jesse gradually became more aware of his surroundings, and soon sat upright. He felt the top of his head, and around the bulky bandage. They gave him a wet cloth, and he wiped his face of the dried throw-up. "Damn! Yuk! Barf!" He spat and tried to clear his mouth of the taste of his own bile. He took a pull from the water bottle Jake handed him, sloshed it around his mouth, and spat. He looked around the cavern. "How'd I get over here?" His pale blue color had brightened to pale white, but his lips were pink again.

"We pulled you through. Can you remember what happened?" Jake probed.

"I climbed out of the water and sat on a ledge while you guys went up the lead. Once you were on dry surface, I didn't think you would need me to pull. I secured the ropes and climbed up on a ledge. I watched the iPad screen, but I didn't see anything but you guys moving through the dark. All of a sudden, I saw a bunch of flashes as the camera popped off, and heard a lot of yelling and running. Then you," he pointed at Jake, "came out of the opening like a bat out of hell, and screaming like a banshee! You dove in at full speed and swam for the other side. I think you went right through the tunnel without even surfacing! I packed the screen away because it went blank anyway, then I saw Tom come rushing out. He jumped in the water and swam for the other side. He wasn't wasting any time either. It all came down so fast; I was still on the ledge. It was as if something was chasing you. I kept expecting the croc to come out any moment, so I held up before I jumped in. I didn't want to end up in the water at the same time with that thing! Besides I thought maybe I could get a picture or two if it showed up. It didn't come, so I hopped in the water and decided to swim over here with you guys. I was walking across the pool, when all of a sudden the water right behind me began to boil, like it was hot! Little balls of water bounced on the surface like little BBs. It was unreal, man! I could feel a heavy current sweep against my legs! Really strong! I just knew it was the gator behind me somewhere!"

"Believe me." Tom assured him. "It was! He must have come in from a different direction, if he didn't slide out of that passage. There must be an underwater channel down below somewhere."

"Anyway, I've seen croc shows on TV, and I knew they did that water dancing thing. I tried to dive and swim through the tunnel, but missed the opening – hit my head. I came up, clipped a line to my belt, and tugged twice, hoping ya'll would help pull me over. I passed out. That's the last thing I remember."

"You are lucky you aren't croc meat!" Jake shuddered.

"You are lucky you didn't drown!" added Tom.

"I'm just lucky all the way around! What now?" Jesse laughed between coughing.

Jake was quick to speak. "Now, we get our asses out of here while we're still alive!"

Tom extended his hands, palms facing out. "Whoa! Wait a minute. We're not done here yet. We need pictures."

"Pictures!" Jake shot back. "Pictures? You got pictures man! You must have snapped half a dozen. The flashes almost blinded me as I ran down the tunnel!"

Tom scanned the pictures on the GoPro. "What pictures? All we got is what looks like a wet, wall. See that? You can't tell what that is. It could be anything. We've got to get a picture of its head!"

Jake pointed to the underwater tunnel. "Be my guest! He's right over there on the other side of this wall. Go for it!"

Jesse stumbled to his feet and pointed directly at Jake. "Listen, Jake," he said between coughs. "We have to finish the job. We can't pretend we didn't see it, or that none of this happened. What if this thing got out of here? If that croc gets loose, it could kill a lot of people. People have to know. Who's going to believe us if we don't have proof? No one! They might believe the professor here, but not us. Then someone would have to come back in here and try to get the proof. We're here; let's do it. I'm scared too, but we're dealing with something no one has ever dealt with. I don't know about you, but I'm in! I'm with Professor Morrison. We figure out some way to get a picture of the head. We get that – we're done! That's all. Then we can leave and sound the alarm."

Jake thought long and hard. He had no argument against pure logic. "How do we do it?" he asked Tom.

"We go back to the other side," Tom involuntarily shuddered. "Is there another way in?"

"None that I know of," Jake answered. "About five hundred yards beyond here is a charted lead. It's on the same level as this one, but no one has been to the end of it yet. If it doesn't go off on a tangent, it is headed back in this direction. It may be the dry lead we crossed on the other side of the pool."

"Ok. Let's go check that out. It's safer than going back through this hole. Jesse, do you feel like you can travel?"

" I guess so," Jesse nodded, his voice still raspy and raw.

Tom handed each of them a GoPro. They lifted their equipment bags, and followed Jake farther into the cave. They passed several openings of various sizes. Along the way, they entered a huge room, filled with sparkling formations. They were snow-white, and the crystals on the stalagmites glistened in their light. One group of pillars looked like a crystal throne, which could have served a king – if the king were fifteen feet tall. It was gorgeous. Jake said the cavers had named it "Landry's Chair" for the famous Cowboy football coach Tom Landry. Morrison took a picture before they moved on. Someone before them had left an old checked fedora behind on the seat of the formation.

After a short time, Jake stopped walking. "This is it."

The smell of rotten eggs filled the air. "Yuk! I think I'm going to throw up again! I forgot about this place," Jesse wailed. He crouched and covered his face with his hands.

Jake explained to Tom that a vein of Sulphur came into the cavern near them, polluting the water, and giving off the foul odor. The first cavers to find it feared it might be Hydrogen Sulfide, which can kill a person. Tests showed, however, the concentration was below a toxic level. The stuff just made the water stink. So far, it was contained to this section of the cavern. "It's only bad here. A little further on the smell goes away. So come on, let's move on, and get out of this stink."

Jesse rose and followed the group deeper into the tunnel. The odor dispersed quickly after they had walked some fifty yards. Jake looked at Jesse. "Feeling better? If you want to sit down now, we can take a break here."

They dropped their bags and sat on the rock floor. Jake broke out some crackers and passed the package around. "Honey Grahams," he smiled as he ate, exhaling dry cracker crumbs.

They had not realized how hungry they were. "You lose all track of time in a cave," Jesse told Tom. "Sometimes you get so carried away, you forget to eat. You don't know if it's day or night outside, or even how long you've been underground. Unless you kept a log and wrote it down, you wouldn't know. I've come out after what I thought was eight hours to find out I had been in for over twenty-four. It's weird."

"How long have we been in here?" Tom asked.

Jake grinned, and checked his notebook. "How long do you think?"

"Oh! Probably eight or nine hours," Tom guessed.

"We came in Tuesday night just after 9:00 p.m. Right now, it is nearly noon on Wednesday. We've been in here fifteen hours. With no sleep. Why don't we get some rest? Take a snooze for a few hours. If you don't take care of yourself down here, it can lead to serious problems. I've seen guys start to hallucinate from lack of sleep. People have drifted off to sleep on their feet and fallen into deep holes before."

Jesse nodded at Jake, "I knew a guy once who thought he saw giant alligator down here!" They all laughed. They got their blankets out, and used their bags for pillows as they settled in for a nap. One by one, they turned their lamps off, and the thick, darkness crowded in upon them.

Jesse was drifting off into much needed sleep, when he heard a far off echo. His sat upright in the dark. "Did you hear that?" "What was that?" Jake turned on his light. The sound came from deep inside a dark lead on their left, away from where they planned to go. In the quiet, darkness, the sound came again. It was unmistakable. Somewhere in the deep dark cave, someone was screaming.

Chapter 13

Clint was in the deep weeds. He had intently studied Pawson's notes and instructions dozens of times. Nothing in anything he read indicated how long it might take the chemicals to ignite. He knew the heat would build inside the aluminum canister until it melted away. At that stage, heat would strip the oxygen molecules from the aluminum sulfate and feed the reaction, which would create a fire that no one could smother. That stage was way past the point of no return. The point of no return was when you pushed the red button on the remote. Clint knew Pawson had not used a remote control igniter. Auto door locks did not become popular until the eighties – two decades after Pawson. Bar-b-que lighters did not come around until many years after. The original plans ignited the fuse with a match, with a fuse "sufficiently long enough to allow you to take cover." Pawson had not defined 'Sufficiently long enough'. Clint concluded from the instructions, the reaction was not immediate. Clint knew white phosphorus flashed, but Thermite was hard to ignite. Logically, it would take some time for the heat to build high enough to set off the Thermite. But how long? Pawson did not say. Pawson was not a physicist or an engineer, so there were many unanswered questions. Pawson had run his experiments with a few ounces of chemicals in an aluminum cigar tube. Clint was dealing with half a kilo – a little more than a pound in each canister. The amount would make no difference in how hot it burned, but it might make a big difference in reaction time and length of burn. He reasoned the longer it burned, the hotter the surrounding rock would become.

Clint climbed the steel steps to the platform and looked at the wellhead. It was bolted to the pipe through steel flanges with ten, 1-inch, steel bolts. He looked at the blowout preventer on the Christmas tree maze of pipes and valves arrayed along the pipe. The system of gate and butterfly valves controlled the conditions inside the pipe. With valves and pumps, an operator can pull a vacuum or create a positive pressure inside the conduits. To introduce a solid object into a well, the pressure had to be neutral. Clint cranked the wheel opening the gate value one-half, and fully opened the butterfly on the positive flow side. This equalized the pressure inside the pipe to match the ambient atmospheric air pressure, which was currently 30 inches of mercury he read on a nearby gauge. He opened the gate value on the injection port all the way, and unbolted the hatch. He looked inside the pipe and realized that the valve's position would not work. Nothing would stop the capsule from falling all the way down the pipe, and quickly moving out of range of the remote control before he could activate the switch. He decided to close the gate on the port to one-quarter. He cranked the valve wheel and then peered inside again. One-fourth of the gate protruded into the pipe form the value. Now the capsule could rest upon the edge of the gate until Clint had a chance to press the red button and let it drop.

He went to his truck and retrieved the plastic box that held the remote control. He crossed over to the shed and opened the door. He cradled the "bitter pill" in his arms as he climbed back onto the steel grated platform. He checked the pressure in the pipe again, and was satisfied with the result. He placed the capsule into the pipe, and hesitated. Hootie's question "why" haunted him. "Money?" Clint realized he was at a turning point. He could defuse the device and walk away. No one would blame him for the failure of the well – no one but himself. It was not his fault that damned granite dome surrounded the pool of oil. He knew no one else could have done more to get past the blockage. Money was lost – sunk costs – the cost of doing business. So what? This was not the first dry hole he had drilled, and probably would not be the last. The oil business was risky – always had been. The costs are high, but the payoff is much higher. Three hundred feet of hard granite blocked the largest oil strike in Texas history. Like an eggshell, the rock wrapped itself around the black gold. Crack the shell, and the oil would flow long after he was dead and forgotten. Walk away, and TJ loses the business his father spent a lifetime building. Money had nothing to do with it. He flipped open the plastic lid of the box holding the remote control. The round, red button seemed to fill his field of vision. At this moment in time, nothing existed for Clint except the red button. His hands shook, so he rested his wrist against the cold steel of the hatch lid. He slowly and purposefully extended his index finger and crossed the point of no return.

The muffled screaming melded into several voices. "The other team!" Jesse's sudden words startled the other two and they flinched. "Hush!"

For several seconds they looked at each other before Jake spoke. "We've got to go help them." He gathered his gear, and Tom and Jesse did the same. They slowly and carefully made their way down the dark passage toward the noises. Soon after they began, the screams stopped. Nothing more could be heard. They stopped to listen. Nothing.

"Listen, Jake," Jesse began, "are you sure we want to do this? You know what could be waiting at the end of this lead. We could run right –.

"I know!" Jake stopped him. "I know. But … but we've got to do something! What do you think, Professor?"

"Tom." Morrison corrected. "We're all thinking the same thing. Somewhere down this tunnel, those other people ran into the croc. Why else would they be screaming? Some of them may be dead or hurt and need help. I agree with you, we have to go do what we can to help them."

Jake gathered his thoughts. After a few moments, he said, "Ok. Empty your first aid supplies and let's see what we have. From the sounds, I think we're going to need them. Jesse you take inventory, and the Professor – uh, Tom and I will get a plan together."

From the discarded piles of first aid supplies, Jesse sorted and combined the materials while he listened to Tom and Jake discuss what would happen next. Even though Tom was the oldest, Jake had more experience in caves. Whatever happened, Jake would have to take the lead. "We have few choices as I see it. We can all leave together and summon help. We can split up and send someone outside for help, while we try to find the other party. On the other hand, we can stay together and go try to help them. If we need to haul someone out, we'll need all three of us. What are your thoughts?"

Tom looked at the supplies Jesse collected, and then looked back at Jake. "The last one, I think. We need to stay together. If someone goes for help, there is no guarantee anyone can respond quickly enough to help. How are they even going to find us once they get to the cave? This thing runs for miles. Once we find out what we are dealing with, we can send someone out for help then. Then we'll know exactly where they need to go and what needs to be done. If we run into the croc, we may need to help each other."

"What have we got, Jesse?" Jake asked.

Jesse listed off several items, which included tape, sterile bandages, compresses, rolls of gauze, and several instant cold packs. Other items were for eye or finger injuries and would not be much help, but the antiseptic towelettes and tubes of antibiotic ointment would be useful. He listed two bottles of Tylenol and a bottle of Advil along with six emergency space blankets, insect repellent and a chrome whistle."

Jake reached out his hand, "Give me the whistle."

Jesse tossed the whistle into Jake's palm. Jake went a little farther in the tunnel and blew two long blasts on the whistle, then stopped. He listened closely as the echoes died away. No response. He blew two more and listened. Silence. He came back to the group. No response.

"We're all agreed?" he asked Jesse.

"I guess so," Jesse admitted.

"Not good enough," barked Jake.

"Ok. Ok. Yes! We have to go down the tunnel to help them," he spoke evenly and carefully. "Even if we get eaten by a humongous crocodile!" he mumbled under his breath as he turned away.

Jake nodded, "Good enough. Ok. Let's lighten
our load. We cache everything we don't need here. We
pack the meds into one kit, and carry the ropes, slings,
and lights only. We're not going to be doing any
unnecessary climbing so all that stuff can stay behind,
along with the charts and scuba gear. Leave the food
here; we can come back if we need to eat. And whatever
you do, don't..." A long, faint, trill of a far-away whistle
interrupted Jakes instructions.

"They are alive!" he shouted. "Let's get
moving!"

Every time they passed a side passage, Jake
would stop a few feet beyond, and sound the whistle
again. Two long whistles, between pauses of a minute or
more. No response, even after several minutes. Jake
decided to keep to the main channel. At the end of the
narrow corridor, they entered a massive room the size of
a football stadium. The ceiling rose at least a hundred
feet high. Large, roundish, structures, like a forest
covered the area from floor to ceiling. It was not
possible to tell if they were stalactites or stalagmites.
The columns were milky white. Green, mossy lichen
covered the exposed rocks and walls. The reflections of
light from those surfaces gave the room a greenish tint.
This was Sherwood Forest, aptly named. The floor was
hilly, and the center rose several feet above the entrance.
On the other side of the room was the TC Passage. A
winding, path-like surface, littered with crumbled rock,
led around the right side of the room.

Half way around the room, Jake stopped again to
blow the whistle. When he heard no response, Jake
expressed his doubts. "I don't know guys. They could be
in any of these side leads. The team came here to follow
and map the TC Passage to its end. So, I'm guessing

they are somewhere up there. We'll come to it in another thousand feet. The entrance is as far as either Jesse or I have gone," he explained to Tom. "What lies beyond that point, we don't know. They could be another mile or two through the corridor. Or, they might not be down there at all."

"They are probably in TC somewhere, don't you think? It was where they were headed," Jesse assured him.

Across the top of the ridge, the floor slanted down, and the numbers of columns lessened. A stream came from beneath a rock on the left wall, and pooled at the edge of the 'forest'. The center of the room now became a concave basin, holding water in a pool. The way extended around the rim of the basin toward the end of the room. Nearly halfway around the rim, a large dark entry loomed ahead. "TC Passage," announced Jake.

Once at the entrance, Jake blew again but got no answer. They entered the dark passage in single file. Along the corridor, the passage widened, and gradually grew into a larger room, but not nearly as large as Sherwood Forest. They could hear the splashing sound of rushing water in the distance, echoing inside the dark passage. They came to an opening where an underground stream cut across the left corner of the room, disappearing somewhere beneath a dark wall. Across the rivulet, a darkened passage, some twelve feet above, disappeared into the darkness. They looked for a way around the stream, but did not find one. It was too wide to jump, so Jake took off his shoes and stepped in. The water only came to his knees. He waded across without getting any deeper, so the others followed. They climbed the rubble to a flat ledge leading off into the darkness. As they sat and put their shoes and dry socks back on, Jake blew the whistle again. Silence.

They moved farther into the passage, and came to a wider room, with a level surface along a large, dark, still pool. Around the left side, they could see a small, white light, dimly flickering in the distant campsite. Jake whistled again. Still no response. They moved toward the faint quivering light.

The scene they would discover would haunt their dreams for years to come. The campsite was quiet and eerie. Nothing moved. The first body they came upon was unrecognizable, except for his clothes. He had no head. Steve Wilson, a senior from Jesse's class at Texas State, was wedged into a rock crevice upside down. His body was twisted in a grotesque position, with his arms hanging down, minus one hand.

"Why is he hanging here?" Jesse asked.

"Croc put him here. They do that. Left him here to cure and get ripe so he could …" Tom's voice trailed off.

"Could what?"

"So he could come back later and eat it."

The group moved farther into the room toward the little light. Bodies lay strewn around the camp like a Halloween scene in a kid's fright house. All of them were dead. "Who blew the whistle?" wondered Tom aloud. Jake pulled out a notepad and pen, and began to write the names of the dead. Between them, Jake and Jesse tried to remember all their names. As Jake wrote, Jesse and Tom circled the camp area looking for more bodies. Someone floated face down in the pool. Tom waded out and towed it ashore. He turned the lifeless form onto its back, and Jake recorded another name on his list.

Gnawed-off arms, feet, and legs lay in various positions all over the cave floor. It was a bloody mess. Jake racked his memory to recall how many were on the team, so he could know if he had accounted for everyone. One name was missing. Mickey Lawson's name was not on the list. "Maybe he got drug into the water," Jesse offered. "He's not here with the others."

"Tom, does a crocodile make a sound like that?" asked Jake?

"Like what?"

"Listen. Don't you hear it?" Every few minutes, a quiet whooshing sound came from the rocks beyond the campsite. It sounded like a puff; like the noise made by pursing your lips together and blowing hard. It was not loud, but they could hear it in the darkness when everything was quiet. "Whoofff. Whooff. Pufffffth." They heard it repeated several times.

"Three! It's a distress signal! Let's go find him!" Jake lurched up and looked into the darkness. "It's coming from over there." They shined their lights ahead as they clambered over the loose rocks and boulders in the darkness. Jesse's light showed something moving. "Here!" He shouted to the others.

Mickey Lawson had crawled as far back as he could into a hole in the rocks. They could not reach him. They spoke to him and tried to assure him they were here to help. His huge, unseeing eyes were wide with fright. His brows arched, and his pupils were small black dots in the middle huge white orbs. The whites of his eyes were completely exposed all the way around. It looked like his eyes would pop out of his head any moment. He rocked back and forth. He did not acknowledge he even knew they were there. Even the glare of the flashlights did not seem to attract his attention. He did not blink. He kept moving his lips as though he was speaking, but no words came from his mouth. After a minute, he raised a chrome whistle to his lips for a few seconds. Then he would lower the whistle, and blow three times as hard as he could, making the whooshing sound they had heard earlier. Then he would raise the whistle again, and then lower it again before he blew once again into empty air. Three times. Distress signal. All the while, Jake tried to get his attention. He did not respond to his name, or their assurances. He kept mouthing silent words, and staring into space with unseeing eyes.

"He's in shock!" Tom said. "We've got to get him out of there."

Jesse was the smallest of the three, so he got on his hands and knees and crawled into the hole as far as he could. He reached out his arm, and grabbed anything he could clutch. He drug a screaming, writhing Mickey out of the dark hole. Mickey made loud blood-curdling screams of panic and fear. "Noooooooooo!" He clutched the sides of the rocks inside his hole and resisted every inch of the way. His were the most terrible screams Jesse had ever heard. When they got him out, Mickey beat the air with his fists, fighting off anything that came near, and shrieking as loud as he could all the while. Jake sat on the ground and cradled Mickey in his arms, gently rocking back and forth – cooing as you would to a small baby. Jake hugged Mickey as tight as he could to keep him from flailing his arms and fighting them. "It's ok, Mickey. You're safe now. We've got you. It's alright. Shussssh."

Gradually Mickey quietened, and stopped struggling. He looked into Jake's face, and mumbled, "Jake…"

"It's ok. It's ok. It's ok." Jake ran the words together in a whisper as he soothed Mickey. Tom brought a wet cloth from the pool. He moved near to wipe the puke, slobber, and dirt from Mickey's face. Mickey jumped and screamed again, but quickly settled down again. Tom handed the cloth to Jake, who gently wiped Mickey's face. Mickey's heavy breathing slowed, and he seemed to revive a little. Jake kept talking to him quietly, and reassuring him. Mickey looked up and said, "Jake?" "I'm here." Jake soothed him. "You're ok. Just rest."

They finally got Mickey to take a drink of water, which he threw up in a coughing fit as soon as it hit his stomach. After what seemed to be an hour, Mickey seemed to be better, but his breathing was still ragged. He had focused one at a time on their faces, moving from one to the other. He was looking for his friends on the crew. He allowed Tom take his pulse without jerking away. "Mickey." Jake said. "Mickey, we need to move you back over to the campsite. All of our first aid stuff is over there, ok? Let us carry you over there. Ok?"

Mickey shook his head no. "Jake – I – I don't want – I don't want to. No – I – don't want to go over there. No. We – we – we – we – can't go over there. No! We can't," Mickey pleaded. "Mickey. It's ok – it's gone now."

"It'll come back. It'll come back and kill us. We can't. We can't go over there, Jake. You don't understand. We can't. It'll kill us!" Mickey crawled away and tried to get back into his hole, but Jake held on tight. Mickey cried. No amount of encouraging or convincing could change his mind. "Ok. Ok. We'll stay here, ok? Just calm down and rest. We don't have to go back over there, ok?"

"Th-th-th-thank you, Jake. Thank you," Mickey kept saying repeatedly. He lay back down next to Jake. His breathing slowed. He curled into a fetal position, and hugged his knees, using Jake's left arm as a pillow. Jake sent Jesse over to the camp to retrieve the first aid supplies. He wanted to give Mickey some Tylenol to help him sleep.

When Jesse returned he watched as Mickey's eyes grew large. Mickey heaved a huge, rattling sigh deep in his chest, and joined the list of fatalities. Jake used his fingers to close his dead, white unseeing eyes.

Chapter 14

If you are going to hide something, you want to hide it in the last place someone would ever look. A place where no one would stumble over it accidentally. The sinking sun, glowing like a shiny new 3-ball, seemed to grow larger against the deep, purple haze. Hootie broke free from the dense mesquite thicket behind the Pump House Tavern, brushing mosquitoes and spider webs from his face. It was a hot, dirty, place under the misshapen mesquite trees. Everything in Texas seems to have a thorn on it, and this place sure had its share of sharps. Clumps of mesquite, prickly pear, bull nettle, sotol, and Mexican dagger guarded the perimeter. No one would blunder on this place accidentally; you had to want to get in there. Hootie even flushed a few snakes out of the way, as he worked himself deeper into the brush. Besides, it smelled like urine under the Mesquite tree – like where a hundred drunk cowboys took a whiz all at once. They probably had. No one would be poking around that place without a good reason.

The regular, shift-change beer crowd was inside the bar, and no one knew or cared what went on out back. Hootie threw his dirt-caked shovel into the bed of his truck, and paused trying to decide if he should go inside for a beer, or leave. If he did not go in, it might look funny to anyone who may have noticed him drive through the parking lot. He dusted off his jeans and wiped his hands on his butt, and turned to go into the bar.

All of a sudden, it felt like someone slammed on the brakes. Everything stopped. Even the earth seemed to stop revolving, and came to a screeching halt. The jolt threw Hootie to the ground. It was as if he was on a kid's party bouncy house – or a waterbed. The air roared so loud, Hottie clapped his hands to his head in pain. The ground undulated and bucked as he looked across the parking lot. Hootie could see the ground rise and fall back like a cake baking in a hot oven. He had never seen anything like this before. He could hear the men inside the bar yelling and hollering. Glass shattered and flew through the air as the windows along the sidewall of the beer joint popped out one by one. Hootie's truck began to hop like a Mexican low-rider. It took small hops at first, but then the rear end leaped a foot or two off the ground with each leap. Hootie was still lying on the shell and caliche parking lot, holding his hands to his ears, when he realized his truck was bouncing in his direction. He attempted to get off the ground, but he could not gain his feet because everything moved so violently. It was like being drunk. He got to his knees, and reached for the edge of the back porch to steady himself. He was jarred to the ground again when he tried to stand. When he looked again, the truck was still bouncing his way. Hootie was helpless to get out of the way. The truck was bouncing three feet high now. He tried to roll out of the way, but the foundation post of the wooden back porch blocked his escape. He lay helpless as he watched the truck crow-hop nearer with each bounce. One more leap and the truck would land directly on him! Hootie watched, as his truck seemed to rise into the air in slow motion, and start back down. He even had time to think, "So this is how I'm going to die." The truck came down hard with a loud wham! Hootie opened his eyes. He was not dead. The truck rested with the rear tire barely 2 inches from Hootie's face. His nose actually scraped the rubber treads of the tire as he turned his head to the side. The shaking and heaving had stopped as suddenly as it had begun. It was quiet again except for noises coming from inside the bar. Hootie slid out from under the truck and saw the back bumper rested on a corner of the porch, holding the rear wheels off the ground. That was all that had saved his life.

Hootie climbed the steps and went through what was left of the bar's back door. The screen came off the frame when he pulled it open, and hung from the bottom hinge. The light bulb on the porch had broken, and the yellow glass crunched beneath his boots. The damage inside was even more than he expected. Not a single window in the tavern was unbroken. The place reeked from the smell of beer from all the broken bottles and ruptured cans. The jukebox lay on its side, still playing. Over the sink, a fountain of water sprayed all the way to the ceiling. In the front corner, the roof had collapsed. Tables and chairs were jumbled and thrown around, and had landed in all positions. The shuffleboard was poking through the wall and halfway out into the yard. Two roughnecks were lifting it while another pulled Clifton Bates out from under the heavy table. Men were getting off the floor, cursing and inspecting elbows and knees for injuries. Others were holding paper towels and napkins to cuts and scrapes caused by the flying glass and debris. They were asking each other what had happened. Was it a tornado? No one seemed to know.

Suddenly the men's bathroom room door exploded off the hinges, and flew across the room sideways. It crashed against what was left of the bar, and landed with a splat on the wooden floor. The coiled spring, which held the door closed, jumped around like a wild slinky. A big cloud of dust rose from where the

door landed. All three hundred and fifty pounds of
Happy Chambliss oozed out of the bathroom, holding
his pants up where his waist probably was. He stood in
the middle of the room and looked around at all the
chaos. "I'll tell you one damn thing!" he said in that big,
Texas voice of his. "It's the last time I'm drinking
Shiner Bock!"

Joe Kruger moved the throttle of his tractor up a
notch, trying to get as much speed out of her as he
could. If he could make two more laps around the hay
field before dark, he would be through cutting. The
field, scored by concentric squares that grew smaller as
Joe bounced nearer the center of the field, was hot and
dusty. The old John Deere was giving him all it had, but
it just was not enough. He eyed the water temperature
gauge as it neared the red. He backed off the throttle,
and guided the tractor and hay mower under the nearest
live oak tree. Nuts! Now he would have to get up early
in the morning and come out here to finish mowing. He
got off the tractor and uncoupled the mower, and
climbed back into the seat. He wiped his face with a
bandana, and hung his sweaty baseball hat on the
gearshift knob. He would have to sit tight now for at
least half an hour before he could drive back to the barn.
He stretched his arms, and propped his feet up on the
engine cowling. He pulled a wet lump of chewing
tobacco out of his cheek and threw it into the weeds. He
took another pinch from a round can of tobacco from his
rear pocket and looked across the rolling prairie toward
La Pryor shimmering in the distance. Maybe he would
take Mona in to town for a little while. Get something to
eat; go dance a few. Have a couple of beers; hang out for
a while. He would get up early in the morning and finish

this little bit of mowing, and be ready to hitch the bailer by eight when the help showed up. We ought to make a couple hundred bails this time, he calculated.

He looked beyond his fence at the 'thirsty bird' pump jack bobbing its head up and down, endlessly pumping black gold out of the earth. He wished for at least the hundredth time the well had been on his side of the fence. Even so, he got a nice little check every quarter from the oil lease. It was not much, but it came in handy.

Joe suddenly heard a hissing sound in the distance slowly that grew louder than the locusts in the trees behind him. It eventually grew so loud it sounded like someone was power washing the side of the barn with him inside. He felt a tremble through his rear end, and then the tractor suddenly jerked a foot to the left. Hard. He had to grab the steering wheel to keep from falling off. He looked back across the field and could not believe his eyes. An eight-ton pump jack suddenly leaped several feet in the air and came crashing right back down. He saw a huge cloud of smoke and dust rise from the well before he heard the sound of the explosion. He felt the concussion blast cross the field to reach him. Out of the billowing cloud, the steel walking beam with the horsehead still attached, came whipping in his direction. It gyrated and twisted like a giant mowing blade, whirling through the air. The horsehead crashed into the earth, took out his fence, and ploughed a long trench in the dry dirt. The whirling steel Pitman arm from the rig flung through the air like a scythe, scalping the ground and kicking up hay where he had already mowed. Hot hunks of red-hot steel and bits of concrete were falling all around him. The hot steel was setting his hay on fire. Joe jumped from the tractor and ran to stomp out some of the nearby flames. Seconds

after he left the tractor seat, the three-ton counter-weight
from the pump jack came barreling out of the sky and
landed where he had been sitting only moments before.
The impact wrapped his green tractor around a huge
Live Oak tree as if it was made of aluminum foil. Joe
stood dumbstruck as he looked at his wrecked tractor.
He realized ironically that most of the pump jack was
now on his side of the fence. He did not see behind him,
as several joints of well-casing pipe arched through the
air toward him like glittering spears on a Greek
battleground. The crushed tractor was the last thing Joe
ever saw.

Forty-two miles away on a drilling rig in
Sabinal, the mast tower vibrated forcefully. "Man! This
ain't right!" the driller yelled to his foreman. Suddenly,
the drill pipe shook uncontrollably. "KICK!
BLOWOUT!" the driller yelled seconds before a large
jolt knocked him off the platform to the ground below.
All hands evacuated the rig and ran for the nearest
cover, expecting a blowout at any moment. Two
roughnecks grabbed the dazed drilling supervisor under
each arm, and drug him into the corrugated pump shed
nearby. The rest of the hands took shelter wherever they
could. Any moment now, they expected huge amounts
of crude oil to gush from the wellhead and spurt high
into the Texas sky. Once they pulled the drill bit and
installed a valve, they would be able to start pumping to
the crude tanks nearby. It would be a good day.

Today would not be a good day. This was no oil
gusher. Thousands of cubic feet of air and natural gas
rushed up the well tube with such force it ejected the
entire drill string from the bore. Joints of crinkled and
twisted casing pipe flew through the air, as the well

upchucked everything in the borehole. Suddenly, there was an unexpected second blast. In an instant, the sparks from metal framework crashing into the drilling tower set off a massive gas explosion and fire. The force of the blast sounded like a tornado – but much louder. In the extreme heat in the middle of the fireball, the steel tower slumped over and melted like ice cream. The hellish heat immediately ate away parts of the steel tower supports. Globs of white-hot liquid steel dripped from the blackened wreckage. A huge cloud of steam, fire, and gas erupted into the sky, and swirled black and red like a brocade bedspread. Clouds of thick sooty smoke rose even higher from the enormous fiery cloud.

Deep in the well, oil and gas laden fluid entered the well bore through the perforations in the pipe, bubbled up, then overflowed into the annulus. With the collection pipe blown off, a pure jet of natural gas vented through the opening, and burned like a giant blowtorch. The site was now a wild well fire burning out of control.

With the second blast, the catwalk and the V-door flew through the pump shed, leveling it. Five men inside the shed we killed instantly either from being hit by the framing or from the hellish heat from the fire. A thirty-foot joint of drilling pipe speared through the office trailer, came out the other side, and embedded itself in the engine of a nearby truck. Behind an earthen berm surrounding the waste pit, a small group of men huddled in agony and fear. They had suffered multiple broken bones and injuries. The jagged end of one man's ulna protruded through his forearm, dripping blood onto his pants. Others had open wounds and burned singed faces. The dam they lay behind directed most of the heat around and over them, but it was still deathly hot. The heat seared their lungs as they breathed the hot air. Scorched, they were screaming in pain and panic.

Some of the men tried to escape by running as fast as they could. The blast lifted the mud logger in mid-run fifty yards away, and tossed him bodily into a cedar tree, his left leg torn off at the knee. Another worker, trapped in the open with no place to hide, succumbed to the heat and fell in a crumpled heap. He watched curly smoke rise from his clothes and then burst into flame. His skin bubbled as he died in extreme agony. A heavy equipment operator, working on a bulldozer a quarter-mile away, was able to say a short prayer for his family before the tongue of heat reached him and snuffed out his life.

Rita and Katie sat on the knob of the summit of Enchanted Rock. They looked out across the valley as the sun faded into a watermelon sky. Fluffy dark clouds, rimmed in silver, floated up from the Gulf – as if someone had taken a silver magic marker and traced around each one. A cool, gusty spring wind blew from the south. Rita could not remember a prettier sunset. She wished Jesse were here to enjoy it with her. No sense wishing that. "If frogs had wishes…," she thought.

"This is where we would be popping a champagne cork," she told Kate. "If we had champagne! You did a great job! I checked you off. You are all ready to go to Colorado this summer."

"Woo-hoo! Time to celebrate! Let's go to Austin!"

"Sure. Why not?" Rita agreed. "Let's go get some real food instead of this camp grub. Better yet!

Let's go to my place, grab a hot shower, and get some great enchiladas."

"Mi Tierra?"

"That's the place!"

As Rita stood to stand, it seemed as if the entire mountain suddenly shifted to the north a few inches. The sudden, unexpected jolt threw Rita back to the ground. A wide-eyed Katie yelled, "What the hell was that?"

"I don't know," Rita got to her knees. "It felt like the whole mountain moved! Could be an earthquake! Grab your gear and let's get off this rock!" Way off in the south, a greyish haze rose high from the earth, barely visible in the gathering darkness.

Ninety-six miles to the east, on Austin's Disch-Falk Field, Longhorn center fielder David Nunez settled himself under a routine fly ball. Radio announcer Bill Fleming called the play. "High fly to center field – won't carry. If Nunez doesn't have a heart attack before the ball comes down, it's all over folks. Longhorns win over the Rice Owls 3-2 in this close…. What the hell?" All of a sudden, it felt as if the earth hit a speed bump. The baseball landed untouched as Nunez rolled on the ground. The Rice runner on third base forgot to run home as the stadium erupted into panicked screams and fans rushed for the nearest exits. Pure bedlam erupted all over the city as people tried to understand what had happened. There was not much damage, only a few broken windows. No one could recall anything similar ever happening before, whatever it was. Speculation ran high; since earthquakes were rare in central Texas, it was not the first thought. Maybe it was a crash at the airport, or a sonic boom.

In San Marcos, the jolt woke Sara as she napped in a chair next to Cody's bed. She looked up to see the liquid in his IV bag ripple, and looked toward the window in the evening light. She fumbled for the TV remote control next to her chair.

A few miles outside Cotulla, Clint had sat in his parked truck for hours. He waited for something to happen, but nothing had stirred. Not even a squirrel farted. He had been alert at first, but now, after several hours, he had grown bored and drowsy in the afternoon heat. He reached for his cell phone to call Hootie, and then on second thought put it back down. He guessed he would have to try the second bitter pill after all. For the thousandth time he asked himself if he truly wanted to go through with it. Maybe this failure was a sign to stop. They had given it their best shot, and it just was not in the cards. He had tried his best, had gone way over the line, apparently for nothing. On the other hand, he still had a final cylinder. He would need to get rid of it somehow – might as well give it one more shot. He had gone this far already. He decided he would go into town for a burger before he called Hootie, and try one last time tonight after dark. If that did not work, he did not know what else he could do. He put his truck in gear and rolled down the rough rocky road toward the highway. His rear tires fell off a large rock ledge on the road, and he bottomed out in his truck. He did not feel the jolt deep in the earth at exactly the same moment as he bounced down the rock-strewn road. He rolled into Cotulla in search of Dairy Queen.

In downtown Houston, the slight jolt pulled TJ away from his sleeping father's side to the nearest window. He scanned the sky looking for what might have caused the building to shake. He saw nothing outside that gave a clue. When he turned back around,

Wilson was awake. He had raised himself up on one elbow, and he shook his long, gnarly finger directly at TJ. Water welled in his father's steel grey eyes, as they burned deep into TJ's. Wilson caught his breath, and croaked in a hoarse raspy voice, one word at a time, "What … have … you ... done?"

Chapter 15

It started as a low deep rumble, far back in the black. They heard it as Jake and Jesse covered the last of the bodies with whatever material they could find. They retrieved poor Steve Wilson from the crevice, and laid him with the other lifeless bodies. Jesse and Tom lined the bodies in rows, and helped identify them. Tom made ID cards for each, which they attached to the bodies. Tom heard a noise as he looked up from the last card, "What is that?"

"I don't know." Jake tilted his head. "It sounds like … thunder." The rumble grew louder as small bits of rock and dirt fell from the ceiling of the cave. "Cave in!" Jake shouted. "Get under something large, and cover your head! Quickly!"

They crowded into the narrow crevice, which moments before had held Steve Wilson's body. They huddled together as a great cloud of dust and dirt filled the air. The noise grew louder, and seemed to go on forever. It sounded like several freight trains were rumbling right through the cavern. They could feel the ground move and shake beneath their feet. The dust cloud become so thick, they could not see each other, even crammed together as they were. Luckily, only small parts of the ceiling crashed down on top of them. The protecting walls of the crevice shielded them from larger objects. They heard the unmistakable sound of large rocks tumbling all around them in the darkness. They covered their faces with bandanas, but the choking dust was everywhere. After what seemed like a long time, the shaking and rumbling stopped, and everything was quiet again.

Jake peered at Jesse through the dust cloud. He could barely make out Jesse's face three feet away. "Did anything about that seem odd to you?" Jake asked, spitting dust.

"Anything! The whole damn thing was odd to me! What are you talking about?"

"I don't know. It seems like this was more than a cave in," Jake observed.

"Man! I don't know," hacked Jesse, "I've never been in a cave in before. I'm just glad we're alive."

"What do you mean by that, Jake?" Tom asked.

"I don't know..." Jake paused, "I've never been in a cave in before either. But it just wasn't like I expected."

"How do you mean?"

"I don't know," Jake shook his head. "The ground moved more than I thought it would. A lot more! It seemed like more than rocks falling and tunnels caving in. Almost like – an earthquake."

"Well, whatever it was, it's stopped now. We need to get out of here," Jesse moved out of the crevice hacking and clearing his throat.

They looked at what they could see of the larger room. Dust and darkness obliterated their view of most of the chamber. Jake immediately took charge. "Maybe it wasn't as bad as it sounded. Jesse, you go around that way," he pointed, "and poke your head in all the tunnels and see how far we can go in them. Tom, if you will, you go around the other way. I'll check the tunnel we came through. We'll meet back here in thirty and compare notes. Hopefully we can find a way out through one of those leads."

Half an hour later, they reassembled to share their mutual bad news. The cave in had blocked every tunnel and corridor with mounds of debris. They found themselves trapped in the cave with no way out. At least by now, the dust had settled some, and they could see better. They washed their faces in the pool. "At least we won't run out of water," Jesse mused. "We'll be ok for a while."

"Until the croc comes back to finish his meal," Tom added.

Jesse snapped his head toward Tom. "You could have gone all day without saying that! You know what? If we can't get out it's probably a cinch that damned croc can't get in!" Jesse reasoned.

"Look! Guys!" Jake spoke. "We can sit around here and do nothing and die, or we can find a way out of here."

"Like how? We're trapped," Jesse threw up his hands.

Jake rubbed his palm across his forehead, and smoothed his hair back. "Ok. Ok, ok, ok…" he repeated. "Let me think!" he racked his brain. "Jesse! Every large crew carries a crow bar."

"I know. You guys made me carry it last time we came in here."

"Well, someone has it in their gear here, somewhere. Go search the bags and bring it back here when you find it. Someone also has a bottle jack. See if you can find that too. Then go gather up all the batteries you can find, and put them in a kit bag. Tom, you go around and gather all the food you can find. I'll get the water bottles filled. We're gonna find a way out of here!"

They found the crow bar in Mickey Lawson's bag, along with a six-pound rock.

Rita tossed her cell phone onto the bed. She bent her head forward and rubbed her wet hair roughly with a towel as Katie stepped out of the shower. "That causes hair loss, you know."

"Bull!" Rita kept rubbing. "I can't reach Jesse. He's still down in the cavern, I guess. Besides, all the phone lines are down anyway. Sounds like it was a pretty big earthquake. Everyone in the parking lot is talking about it."

"Yeah. I just talked to my Dad while you were in the shower. He was ok, but he seemed anxious and distracted. I guess he was worried about his men, and the oil well."

"How did you talk to your dad with all the phone lines out?"

Katie proudly held up her yellow and orange cell phone. "ISatphone Pro! Satellite link. Even if the towers go down, the satellite will still be up there. You have to have a clear line of sight to the satellite for it to work, though. Daddy got it for me."

"Must be nice! You rich kids! Hell, I don't even have cable TV!"

"Knock it off! You want one? I'll get you one. It's even solar powered. Only a few hours a day of sun keeps it charged up." Katie made a little girl voice. "Daddy gives me everything."

"Yeah, and you work it too, don't you? You spoiled brat, rich girl! No one is ever going to marry you – they can't compete with Daddy."

"Shut up!" Katie laughed. "Now, I won't get you one for that! But I'll let you use mine to see if you can reach Jesse or Jake."

"How does it work?"

"Same as a regular phone. You have to wait for the link – a little green light goes on. Then you can dial. If you don't wait for the link, you are on regular cellular."

After several unanswered rings, Rita gave up. She suddenly realized how hungry she was. In the parking lot, they ran into a group of friends gathered in an excited knot. "We're going to town to have some Mexican food. Anyone want to go?" offered Katie.

"You can't get to SA! Haven't you heard? They've shut down all the highways and roads. No one can get in or out!"

"Sure, we heard, but we thought it was just a little tremor!"

"Little tremor?" they laughed. "Try major earthquake. The largest earthquake to hit Texas in history probably."

Katie turned to look at Rita, and saw only her back as she raced down the sidewalk toward her apartment. When Katie caught up, Rita was literally throwing stuff all over the room as she dug through a duffle bag Jesse had left behind in camp. "What are you doing?"

"Jesse and Jake are trapped in the cave! It must have caved in on them during the earthquake! We have to go find them!"

"Find them? Have you gone crazy? How are we going to find them? You told me yourself that cave is fifteen miles from one end to the other! And even if you could find them, didn't you hear? Everything is shut…"

"Here it is!" Rita went to her kitchen table unfolding a huge map of the cave system. She spread it out over her tabletop. "They left in such a hurry, Jesse left his map behind. Before he went back in the cave, he showed me where they found that skin. He marked it somewhere here on this map. Where? Where is it?" She ran her fingers over the map, looking for Jesse's mark. Rita jabbed her finger down on the map, and looked at Katie, "Here! Hold your finger here!"

Katie placed her finger on the spot, and shook her head as Rita rummaged through a kitchen drawer behind her. "Ok. Maybe that's where they found the hide, but so what? That doesn't tell us anything about where they might be. Might as well find a needle in a haystack!"

"Yes, it does!" Rita insisted. Rita pulled out an ice pick from the drawer, and ran back to the table. She stabbed the map right in the exact location, a fraction of a second before Katie jerked back her finger. The map was pinned to the wooden tabletop.

Katie yelped, and jumped back from the table. "Have you gone crazy?" Rita had a wild look in her eyes, as the ice pick wobbled in the middle of the table.

"No! See what the scale on the map is, and measure the distance from the entrance of the cave to the ice pick!" Rita yelled over her shoulder as she ran from the room. Katie could hear things flying against the walls of Rita's bedroom. Rita found a measuring tape in the drawer and measured from the entrance of the cave to the ice pick. Seventeen and three-quarters inches. Rita came running back into the room and spread another map out on the floor next to the table. It was a topological map with brown and green swirls and curves covering the area. "What was the scale?"

"1:2400."

"Ok. Great! Get a ruler and protractor from my desk. Top left drawer! Hurry!"

When Katie came back with the ruler and protractor, Rita told her to draw a straight line from the cave entrance to the ice pick. Then she had Katie measure the angle from true north on the map. 170 degrees from north. The entrance was 17 ¾ inches from the ice pick.

Rita laid the ruler on her map, made some calculations, and drew a red circle around a point on the map. "Here is where they are! Right here! Government Canyon!"

"Government Canyon? We've been out there before," Katie recalled.

"I know! Remember? We went mist netting for bats out there one night with some professor doing a study for the parks service. A couple of years ago."

"I remember."

"Grab your stuff, and let's go! Fill up your water bottles first." Rita stood and ran back to her bedroom.

"Where are we going? Don't you know there's an earthquake going on?"

Rita hollered back through the apartment. "Government Canyon. We're going to get Jesse and Jake out of that cave!"

Katie stood with her mouth open. "You have lost your ever-lovin' mind!"

Sara's hands trembled as she stared in astonishment at the television. A flashing banner reading "News Alert" scrolled across the bottom of the screen, as the station's "Breaking News" theme music signaled important developments.

"We interrupt regular programming for this live news bulletin! What seismologists describe as a major earthquake has struck central Texas. Initial reports measure this disturbance at over nine on the Richter scale, making it the largest earthquake ever to hit Texas! We go now to meteorologist Stan Kurtz, standing by at the Center for Geological Research on the campus of the University of Texas. Stan, are you there?"

The scene cut to a jittery screen showing a field reporter holding a microphone. "I'm here, Mike! I'm here at the UT Center for Geological Research, talking with Dr. Vicky Garner, Director of the Center, and an expert on earthquakes. Dr. Vicky, what's happening?"

The camera centered in on a smallish brunette woman in a lab coat. "Stan, we are measuring disturbances in South Texas that are astounding in their magnitude! Nothing in Texas has even come close to this level of activity. This is a major earthquake, measuring a 9.3 on some scales. The epicenter seems to be south and west of San Antonio, near the small town of Brundage, just outside Carrizo Springs. This is a huge one, Stan!"

"What does that mean for people in the area, Dr. Garner?"

"I can't speak for authorities, but I expect major damage all along a line stretching from Uvalde, right through the major populated center of San Antonio. Seismic meters are jumping off the scale all along that line. These tremors are being felt as far away as Oklahoma City to the north and New Orleans to the east. This quake is more powerful than the 9.2 Great Alaska Earthquake. Stan, this earthquake is many times larger than any ever felt in Texas. The effects of this tremor are going to be horrendous!"

"To date," Dr. Garner continued, "there have only been five earthquakes in the world over a 9, Stan. This is the sixth, and it is going to be ..."

The studio anchor interrupted, "Dr. Garner, we are sorry to interrupt you. This is Mike Hardesty in the "NewsLive9!" newsroom. Stan, we're getting a preemptive feed from the Texas Department of Emergency Management on the Texas Emergency Network concerning this disaster. We have to cut away! I'll get back with you shortly if I can."

The screen suddenly cut to a government official standing in front of a wall bearing a large State of Texas seal, and several Department of Public Safety troopers positioned prominently behind him. He was in mid-sentence, as he delivered his hastily prepared briefing,

"…nothing short of devastating. All traffic into and out of San Antonio has come to a dead stop. The governor has activated the Texas Emergency Management Plan. Communications with the Emergency Operations Center in San Antonio has been disrupted. The Governor has declared fifteen counties from Bexar to the south and westward as a disaster area. Again, the Texas State Emergency Operations Center has been activated, and is now controlling the disaster response from Austin."

"The earthquake is being reported as 9.3," the official was handed a paper from off-screen, "with an epicenter eight miles east of Carrizo Springs. Residents in the area are cautioned to seek shelter immediately, avoid areas where structures may topple or live electrical wires may be down, and to be alert for fires and gas leaks. Stay tuned for further announcements. In the meantime," he urged, "please shelter in place, as aftershocks could happen without notice. Stay off area roads so first responders can get to critical areas. Above all, cooperate with local authorities. This concludes our initial briefing. We will release additional information and further instructions throughout this emergency. Thank you." The official left the podium ignoring the questions reporters shouted over the noise of the crowd. Photo flashes illuminated the room like lightning.

Awkward moments of silence followed as audio/video technicians returned control back to local stations. Mike Hardesty was talking to someone off-screen who handed him a paper. The producer caught his attention, and Mike suddenly realized he was back on the air. "We are now getting word that all air traffic to San Antonio International Airport has been diverted to Austin, and other airports. We are also getting reports of wide-spread utility and communications outages in the area." Maps suddenly appeared on the TV screen as

Hardesty walked in front of them. "The pictures you are seeing on your screen are from the live Transguide cameras posted in and around San Antonio. Most of the images we can see come from outside the 410 loop," Hardesty said, "as the inner-city cameras are not transmitting at this time. However, as you can see in these images just outside the city center, a huge cloud of smoke and dust hangs over the city. I can only imagine what is going on down there right now as we try to get crews to various parts of the city to get a better idea of what's happening."

The camera switched back to a close-up of the anchor. "Also, as we try to get the bigger picture of developments, we want to remind you to comply with all instructions of local and state authorities. As you heard moments ago, the Texas Department of Emergency Management has activated a statewide crisis plan, and is staffing the State Emergency Operations Center in Austin to handle this emergency. State authorities are asking the public to stay in place, to avoid road travel, and to avoid entering buildings which could be unstable or leaking natural gas."

The television switched to flicking high-altitude pictures of parts of Central and South Texas. "We are now looking at a satellite image of areas around San Antonio." Hardesty walked into the screen and pointed to areas on the large photograph, "The darker areas appear to be smoke clouds rising from a long line extending south and west of San Antonio toward Uvalde. We have not yet received official reports of damage or fatalities, but this area looks to be over a hundred miles long! No official reports of damage or fatalities have been received, but judging from these visuals I don't see how we can escape without terrible consequences." The camera followed Hardesty back to the anchor desk as he continued to talk.

Co-anchor Lisa Carruthers, who had been off-camera compiling fast breaking developments, rejoined Hardesty on the set. "Mike, we are getting brief, still unconfirmed reports of some sort of aircraft mishap now at San Antonio International. Word of this and other developments, are coming in so fast it is hard to sort them all out. We are continuing to try to get someone on the scene to tell us what is going on, but communications are extremely limited." The space at the bottom of the television screen scrolled information that had already given about the location and size of the disaster.

"As we heard, just moments ago," the camera zoomed into a close up of Carruthers, "the Governor has declared fifteen counties, including Bexar County, major disaster areas. The statewide SOC has been activated, and hopefully we will be able to get some reports soon." The camera returned to a wide-screen shot of the set as crewmembers rushed around in the background.

Mike announced, "We are hearing an emergency medical hospital is being erected at Randolph Field, with ANG and Air Force field units responding to the emergency. We are told the runways are open at Randolph, but not at San Antonio International. We have had no word on the status of Lackland or Fort Sam Houston at this time."

"Hold on!" Lisa excitedly broke in again with her hand pressed against her ear. "We're getting a live report from Austin Airport coming in right now! Sandra Quillin is standing by – Sandy, can you hear me?"

The scene switched to a well-dressed woman with a "NewsLive9!" microphone standing near an obviously tired and haggard man wearing jeans and sweatshirt. "I hear you Lisa. I'm here with Mr. Grady Prichard, a passenger on a major airline diverted here to Austin. His flight had been scheduled to land in San Antonio earlier today. Mr. Prichard, what can you tell us?"

"Yes, ma'am. We were coming in on our final approach to San Antonio. The captain had just made his announcement to put away our tray tables, when we suddenly pulled up – real hard. We must have been close to landing when they waved us off, and diverted us here to Austin. We were pretty low, and as we pulled away, we banked really hard to the left. We all thought something had gone wrong, and several of the passengers panicked, thinking we were going to crash. I raised my window shade, and I could clearly see the San Antonio airport. There is definitely an airplane down there on the ground, burning. Fire trucks and pumpers were spraying it with foam and water as we flew over. The entire runway is blocked."

"Did you see anything else, Mr. Prichard?"

"Not really. Like what?
"Sir, we are getting reports of a major earthquake outside San Antonio. Did you see anything coming in or flying over the west side of the city?"

"No, not really. As I said, my window shade was down until the engines revved up and we went into that steep climb. That's when I looked out to see what was happening. They didn't tell us anything except that we were coming here to Austin."

"There you have it. Thank you, Mr. Prichard. For "NewsLive9!" this is Sandra Quillin. Back to you Mike."

"Yes, thank you, Mr. Prichard. Folks, we are still piecing together what has happened in San Antonio. We have just received an eyewitness account of an airliner on fire at San Antonio International. We have not received reports of a crash, so the cause of that fire is unknown at this time. So now, let's take a moment to re-cap what we DO know…"

Over the hospital intercom, Sara could hear the announcement, "Code Blue! Code Blue! Room 1121. All CRASH team members respond. Code Blue – 1121 STAT!"

1121? That was Cody's room! Suddenly, the room was flooded with nurses and medical technicians. Sara, still shocked by the television reports, thought they were responding to the disaster, until they gathered around Cody's bed. Sara watched as they stripped all the bedding off and kicked it under the bed. They ripped off anything attached to Cody, and threw it out of the way. The IV pole went crashing to the floor. The nurses began emergency lifesaving actions on Cody, including CPR. One nurse was on the bed applying violent compressions to Cody's chest. Another prepared the defibrillation paddles. One nurse yelled "Clear!" and the nurse leaped off Cody's bed, just before the paddles slapped against Cody's chest. Sara watched as Cody's body heaved in response to the electric charge. The convulsion was so violent it caused Cody's feet to jerk up into the air and drop back onto the bed. It was a horrible thing to have to watch your child going through, but Sara knew it was necessary if they were going to revive Cody. She knew he would be bruised black and blue after they finished with him. Then it dawned on her it may not matter.

Sara felt like she was in a nightmare. "What's going on?" she pleaded, knowing the answer.

A nearby nurse responded. "Please Ms. Hughes! Please, go over by the window and stay back out of the way."

"What's happening to my son?" she insisted.

The nurse barely looked at her as she prepared an oxygen mask. "Code Blue. Your son flat lined!"

Chapter 16

Long before dawn, Rita bounced into the caliche limestone parking area of the empty Government Canyon State Park. Katie stretched her arms above her head and looked around. The painted iron pipe normally blocking the entrance to the park stood upright in its mount. Someone had neglected to put it down. The nightlights inside the building cast a pale yellowish square on the wooden porch. The headquarters was a log cabin structure at the edge of the brushy clearing. There was no overnight camping allowed in this section of the park, so no one was around. Rita parked her car near the corner of the building. The unwashed dented park pick-up was under a nearby tree. The old truck had so many scratches you could barely see the Texas Parks and Wildlife emblem on the door. The truck did not have any windows for a reason. Rita knew the park only used the 4-wheel drive truck for one main purpose – getting into and out of the deepest recesses of Government Canyon.

Rita was thrilled to see this dented old truck. They always park it under the tree and leave the keys inside. She knew her own little car would never get very far into the outback. She walked to the open driver's window, and flipped down the visor. The truck keys fell into her hand. Park guys are so predictable she thought; thank goodness! The girls quickly transferred their gear to the park's truck, and fired up the engine. They bumped off past the building down a rocky slanted road in the dark.

"You wanna tell me where we are going?" Katie yawned.

"Yeah. Remember the last time we came out here a couple of years ago?"

"I do. If I remember right, that's when you and Jesse started dating. AND," she pointed at Rita, "if I remember right, you two were missing from the group for a couple of hours. In the middle of the night," Katie added with an arched eye and a knowing smile.

"Yep."

"Woo –woo!"

"Woo-woo yourself, you nit! I'm not like you! You and Jake were making out down by the creek! So don't start with me! Jesse and I were doing something a lot more important!"

"Yeah? Like what?"

"Jesse had a topo map, and it showed a depression about a thousand yards away from the creek. Cave Creek. We went to look for it. It sits beneath a high cliff on the west side of the ravine. He was looking at the cave, and I was looking at the rock cliff. That cliff is where we are going. To get back there, we have to go far back into the primitive area of this park. Way past the Zizelmann homestead."

"How in the world are we ever going to find it? In the dark!"

"I picked up a park map on the porch while you were loading your gear. The Zizelmann place is marked. This road leads right to it, if we take two lefts and a right. Past there, we can take a shortcut, if we can get on Little Windmill hiking trail; that is if the truck will fit

Otherwise, we have to take the northern loop. Windmill will cut out nearly two miles. Windmill will take us past La Subida, which will take us right to Cave Creek. From there it is only a couple of miles up Cave Creek trail. If the trails are blocked, we'll have to take the creek bed. Cave Creek is in a protected habitat area, hiking only, but we don't have time to walk."

The truck bounced down the rocky roads in the shadowy night, the headlights slicing through the dark woods. The red glow of their taillights behind colored the dusty road a pinkish red. The cedar and scrub oak brush along the side of the road continually scraped the sides of the truck, and limbs and vines often poked in through the open windows, snatching for them like dark monsters. That is why there was no glass in the windows. The truck came so close to trees beside the rutted road, Katie's arm would have been broken or drug off had she left it outside the window. They scraped bottom a few times, and more than once bounced over rocks so hard they bumped their heads on the inside of the cab roof. The cab headliner was gone and the roof of the cab was bare metal. Katie wished she had put on her climbing helmet.

It was past midnight when they found the Windmill trailhead. The entrance to the trail was blocked by short cedar posts embedded into the ground and linked together by rope. Rita backed the truck up to the posts, and got out. She pulled a rattling chain from the bed of the truck, and looped it around two of the posts. She roared off and ripped the posts right out of their cement and rock footings. After throwing the chain back into the truck bed, she turned the truck around and plunged down the narrow trail at a break-neck speed. Katie prayed they would not run off a cliff.

When they reached the old windmill, they turned north again onto an equally narrow, unmarked path. A mile further, the trail merged into Cave Creek hiking trail. Long wisps of Spanish moss hung like witches hair from the oak branches growing over the dark spooky lane. A few minutes later, they parked the truck by a streambed, which cut into the side of a tall rocky cliff. "The cave is right over there, right across the creek!" Rita pointed. She turned her flashlight on before she cut the truck headlights, and grabbed her gear from the truck bed.

Katie followed Rita across the shallow streambed, and up the other side. When Katie caught her, she stood looking at a narrow, slotted opening barely two feet high. It disappeared into the dark hole beneath the wall. It was half past two a.m.

"Are you nuts?" Katie asked. "Do you even know where this cave goes? Can't we wait until it gets light?"

"No. It's unmapped. Jesse said he was almost certain it connected to a vast underground system connected to Honey Creek. I calculated their position to be near this very spot. If Jesse was right, we should be able to get in from here, and find them rather quickly."

"If that is true, why didn't they just come out here?"

"Actually, I was hoping we would find them hunkered down around here. Too bad they are not. It's easier to find your way in, than it is to find your way out. There is a maze of tunnels in a cave; finding the right one from inside leading to here would be difficult."

"Then what makes you think we can find our way in?" Katie wailed. "You don't even know if it goes through or not!"

"Did you ever work a maze? The easiest way to solve it is to work it backwards. By going in here, we are working the maze backwards. Once we get inside, we'll have to leave trail markers so we can find our way out again, because there are no maps. It's all uncharted, but I'll pencil our route on Jesse's map as we go along. If Jesse was right, and if it goes through, we should be able to locate the spot where they found the hide. They won't be far away from there."

"Sounds simple enough. Too simple!" Katie shouldered her gear, "We're going to get lost in a cave and die!" Katie moaned.

"Come on," Rita urged as she moved toward the narrow opening. She flashed her light around inside the deep hole. The beam of light cut through the gloom like the blade of a knife. It was dark. Rita took a deep breath, and wiggled into the hole. All of a sudden, something was on her face! Rita let out a loud scream. A spider web spread across her face like a death mask. Rita lost control. "Pull me out!" She yelped. "Pull me out! Oh, God! Pull me out!"

Katie drug her shrieking friend from the dark opening. "For crying out loud! What's wrong? Are you hurt? Was it a snake?"

Rita stood and wiped the spider webs from her face, as tears mingled with the clammy spider webs on her cheeks. She sank to her knees with her face in her hands. She wept hysterically. Katie could barely make out the words she bawled. "For the love of God! I can't!" Huge tears ran through her fingers. "I can't go in there!" She blubbered. She fell forward onto her face and cried loud, body-wracking, sobs. Katie had no idea what was wrong, or what to do. She finally did the only thing she knew. She knelt near her friend, and slowly rocked her back and forth. A light mist fell as the two women clung tightly to each other in the dark, heavy night. One woman bewildered beyond comprehension; one heartbroken beyond words.

Sara visually traced the tangled tubes and wires extruding from her son's body toward their terminus on some medical apparatus. What were they all for? Which one was the breathing machine? Her poor, precious baby had taken a torturous beating from the nursing staff, but at least he was alive. His blond hair lay across the pillow beneath his bandaged head. Code Blue had been a nightmarish flurry of frantic activity as they tried to revive Cody. When the frenzy was over, a giant tube snaked down Cody's throat, and a machine whooshed and clicked with his every breath. Another machine beeped and traced a green peaked line with every heartbeat. Through it all, he had not gained consciousness. Had taken a beating, but he was still alive.

Was he in there somewhere? Did he know what was happening to him? Was he aware she was here? None of her questions could be answered. With all of the intelligent, trained, professional people around, no one seemed to have any answers at all. No one knew anything.

They did say Cody had the additional risk of developing pneumonia – most ventilator patients did. The staff seemed to expect it. The nurse left her a pamphlet explaining mechanical ventilation. A pump sends air down a tube into the windpipe, forcing oxygen into the lungs. 'A breathing machine', thought Sara.

After the danger had passed, they had asked her if she wanted a feeding tube installed. She did not know. They told her, because he was intubated, the feeding tube would be inserted surgically though the abdomen. Her first reaction was, "No." He had enough tubes and machines already. The nurse backed off, and said if Cody stayed on the vent more than a day, he would need feeding. "So, prepare yourself," she said ominously.

Where was Dr. Bryan? The nurses on the floor did not know. When morning came, along with shift change, the case manager came by the room. The conversation did not go well again. Sara, weakened by the excitement of the night and the trauma of seeing her child nearly die right in front of her, sat exhausted and listened to the case manager explain the procedures and what Sara could expect. It was not good news, but at least someone finally had some answers. Sara felt grateful, even if they were not the answers she longed to hear.

TJ wearily dialed Clint's number. A tired, equally weary Clint answered, "Hello?"

TJ relayed the sad news he had already given his mother and sister. "We lost him early this morning."

"I'm so sorry, TJ. He was a good man."

"He died peacefully in his sleep early this morning." Clint wanted to hang up, but it was clear TJ needed to talk. "He was awake last night. I stayed over because he was uneasy and restless. Along about the time we felt that tremor, he got agitated about something. By the way, are you ok? Is everything ok down there with the site and the men?"

"We're all fine. Everyone was on standby. No one was hurt as far as I know. I haven't heard from Hootie, but I'm sure he's ok. I don't see any damage to the site here in Cotulla, I don't know about #2 in Dilley. Not that it matters much now."

"Clint, did we cause all of this? All this earthquake stuff? Do you think?"

Clint threw caution to the wind and decided to risk talking on the open line. It didn't much matter anymore. He tried to speak as obliquely as possible. "I don't know, TJ. After I dropped it, nothing happened. Not a sound, a wisp of smoke, or anything." Clint sighed, "I don't know if it ignited or not. I had a backup, and I was going to try it, when all hell broke loose down here. Your guess is as good as mine is, but it would be a hell of a coincidence if not. All communications are out; I can't reach anyone in San Antonio. All the local radio and TV stations are off the air. Electricity is off. If I didn't have a SAT phone we wouldn't be talking now. It's a mess down here. A giant black cloud of smoke and dirt covers the whole area. I don't see how, if it was us, it could have been so wide-spread. Nothing came back up our pipe, so maybe it wasn't us. I just don't know. I'm thinking I should vacuum and flood the well, and see what happens just in case there is a fire down there."

"I guess with daddy gone, finding the oil doesn't much matter now. Whatever you do, you be careful."

"I'm sorry, TJ. Sorry about your daddy and sorry we lost the company."

"Can't be helped. It was meant to be. You and I
will start over with Rio Frio. I'll probably sell my shares
of HNH to Nobles – if he'll buy it. Wrap up down there,
and come on in. Funeral is Saturday. He would want you
to be here. Get all the men out of danger if you can.
Don't try to recover anything, we'll mop up after all this
is over."

Jesse looked at the massive mound of rock and
rubble blocking the passage. Escape seemed impossible.
He wondered how deep the pile went and how many
rocks would they have to move until they could squeeze
through. It was like a massive game of Stacks. How
many rocks could you pull out before the whole pile
toppled down on top of you? There was only one way to
find out.

The crowbar and the jack helped. Gradually, they
cleared a man-sized indention in the rubble pile.
Everything seemed stable so far, with only a few smaller
rocks falling in when they pulled a larger one out. Jesse
levered the crowbar, while Jake pumped the hydraulic
bottle jack. Tom scooped the loose stuff into a bag and
hauled it out of the way to dump. After an hour of heavy
grunting, they sat and wearily looked at each other. They
were exhausted. Jake kept trying to think of another way
out. Getting out through this blockage was their only
option. After two more hours, the indention in the rubble
was the size of a small garden shed. In the deepest part,
Jake saw an open space in the pile of rocks. He
tentatively put his arm into the dark hole. It went all the
way in, up to the shoulder. "Guys!" he shouted. "I think
we've reached the other side." They shined a light
through the opening, and it seemed to go on forever.
With new energy, they eagerly pulled rocks away from

around the hole until they had a space large enough to crawl through. They wiggled in one by one, and slid down a rocky incline on the other side. They found themselves on the edge of Sherwood Forest. It was close to where they had cached their gear.

Jake consulted his map. "If we go right, it should take us to the main passage. If we go left, that will take us to the pool where Jesse got hurt."

"Lake Placid!" Jesse volunteered. "Like in the movie. One big, fat-assed crocodile lives there!"

"Jesse, it's closer. Besides, the croc is not in there anymore. Remember? He's way to the north at TC. Going out through that pool will get us out of here an hour earlier. We're going left," he decided.

"I'm with Jake," Tom added.

Jesse was so mad he was trembling. "You're with Jake? You're just looking for another chance to take a picture so you can get famous!"

Tom turned on Jesse. He loomed a full foot taller than the youth. Tom clenched his fists and pushed Jesse against a rock wall. His chest pressed Jesse into the wall. Jesse twisted away, and moved backward along the wall. Tom backed off. Tom unclenched his fist. He was tired, and his nerves were frayed. There was no sense taking it out on Jesse. When he spoke, he made his voice calm, and he measured his words well. "Jesse. It's true I want a picture, if we can get one. But not at the risk of anyone else getting hurt. We've got eight bodies back up in this cave, whose families are going to be devastated. We need to get out so we can summon help. One way is faster, the other way is safer." He found himself arguing against himself. He turned and looked at Jake. "I'm changing my mind. I agree with Jesse. Let's go the extra mile and not take the risk."

Jake yanked his hair with both hands as he walked in tight circles, mumbling something about leadership by committee. Nevertheless, he finally shrugged and said, "Alright. I know when I'm out voted. Let's go."

The longer passage led past their old base camp, which nestled next to another body of water. When they arrived, they were exhausted. Jake suggested, "Let's take a break and eat something. We haven't stopped in eighteen hours. We've got stuff here; coffee and provisions. A short rest, and we can be on our way. I don't know about you guys, but I'm dead on my feet."

Getting agreement was not hard. They had not slept in two days. They fired up the charcoal hibachi. Jake fried some canned Spam, and they suddenly ached with hunger pains. They could not remember when they had last eaten.

"I don't think I need this anymore," Jesse decided, flinging the crow bar to the side. Jake threw the jack aside as they settled down to hot coffee, fried Spam, and crackers. They were so hungry they did not notice the slight movements in the black, watery pool at the edge of their camp. Had they shown their lights across the calm water they would have seen it. Not twenty meters away, upon the dark surface of the water rose two knobby bumps, and two red, glowing eyes watching their every move.

Chapter 17

Katie was unsure what to do next. She had never seen her friend so distraught. After several awkward moments of holding Rita close, and rocking back and forth, she thought Rita had fallen asleep. She slowly drug an equipment bag from behind her body. She shook and arranged the bag to form a somewhat comfortable support, then quietly and carefully laid Rita's head down on the makeshift pillow. Rita stirred, but did not awaken. Katie covered her with a silver emergency blanket from her own kit bag. She went back to the truck to get provisions, thinking she should have some coffee ready.

When Katie returned, Rita still slept a fitful troubling sleep, jerking and trembling almost spasmodically. The light mist turned into sprinkling rain. Rita unfolded a woolen blanket she found behind the truck seat. She sank to her knees beside her friend, and softly covered her face and head with the blanket. Rita's eyes immediately snapped open! She screamed, and wildly flailed her fists against the cover. "No!" she screamed pushing Katie away. "No! This is not going to happen again!" Confused, Katie scooted back from her delirious friend. "What's wrong?" she tearfully asked.

Rita did not answer. She lay her head back down, but her eyes were vacant. She stared, unseeing, past Katie – through Katie. Rita moved her mouth, wordlessly saying something Katie could not hear. Rita's open eyes were seeing something Katie could not see. Wherever she was, it was not a good place. Whatever she was seeing totally traumatized her.

It is as dark as a tomb. It is so dark you cannot see your hand at the end of your arm. Darker than the far side of the moon. Not just dark, blacker than dark. A dark beyond pitch – beyond perception. It presses in all around you and steals your breath away. It squeezes you into something microscopic. The dark sucks all awareness into a void where nothing exists.

It is happening again! Rita is nine years old. She is smothering. She cannot breathe. She feels hairy gnarled fingers forcing a hot woolen blanket tightly against her face. The bed jerks and shakes and a heavy weight lies across her body so she cannot move. Gradually, almost in slow motion, a corner of the blanket slides down her face uncovering one eye. The streetlight outside flashes brightly on the blade of the knife. The light shimmers and gleams, then shifts to reveal the reflection of his mouth and grizzled chin. She recognizes him! But she cannot recall his name no matter how hard she tries. She sees his lips draw back in a toothy sneer, and she hears his raspy whisper, "You see this butcher knife?" "Un-huh," She whimpers. It IS a butcher knife! The word "butcher" sends shivers through her body. "If you scream," he growls, "I'll cut your throat. Do you understand?" "Un-huh," She snivels. "If you tell anyone, I will kill your sister, and your mother, and everyone you know! Do you understand me?" The knife shifted and she could no longer see his cruel mouth. "Yes," she weeps, as a snot bubble forms at the end of one nostril. The blanket jerked back over her face and head. She cannot move. She is suffocating. The bed jerks and creaks in the darkness, until finally the weight shifts from her body as he rises from the bed. He slinks off into the dark, leaving his wet sticky trail across her stomach.

"Rita." Someone is calling her.

Rita opens her eyes to see the face of her friend Katie, who sobs. "Oh, My god, Rita! I never knew. I'm so sorry that happened to you."

"You know?" Rita asks, bewildered. She was not supposed to tell.

"You told me … everything. Everything, except who he was."

Rita's sad eyes looked to the sky, as the salty tears rolled down her cheeks in streams. "He was my foster-father. I can't remember his name..." her voice died off into blubbering sobs. "I swear I can't. I've tried," she bawled, her fingers to her mouth. Her body heaved with heart-wracking moans. "I wasn't supposed to tell."

"It's ok, honey. It's ok now, Rita. You're safe. We don't have to go in the cave. We tried. We'll get in the car and go home. Ok?" Katie pleaded.

Rita looked puzzled. She looked at her friend, "What?" She stopped crying and shook her head as if she had not heard what Katie said.

"We can go home," Katie repeated in a soothing voice.

Rita bolted upright. "No!" She shouted. "No! We're not going home, damn it! We can't!" Rita got to her feet and stomped around in circles, "That son-of-a-bitch has kept me afraid for ten years! No more!" she yelled in an angry voice. "No!" She pointed at Katie, "He's not going to make me afraid any more. He's not going to keep me away from Jesse!" She wept in anger now. She went around gathering her gear as she ranted on about her attacker, calling him every foul name she knew, plus a few she invented. She abruptly stopped and looked directly at Katie. "You know what? Fear is not the problem! I've been afraid a long time – I still am." She looked at Katie and wiped her eyes with the back of her hand. "The problem is what fear keeps us from doing! Get your stuff. We're going in there and get Jesse out!" She turned and walked off toward the cave.

As Katie grabbed her gear and followed her friend, Rita shouted back over her shoulder, "And, his name was Richard! And he is in hell where he belongs!"

Jake woke with a start. He thought something had moved in the water, closing in on them – stalking them. He looked out on the dark pool as he flashed his light across the calm surface. Nothing moved now; it must have been his imagination. He looked at his sleeping companions. 'We must have been totally exhausted,' he thought. They had intended to only rest and eat, but everyone had dropped off to sleep. How long had it been? He looked at his watch. Nearly three hours. It will be dawn outside soon. Actually, the delay was not too bad. They needed the rest. They could still be out of the cave in two hours if everything went well.

He roused Jesse and Tom, and they quietly gathered their gear, and readied themselves to move out. To get across the pool, they would need to traverse a narrow ledge, barely a yard wide that ran around the left side of the lake. The ledge ran some twenty feet, widened out on the other side, and then stepped down onto the level cavern floor. Jake looked wearily at the dark watered pool. He would feel much better with this pond behind them.

Jake went first across the narrow ledge, followed by Tom. Jesse held the light and brought up the rear. After he and Tom crossed, Jake illuminated the path for Jesse. Suddenly, without warning, a huge splash erupted from the surface of the water. A hard fleshy tail slashed out and created a huge wave that slammed Jesse against the rock face of the cavern. A flash of pain jolted through Jesse's left arm and side. Jesse teetered on the edge a moment, waving his right arm in an effort to regain balance. Jesse bent forward to catch his balance, bumped the wall with his rear end, and tumbled headlong into the water.

Jesse popped up as quickly as he could. "Jesse!" Tom hailed in the echoing cavern, "Stop! Stay still! Do not move! Don't panic!"

"Don't move? Are you crazy?" It took all of Jesse's will not to swim as fast as possible to get out of the water. He had never been so scared in his life! The entire left side of his body from waist to shoulder throbbed. Where was the croc? Jesse was afraid he had broken his arm; he could not move it at all. He looked around the surface of the pool. Nothing stirred; except the ripples of his own splash. He could hear Tom coaching from the far bank. "It is waiting for you to move. As soon as you do, he is going to grab you. Remember what I told you earlier what to do. If you can see him, tell me where he is. He needs to be a few meters away before you move. That may give you a couple of seconds to get out of the water, but make sure!"

"I can't move my shoulder! I think it's broken. I can only move my right arm."

"That's not good," Jake placed his hand on his forehead.

"Not good at all." Tom said softly so Jesse could not hear. Then to Jesse, "Quiet down and see if you can find where the croc is. We need to spot it, if we can."

"There it is!" Jake aimed his light to the far side of the pond.

"Listen, Jesse. He is fifty feet away from you on the other side. Move as slowly as possible toward the ledge. I'll be there to help you out. Slowly! Try not to make any waves."

Tom edged out onto the narrow ledge, and quickly walked to the spot where he would be able to reach Jesse. When he was almost there, Jake shouted, "He's on the move!"

"Jesse! Get out! Take my hand!" Jesse raised his good arm, and Tom grabbed his forearm and yanked him from the water. Tom dragged Jesse across the ledge toward safety, as the huge crocodile lunged from the water and crashed snout first into the rock wall, narrowly missing them. Bits of rock and several crocodile teeth bounced from the wall and fell onto the shelf, as the huge croc flopped back into the black water. Tom literally ran, dragging Jesse to safety, before dropping him onto the floor on the other side. He helped Jesse get to his feet, and they all moved away from the edge of the pond, back into the blackness. The croc swam in tight circles, looking for its prey, and making huge waves lap up onto the narrow ledge and splash against the wall.

Jesse glared at Jake. "Up at TC, huh? TC my ass! Owww…" Jesse's left arm ached as if it was falling off.

Tom examined his upper arm and shoulder. "It's dislocated! I don't think it's broken. But this is going to hurt!"

"What are you going to … Owwww! Damn! Are you nuts?" Jesse screamed as Tom jerked his arm as hard as he could. Tom heard a satisfying pop as the ball and joint popped back in place. "At least now we know it's not broken!"

"My side is killing me. I'm gonna pass out!" Jesse moaned.

Tom examined Jesse's left side. "I think you have some broken ribs,' he announced. He took tape from the bag and wrapped Jesse's torso tightly. "Here. Take these!" he offered some white pills.

Jesse could move his arm now, but there was a lot of pain. "What is it?"

"Tylenol. Take five of them. I'm going to put your arm in a sling, and ice it down. The ice will help your ribs too." He popped an emergency ice pack and nestled it into a sling he tied behind Jesse's neck. "Try not to move it for a while."

"No problem with that," Jesse winced.

Jake looked nervously toward the pool. "Let's get out of here. Jesse are you going to be able to swim out of the cave?"

"You get me to that exit, and I'll get out if I have to walk on the bottom!"

They moved down the tunnel toward the Honey Creek exit. Half an hour later, they were nearing the pool where they had rested only a few days ago; it seemed like years. As they moved past that place and rounded a turn in the cavern in the dark, Jesse heard Jake exclaim, "Oh, no!" Jake even threw the f-bomb, which he rarely used.

"What? What's the matter?" Then Jesse looked ahead to the end of Jake's light beam, and he could see for himself. Heavy rocks and boulders completely blocked the passage. His heart sank. How big was this one? It was impossible to tell. There was no way past it. He looked in horror at a huge pile of rock and rubble obstructing their way. With no crowbar or jack, and only two able-bodied men, getting past this barrier was going to be nearly impossible. Suddenly, their obvious predicament occurred to Jesse. "We're trapped! The only way out is … back there," he turned and pointed with his light, "Back past that thing!"

Sara watched through the hospital window as rosy dawn colored the sky. She watched yet another helicopter, lights strobing blue and red, land on the hospital helipad. She saw hospital staff push a gurney underneath the whirling props and unload the patient from the Air Life unit, before rushing back inside. The stream of helicopters had been coming and going for hours. The hospital was a flurry of activity, as a convoy after convoy of ambulances, with their lights flashing, came lurching under the overhang at the emergency room door.

No one had come by to check on Cody since he had placed on the machines. When his I-V bag went dry, the alarm went off and beeped for five minutes before Sara went out into the hall searching for help. She flagged down the nearest nurse. "My son's I-V is empty. The machine is beeping."

As the nurse changed the bag, she explained that the hospital was flooded with casualties from the San Antonio earthquake. Every hospital between New Braunfels and Dallas was overwhelmed. Many of the staff doctors and nurses were out, helping with the response. National Guard and Reserve members had been called to duty, leaving the hospitals short staffed. The hospital was calling in all available personnel to help. They were drafting all local doctors and medical personnel from the community when possible. There were not enough doctors to go around. The nurse said she had been told there were thousands of injured, and hundreds dead.

Where was Dr. Bryan? "Activated," the nurse responded. "He is a reservist, and was called to active duty. The Army takes first priority you know. He is treating head trauma victims at the field hospital at Randolph Air Force Base, outside San Antonio." The nurse did not know when Dr. Bryan would be back. "Sorry, I've got to go," the nurse said as her pager beeped and she hurried out of the room to attend an urgent care need on the next floor. She assured Sara she would be back to check on Cody as soon as she could.

Sara forlornly sank into the chair near Cody's bed. She felt completely dejected. What was to become of her beautiful son? Her pride and joy? Were they just going to let him die? What would happen if he had another attack, and no one was here to help him? He would die in pain and misery. He was the one person in this life she loved more than anyone else. With Frank gone, Cody was all the family she had left. It was killing her to see him like this. How would she ever be able to stand by and just watch him die? On the other hand, could she stand seeing him pounced upon and

pummeled by another emergency Code Blue? That had
been horrible. She could swear she heard his ribs crack.

She closed her eyes and watched the memories,
like a movie in her mind. She wanted desperately to
leave the here and now. Eight-year-old Cody stood at
bat near the baseball tee. She could hear the loud pop as
his bat hit the ball, and the crowd cheered as the ball
rolled past the center fielder all the way to the fence.
Run, Cody! No, Cody! Run the other way! She laughed
through tears as she visualized how her son ran the bases
backward from third to first, and then to home with his
first home run! His blond hair flowed from beneath his
red baseball cap. The shortstop stood on the infield with
the ball in his hand, as the coaches left the dugout
benches and consulted with the umpires gathered around
home plate. What was the ruling? Was he safe or out?
As Cody's coach pleaded his case with the umpire,
someone must have told Cody to run the other way.
Cody took off and loped around the bases once again,
this time in the right direction, unnoticed by the men
gathered at the plate. The shortstop, still unsure what to
do, watched Cody gleefully run past without attempting
to make a tag. Cody rounded third and headed for home,
as the coaches and umpires finally noticed what he was
doing. They moved aside as Cody triumphantly jumped
from three feet away and landed with both feet flat on
home plate! That set off another round of arguments and
rulebook checking. Meanwhile Cody did jumping jacks
and cartwheels all the way back to his bench. The
coaches and umpires finally agreed that since Cody did
eventually touch all four bases, twice, and no one had
tagged him out, he was safe! After all the running, and
the jubilant celebration, and the look of pure joy on
Cody's face, the coaches and umpires did not have the
heart to take it away from him. Home Run!

She ran through other scenes of Cody's youth. Of his first bicycle, then his first roller-skates. The first skateboard scared her to death. She was sure he ditched the helmet as soon as she was out of sight! She went through the lengthy history of scraped knees and elbows, cuts and bruises. He was a very active little boy. He got his first broken arm on his BMX when he was ten. Even a broken arm did not slow Cody down. He missed a week of races and then got back on the bike, cast and all. At first, when he got hurt, he ran for his mother. Then, as he grew older, he grew more independent. His father, Frank, always told him, "You can do anything you are big enough to do!" Cody believed him. By the time Frank died, Cody was not a mamma's boy anymore. He was a little man. He grew up lean, fit, and fearless. She was so afraid for him, but at the same time so proud of him. He was so independent; he barely needed her at all. She barely got a hug anymore. When Sara had the opportunity to run for the Texas house, Cody was her strongest cheerleader! He was in his last year of high school then, but he was so solid and dependable, he did not need constant supervision. He spent every weekend putting up signs all over their neighborhood. She was gone a lot, that first year, but he made great grades and received a full scholarship to Texas State. He played on the Bobcat baseball team.

Nevertheless, she sometimes missed her little boy, especially since Frank had died and left them on their own. Now she was losing Cody too, and there was nothing she could do about it. Nothing! Deep in her heart, she knew her son would not want to live tied to a machine; unable to run, ride, or climb. She went to his bedside, and lifted his lifeless hand. She held it for several moments, and then gently placed it back on the cover. She stood by her chair deep in her thoughts. With tears flooding her eyes, she picked up a pen and reached for the DNR order. Through sobs, she signed the form and softly whispered to her son, "Please, get well, son. You can do anything you are big enough to do!" She prayed herself to sleep.

Clint's first instinct was to try to stop whatever was going on down in the well. He was not sure his bitter pill had even ignited. He did not believe it had. Nevertheless, guilt flooded his mind as he asked himself once again, had he caused this tragedy? He did not know. Wouldn't he have seen something come back up the pipe? This earthquake thing must have been a coincidence. How could something he dropped into a well in Cotulla set off an earthquake as far away as Uvalde? One hundred miles away! It just did not seem possible. He agonized over the thought that he might have been at fault. Had he caused all those people to die? Something inside told him he had. How could he live with that?

He knew the white phosphorus would continue to burn until it ate itself up, or smothered out by lack of oxygen. He could shut off the air pump, cutting the air supply or try to smother the fire. On the other hand, he could take a chance and flood the well with water, putting out whatever fire might be down below. Clint decided to do both, relying on gravity to pull the water into the well. It was not a good decision.

Clint shut down the air pump, and slammed his palm against the red Emergency Flush button, instantly flooding the hole with tons of water. Within seconds, a thousand gallons of water washed down the pipe, pulled deep into the well by weight and gravity. It only took a few seconds for the water to reach the bottom of the well. When it did, the super-heated white phosphorus vaporized the water into ten-thousand cubic feet of white-hot steam. A cloud of steam screamed up the well casing, ripping a half-ton cast-iron pump off its encasement as if it were a plastic toy. Clint was not aware of it by then. In an instant, the intense heat literally melted the skin and meat off his bones before it carried what was left of him aloft with the rushing steam.

Far beneath the well, a huge crack the length of a freight train opened in the granite dome, and the escaping natural gas flash ignited in the extreme heat. The underground fire raged out of control, as burning gas blasted up the well bore, and incinerated everything within half a mile of Dilly Chalk No. 1. The heat in the pyrotechnic cloud was so intense, it created its own plasma lightning. Ragged streaks of jagged lightning jutted from the red and orange mushroom cloud, glowing as bright and hot as the sun, as it rose hundreds of feet above the well site.

The head blew completely off the well as one hundred fifteen joints of drill pipe soared sky-high. The steel drilling platform, glowing red hot, was lifted in one piece high over the tower, then came crashing down on top of the tin roof of the pump house, collapsing it inwards. Slivered steel pipe littered the ground. Later, they would find pieces of well casing over a mile from the well site. They never found Clint's remains; his body instantly disintegrated and ceased to be in the heat of the fierce flash explosion.

Chapter 18

Several meters into the darkness, Rita and Katie came to a steep drop-off. They shined their lights from the cliff to the deep bottom, and judged the distance to be about forty feet. Rita anchored a rope to a large rock, and using her descender, rappelled over the edge. When she reached the knot on the end of the rope, her feet were still dangling in midair. She swung her foot around in an arc, trying to touch something. Anything. She found a toehold and tested her weight on the small crevice she found. Satisfied it would hold her, she let go of the safety rope. She found a handhold, and stretched her other foot as far down as it would go. She found the floor fifteen inches below, and dropped from the wall. "The rope ends about six feet from the floor!" she called to Katie. "When you get to the knot, just let go! The floor will be only a foot or so down." Katie came rappelling down, and soon landed on the floor beside her.

They felt their way along the gloomy corridor in the feeble light. They kept to the passage as long as it led in the direction Rita wanted to go. If they could stay on course, the tunnels would take them to the place she had plotted on the map. When one passage died out, or turned off in a direction they did not want to go, they backtracked and took the next promising passage farther on. They followed the new one until it also went off on a tangent, then came back to try another. They repeated the process at each stop. At each path change, they took down old trail signs consisting of three increasingly smaller rocks stacked one upon another, and left a new one. Those markings would help them find their way out on the return trip.

After several long hours of trekking though the dusky cave, they came upon a trail sign they had not laid. At the entrance to a side passage, a pattern of rocks in the shape of an arrow, pointed down the new passage.

"Someone's been here before!" Rita said triumphantly.

After a few miles, they entered a large room alongside a pool of dark water. A well-used campsite sat on the shore. They could still smell the smoke from a recently used hibachi, which was still warm to the touch. "Someone was here recently. How long have we been in here?" Rita asked.

Katie looked at her watch. "It's hard to believe, but we've been in here over twenty hours! No wonder we're so wasted! Let's take a break and eat something."

The girls dropped their equipment, and opened up a food packet of peanut butter, cheese and crackers. It was better than nothing, and it was quick. As they ate, Katie waved her light around the dark room where they sat. A narrow ledge hung over the water, like a shelf, running along the left side of the cave against the jagged rock wall. It led the entire length of the pool and ended where the tunnel stretched on into the darkness. It was an easy way around the pool without getting wet, so they decided that was the way to go. After they ate, they felt refreshed, but still tired. "I think we are close," Rita said consulting the map once again. "If this is right, we should be only about an hour away from where they found that skin. They should be just ahead of us. Let's try to get there before we rest. We can sleep when we get there. Ok?"

"I think I can make it," Katie agreed half-heartedly.

Rita held the light as Katie gingerly stepped out onto the narrow shelf. Once Katie made it across, she would hold a light until Rita crossed. As soon as Katie began to walk, something rippled the water out in the darkness. Rita swung her light out onto the surface in the direction of the sound. A wave of water headed straight for Katie! "Katie! Run!"

"I can't see! You took the light!" Katie squawked. Before Katie could move, the ripple became a rushing wave. The huge breaker swamped the ledge, and knocked Katie against the wall. She fell splashing into the dark, foreboding water! The water splashed and roiled, as a dark angular form grabbed Katie, and drug her underneath the tumultuous waves. Rita realized Katie was caught in a life or death struggle with something huge. What was that? A large crocodile? Rita ran into the shallow edge of the water waiting for her friend to surface. She might have a chance to snatch her friend from danger.

Beneath the water, Katie fought for her life. Her arm was trapped in the huge jaws. Other than the tight pressure, it didn't hurt much. Her arm was wedged between two of the giant teeth, but she could not free herself from the powerful grip. She was running out of air. She was drowning. Suddenly, the croc began slowly to roll to the left. Katie had never seen a crocodile in the wild, much less wrestled one. She felt herself being pulled end over end as the huge beast twisted and screwed deeper and deeper into the water. Another few seconds and she would pass out. Suddenly, miraculously, she found herself on the surface. She gasped large gulps of air. Her arm was free of the crocodile's massive jaws. She realized the thing must have let her go to get a better grip. She wiped water from her eyes and looked around. Even in the dark, she could see the glossy yellow eyes of the huge crocodile, as it swam directly toward her. It knew she was helpless. Katie saw Rita's light flash by, and swam as hard as she could for the edge of the pool, with Rita urging her on. The massive croc intercepted her escape and grabbed her once again. She felt a burning flash of pain as the creature pulled her back out into the deep water. This time one of the massive teeth had sliced into the meaty part of her upper arm; blood was flowing back down her arm toward her face. She was wedged into its mouth so tightly she could not withdraw her arm without ripping the flesh. She knew in moments the beast would carry her under, and she would surely drown.

With her free right hand, she searched her pockets and equipment belt for something she could use as a weapon. Anything. As the crocodile drug her further into the darkness, Katie dug her feet across the slick rock bottom of the pool, and began to pound on the giant snout with the only thing she could find of any heft – her cell phone. With her free arm, she pounded and rapped the crocodile's huge snout until the phone slipped from her grasp. She searched desperately in the water but could not find the phone again. She pulled a metal carabiner from her belt. She grabbed the attached wire loop and began flailing the animal's snout with the heavy steel clip. She wanted to aim for its cold yellow eyes, but they were too far away. The crocodile continued to move backwards, drawing her deeper and deeper into the inky water. She whipped the bony muzzle as hard as she could, again and again. Suddenly, the animal released her once more. She jerked her bloody arm from between the white teeth, and swam as fast as she could for Rita and the safety of the shore. Suddenly Rita was behind her, pushing her from the water to the safety of the dry rocky bank. Katie collapsed onto the rock floor, spitting water, and panting for breath. Blood was flowing freely from Katie's wound so she quickly took off her shirt and wrapped it tightly around her arm. She looked up in time to see the giant ripple coming up behind her friend. She tried to scream for Rita to get out of the water, but it was too late! In an instant, the croc grabbed Rita, and pulled her backwards out into the black pool. Rita was leaning forward trying to keep from being drug backwards, but she was losing traction.

Around the bend in the cavern, Jesse heard the screams, and the sounds of a struggle. "That sounds like Rita!" he yelled at the others as he broke into a dead run. Around the bend, at the edge of the pool, he could see the monster croc dragging Rita out into the dark water. Without thinking, he ran along the narrow shelf and jumped into the dark water headfirst. He immediately realized his mistake. With only one working arm, he was nearly helpless in the water. He surfaced within inches of the hissing animal, which was moving backwards on strong legs with Rita in his massive jaws. With one swipe, the croc whipped its tail toward Jesse, throwing him out of the water and up onto the rocks beyond Katie. Jesse flew through the air in a full somersault. Time seemed to be in slow motion. He saw the hard rock floor rising up to meet him, then nothing but black. Katie screamed as his body landed with a sickening thud and rolled across the hard rock floor of the cave. Jesse's lifeless body did not move from where it landed.

Tom and Jake began to heave heavy rocks toward the croc in an attempt to distract the beast. When Jesse went flying head-over-heels, Tom raced along the narrow shelf and dove into the water feet first, intending to mount the thrashing croc. The croc was too fast for him and whipped away. Without thinking of the danger, Tom lunged to grab for Rita's arm. Without releasing Rita, the animal lashed out with a thick-clawed foot and raked Tom across the chest and belly. Blood seeped through his shirt and stained the frothy water.

Rita struggled as hard as she could as she tried to get out of the water, fighting to gain purchase on the slick bottom of the pool. Every moment the shore receded further and further away as she found herself in deeper and deeper water. She felt no pain, and she realized the crocodile had grabbed the tail of her loose shirt. Her hands searched desperately for something to fight with – a rock or anything. Her hand touched something hard and long just beneath the surface of the shallow water. She grappled for it beneath the water. It felt like an iron pipe! She seized it in her grasp.

She suddenly realized adrenalin was coursing through her body, as she was flooded with endorphins. Her heart pumped hard, at nearly 180 beats a minute; three times her normal rate. She could hear her heartbeat in her ears. The flight or fight response was giving her strength beyond her normal ability, but she knew it would not last. Within seconds, she would be exhausted, and drowned as the beast drug her beneath the water. She could feel herself sliding across the slick rock into the deep dark. She was aware of splashing in the water nearby, but the croc was so loud she could hear nothing but its roars and hisses.

Katie waved her light across Jesse's lifeless body and screamed. She whipped her light back toward the pool, just in time to see a tall man dive into the water. She saw the croc lash out with a webbed foot, raking the man across the torso. Katie saw blood drench his shirt as he fell back into the dark water and sank. Surely, he was dead. Katie imagined his intestines spilling from his torso, only held together by the confines of his bloody shirt. In the flashing of Katie's light, Rita could see the croc's dead, yellow eyes frothing and bubbling, as he continued to pull her backwards out into the deep. She could see Rita try to aim the crowbar for the spot between those large yellow eyes, on top of the knobby head. However, her arms were not long enough to land a blow that high up on its head.

The bar kept bouncing off the thick, bony snout, sending vibrations down the iron crowbar through Rita's arm, like when you hit a softball with a bat and you don't hit it cleanly. The golden-flecked eyes blinked and turned milky white as a sort of membrane came down to cover them. Rita knew the croc was about to go under with her firmly trapped in his mouth. The crock shook his head violently, and Rita's shirt ripped open. She twisted free of the cloth, turned, and aimed a blow as far up on the snout as she could reach. She aimed for the right eyeball. It was too still far away, but she must have struck something sensitive. The croc opened his mouth and roared so loud Rita's ears ached. Rita trembled at the sight of the sharp, flashing white teeth gleaming like butcher knives in the flashlight.

Realizing she was now free, Rita crawfished backwards through the thick water toward the safety of the shore. She turned and ran as fast as she could through the heavy water. She heard Katie scream, "He's coming again!" Rita turned and faced the huge, open, tooth-lined mouth. The massive jaws gaped open so wide Rita could see all the way down its throat. The mouth seemed large enough to swallow her whole! "Run!" Katie's screams echoed from the walls; but Rita stood her ground, mesmerized by the gaping maw of the animal's throat. The giant teeth were snowy white, gleaming in the dim light. They seemed as long as her forearm. The long, slimy, orange-yellow tongue undulated inside its mouth. Huge bubbles gargled inside its throat, and flowed out of the sides of its mouth. The animal hissed and bellowed! Rita knew in seconds, it would crush her to death in those massive jaws. Her mind raced. 'This cannot be real! This can't be happening. This is not the way I'm supposed to die!' As the words exploded in her mind, she kept seeing vivid pictures flashing through her brain. How could it be? She was looking right at the animal. The real scene and the imagined ones appeared at the same time in her brain. How odd. Pictures and scenes from her past flashed through her consciousness as the awesome gaping mouth towered above her; flooding her mind simultaneously. Almost in slow motion, she could see the horrible jaws begin the close upon her upper body. 'Why did it move so slowly?' she wondered. As the giant jowls slowly inched down, Rita thrust the crowbar upright into its closing mouth. Suddenly, everything was moving too fast! The mouth crashed upon the crowbar, keeping the croc from closing its jaws completely. Teeth and blood sprayed from the huge thick, bony lips, as the iron rod stuck into its upper and lower jaws. The croc made thunderous roars and unearthly, horrifying sounds that echoed off the cave walls, and amplified through the cavern.

Suddenly, the croc turned and swam away. Rita saw it swim toward a large opening in the wall, as Jake peppered its head with heavy stones. The croc swam through the black water and disappeared into a crevice on the far side of the pool. It dove beneath the surface. With a flip of its enormous tail, it disappeared deep into the dark fissure. Tom reached for Rita and pulled her up onto the dry floor of the cave. Katie grabbed her, crying huge sobs, as the girls crawfished back from the water. Gradually the surface of the water calmed as the waves and ripples disappeared.

Rita and Katie collapsed holding each other close. "I thought you were dead," Katie cried as she pulled Rita to her again.

"Me too!" Rita winced into Katie's shoulder.

"Rita…" Katie began, "Jesse …." she pointed to the dark heap, crumpled onto the cave floor behind them. Rita was looking at the bleeding man beside her. Rita's mind was a whirl. So much happened so fast she could not comprehend everything at once. She watched the stranger beside her peel open his shirt to examine his wounds. "Who are you? Where did you come from?"

Tom looked at her as he wiped flowing blood from his chest and stomach with what was left of his shirt. "I'm Professor Tom Morrison," he said as if he expected her to know.

Rita looked at him in disbelief. "Jesse's professor? Where is he? Is he ok?"

"Rita!" Katie wailed as she directed her light and Rita's attention behind them, to the wet, motionless heap of Jesse Perrine.

Thirty miles west of San Antonio, Medina dam began to crack. The masonry dam was built on the Medina River to collect water for irrigation. When it was finished in 1913, it was the fourth largest dam in the United States. It stretched one hundred thirty feet across a narrow canyon, and rose one hundred sixty-four feet over the Medina River. When full, it held over a quarter million acre-feet of water.

On the downstream side, at the base of the dam, a small crack appeared in the concrete surface. Like a crack on an automobile windshield, it slowly spider-webbed up the outside wall of the dam, growing larger as it climbed higher. Along the surface, small chunks of concrete blew from the wall, causing tiny streams of water to seep from the cracks. Unseen and undetected, the crack spread slowly up the concrete face. The old dam gave way, inch by inch.

In downtown San Antonio, a priest in a long brown robe moved through the streets of the city in the pale dawn light. His robes flowed and flapped in the breeze; and strings of beads dangled from his neck as he bent to pray over the dead, or to administer the Holy Sacrament to the still living. As much as he could, he gave comfort and moved on. He moved from body to crumpled body with a bottle of olive oil. After anointing them and praying, he attempted to relieve their suffering as much as was humanly possible. His eyes were sunken, empty, and dark, above his raw red ruddy cheekbones. Dirt-lined tears streamed down his grief-stricken face, and he slowly rose from each slumped body like a man on the verge of death himself. He moved slowly through the dust and filth. So many needy. Repeatedly he moved from body to body and offered what comfort he could as he worked his way slowly into the distance. When he was gone, a stray dog nosed the bodies, licking at the oil the priest had left on them. A street preacher on the corner of Presa and Houston proclaimed the end of the world was here, beseeching anyone within earshot to "Get right with God before it is too late!" The crowd around him was as oblivious to his presence as they were to the dog, still sniffing and licking the dead bodies.

News Director for "NewsLive9!" Judith Padilla sat at her desk preparing for the mid-morning report of state and local news. The earthquake would take prime billing as it had for the past two days.

"Miss Padilla?" a young, timid voice called her, as if in a question.

Irritated, Judith looked up from her computer monitor. "What?" she snapped at the intern.

"Judith, we've got Carl on a live feed from Alamo Plaza."

Judith jumped to her feet, scattering her work across the floor. "Quick!" She listed a string of orders in rapid fire, "Bring him up on the news desk. Run and tell Thomas we're going live as soon as he can break us in. Then go find Mike and Lisa, and get them back on the set as soon as possible! Hurry! Hurry! Run!"

Judith ran to the news set without even pausing to put on her shoes. She pointed to the overhead control booth and then toward the monitors on the news set. The directors behind the glass windows patched the feed to the studio set. In the flickering screen of the monitor, she could see an untidy Carl Bellow standing in front of the Alamo! He held a microphone in his hand. She bent forward to the microphone on the desk and keyed the button, "Carl! Carl, can you hear me?"

Carl pressed one hand against his left ear, "I can hear you. Judith? Is that you?"

"It's me, Carl. Mike and Lisa are off the set right now. Carl! As soon as we can, we're going live with your report! Are you ready? So far, you are the first to report live from downtown San Antonio! Thank God, you are alive! We've been so worried about you guys! What were you doing down there?"

"We were covering the designation of the San Antonio missions as a World Heritage Site, when all hell broke loose. The crew and I have spent the last two nights here in Alamo Plaza in the satellite van. We are in one of the only places in the city that wasn't heavily damaged! We're all ok. Pass the word; we're alive and well. James is here with me shooting footage, and Wanda is in the van. We are all fine. Helicopters have been dropping food, water, and supplies since yesterday."

"Can you go live with a report?"

"Ready when you are."

"Ok, Carl, live in 5!" Judith watched the news flash scroll across the monitor screen as a producer in the booth counted down with his fingers, "Live in 3 – 2 – 1." He pointed his finger directly at Judith, and like a professional, without rehearsal, her training kicked in as she reported. "This is Judith Padilla in the "NewsLive9!" news room. We have the first on-the-scene report from our reporter Carl Bellows, reporting live from Alamo Plaza in downtown San Antonio! Let's go now to Carl Bellows – Carl, tell us what you are seeing."

"Judith, this is a scene of total devastation! There are horrible sights everywhere you look here on the streets of San Antonio!" The camera panned around the plaza, zooming in on certain areas, and moving quickly past rows of covered bodies. "You can hear the helicopters overhead, as they bring in supplies to the survivors, and take out the critically injured to area hospitals. Here in Alamo Plaza, the Alamo and most of the buildings behind us were spared major damage; but the downtown city streets are ruined. I don't know if you know this, Judith, but the sidewalks around the famed River Walk were propped up on wooden scaffolds and steel braces over deep basements and vacant spaces! Sidewalks have collapsed, and caved-in, carrying pedestrians, and whatever was on them at the time into deep holes. You can see from these pictures the tangled and splintered frameworks that were holding the sidewalks up. Bridges over the San Antonio River in the downtown area have collapsed, and cars and buses have plunged into the muddy river below. Death and destruction is everywhere we look! It looks like a war zone!"

The picture returned to Carl as he continued to report the scene. "The scene is horrible and nightmarish! When this thing hit, at about sunset Wednesday evening, it seemed like the end of the world! It's Friday morning now, and aside from these rescue helicopters, relief has still not reached us. They told us all of the freeway entrances leading to the downtown area are blocked, and no vehicles can get past. The last thirty-six hours have been hellish! People are screaming and calling for help in every sector of this city."

"Carl, tell us what happened when the earthquake hit."

"We were here in Alamo Plaza covering the story on the World Heritage designation for the San Antonio missions, when suddenly the ground began to pitch and ripple beneath our feet. Buildings began to collapse; huge chunks of concrete and bricks began to fall onto the sidewalks, crushing cars and anyone or anything underneath. We were thrown headlong onto the ground. The ground moved so much no one could stay upright. Dust was so thick you could not see. This morning is the first time the sky has cleared enough for us to get a signal through. If we were anywhere else in the city, I do not believe we would be reporting now. In seconds, those streets and sidewalks we showed you moments ago began to buckle and collapse inwards into the basements and open areas underneath. The earth shook for several minutes. Then, explosions and fires broke out everywhere. Emergency response has been non-existent! The downtown fire station itself is on fire, with the pumper truck still inside! How strange it is to see an entire building on fire with no circling fire trucks pumping tons of water on the blaze. There is simply no way emergency crews can get to us. Gas, water, and electricity have been shut off. The fires continue to rage in some sectors of the city with no help in sight!"

The camera zoomed in on Carl's haggard face. "When the shaking began, I saw the Tower of the Americas in Hemisfair Plaza fall over like a tall, majestic tree. It was an incredible, unbelievable sight. It tilted to an unbelievable angle, then slowly timbered downward. The round observation deck at the top came off, glanced off the roof of the Federal Courthouse, and rolled down Durango Street like a quarter on a bar room floor! It looked like a bad digital effect in some disaster movie. The massive wheel rolled three blocks down Durango, then toppled over, crushing cars, buses, and anything, or anyone, unlucky enough to be in its path!"

The camera panned to the east as Carl pointed, "Across where IH-37 used to run, the Alamo Dome collapsed in on itself like a four-poster bed! What would have been shelter for these hundreds of victims is now a useless hulk – even if we could reach it. People are sleeping in the open in makeshift camps here in Alamo Plaza and in Military Plaza down Commerce Street. Every park in the downtown area has been converted into a camp. No one wants to be inside a building right now, Judith!"

The camera returned to Carl, "Then, yesterday morning, at about this time, a massive explosion was felt in the downtown area. A huge mushroom-shaped cloud with a massive fireball rose high over the southern horizon. Shortly after, several Air Force jets screamed over the city headed in that direction. Some of us thought we were under nuclear attack, which caused even more panic. No one we have been able to talk with knows what that explosion was, Judith. Have you heard anything?"

Judith broke in, "We don't know what it was, Carl. However, we are NOT under attack. You can be assured of that. The earthquake set off several oil well fires to the south and west, and as far away as Uvalde. It was probably a refinery, or an oil well exploding somewhere south of you."

"As I said, Judith, helicopters continue to drop supplies and equipment into the city, and to lift out survivors. There are so many injured, they have not even begun recovering the bodies of the dead. Few cars are moving on the streets. Yesterday a group of vehicles tried to leave town, their lights cutting through the dust like light sabers from a Star Wars scene. As they returned disappointed, people rushed to those vehicles hoping to find rescue workers inside. Their hopes dashed, as they discovered that the occupants exiting the vehicles were survivors just like ourselves. There is not a single open roadway out of this city. Several groups have attempted to walk out of the downtown area. We do not know if they were successful or not. You cannot imagine the feeling of hopelessness and inadequacy, Judith, as you realize how helpless you are in the face of utter devastation and horror going on right in front of your eyes."

"Heroic attempts to organize and treat the victims have been amazing to watch. Many more people are trying to help than are trying to take advantage. But I'm sad to report, that element is here too! Gunshots have been frequent, and reoccur night and day around different sectors of the city, Judith. Piles of goods, in their original factory cartons, are piled on sidewalks, as looters realize they have no place to take their ill-gotten goods. Ghouls have been rifling bodies for jewelry and cash. Credit cards are useless in this city, now disconnected from the grid. Relief supplies, stacked to be distributed to the needy, are ransacked and raided by those who seem to have no regard for anyone but themselves. Only this morning, an emergency food kitchen set up here in the plaza was robbed at gun-point by a large gang who hauled off half of what was intended for all the survivors."

Judith broke in, horrified, "Carl that sounds dangerous. You need to get somewhere safe!"

The camera showed the dazed and tortured face of the veteran reporter as he looked blankly at the chaos around him, and then directly into the camera. "Where might that be, Judith? Where might that be?"

Chapter 19

It took hours for Aquasaurus to dislodge the strange and painful object jammed into its lower jaw. The steel bar prevented the crocodile from fully closing its mouth. The flight reflex took over, and its every instinct was to escape the pain. It followed its normal tunnels and escape routes only to find some of them blocked by debris. The retreat was confused and convoluted. As it moved down new watery avenues of escape, some of them were very narrow and confining. The animal, already agitated and nervous from the earthquake, now grew more frustrated with this last strange encounter. The prey had fought back. Nothing like this had ever happened before. The new surroundings were strange and unfamiliar. It preferred familiar hunting grounds, if only it could find its way back. The croc swam through a narrow tunnel in the dark cold cavern. The tunnel was barely wide enough to accommodate its wide body. Eventually, the narrow tunnel widened into a high room with an unfamiliar pool, miles from the encounter where the prey had fought back. No prey had ever resisted before. Confusion was a new experience.

The huge crocodile beached in the shallows to rest. The wrinkled, moldy animal lay with its knobby legs splayed across the cool rock. Its sides heaved from the exertion of having traveled miles in retreat. Gradually, calmness and peace returned. The creature looked around. Fresh air blew gently through the passage from some unknown source. New and strange smells were in the air. It was unfamiliar, but not unpleasant. The crocodile found it refreshing, and soon fell asleep upon a rock in the dim cavern.

The new and unfamiliar space, littered with rocks, which had existed since the beginning of time, sprinkled here and there with organic material. Fresh soil, roots, leaves, branches, and grass littered the slope ahead. When the croc awoke, the aroma of this organic material was a new sensation, and invigorated the animal. The plants did not interest it in the least, however, the croc knew from instinct that where there were plants, there was prey. It gradually moved forward from its resting spot up a jumbled incline. Slowly, purposely it climbed over huge boulders and debris as its stubby, clawed legs scraped the surface for purchase. Deliberately, foot by foot, it heaved forward. The loose soil and gravel, cascaded behind, as it climbed higher and higher. The light was blindingly bright as milky-white protective eyelids slid down to cover the gold-flecked yellow eyes. At the top of the ramp, past recently uprooted trees littering the hole, the sunlight heated the calloused, hard leathery skin. The grey and brown skies, filled with dirt and dust, blocked most of the sunlight. The warmth felt good to the cold-blooded animal. Looking side to side, with great swings of its massive head, the crocodile crawled into a leafy, shallow creek bed. Aquasaurus – a descendent of Carnufex, the Butcher! – crawled out of the cave. For the first time in thousands of years, a true dinosaur roamed the face of the earth.

On the southern, outside wall of Medina dam, earthquake damage was slowly taking its toll. The crack had significantly widened since morning. The undiscovered flaw slowly crawled up the wall, getting deeper and wider as it rose higher. Dozens of streams of water were squirting from the dam wall like golf course sprinklers. In areas where the concrete had blown out from the water pressure, mud oozed from inside the dam, and flowed in long, brown streaks toward the riverbed below. At the streambed level, the crack was not much wider than a finger. As the crack zigzagged up the dam, it grew larger and larger. At the halfway point, it was large enough to put a hand inside the crack. The fracture continued to expand and move upwards. Only a few feet to the top, the fissure was wide enough to accommodate a grown man. Bent and bulging out from the cracks, the steel rebar and metal screening beneath the concrete surface were now visible. It appeared as though the entire structure had bowed outwards from its original position.

On top of the dam, the crossway was behind a locked steel gate to prevent pedestrians from crossing the dam. In the old days, cars could cross the narrow way to reach the ranches on the other side of the canyon. Vehicles had been banned for years. Dam officials allowed foot traffic up until the last few years. Now they kept the gate locked. The area had gone through a serious drought in the last three years as below-normal rainfall had shrunk Medina Lake to barely more than a mud puddle. The previous summer, the lake was only two percent full. Only scattered remnants lay where once a beautiful hill country lake sparkled and rippled in the sun. The receding water exposed old cars, and detritus from years of illegal dumping. Inspections of the dam revealed serious structural flaws caused by years of neglect and countless cycles of alternate years of drought and flood.

With the arrival of fall and winter, the rains came at last. Oh! How they came. It was as though nature was trying to make up for the lack of rain all in one season. North of Medina, floods on the Blanco River washed entire houses away; several lives were lost in the raging deluge. On the Guadalupe River, Canyon Lake, some twenty feet below normal, once again refilled to capacity. In the Medina Valley, there were serious concerns whether the old dam would hold; but it held. Gradually, Medina Lake filled up again, nearly to capacity. Unfortunately, once again, the opportunity to repair the old dam had passed because of the lack of time and funding.

Suddenly, a fountain of water blew out high up on the dam wall. A chunk of concrete the size of a Volkswagen shot out of the crack. It looked and sounded like it came from a cannon. The concrete mass tumbled end over end, and crashed into the bottom foundation of the dam. The weight of the dislodged piece of concrete destroyed one of the buttresses bracing the footing. The dam groaned and creaked, as more and more water leaked through the structure. Water was erupting from a dozen places. The old dam was leaking like a sieve. With a sudden, terrible ripping sound, the dam suddenly buckled and opened up like a water balloon. Millions of gallons of water broke through at once, sending a torrent of water down like a massive waterfall. Tons of water, mixed with huge chunks of concrete and mud, quickly filled the normally calm creek bed below. In seconds, the creek became a tidal wave of brown, muddy water, racing headlong downstream. The riverbed could not hold it all; the flood lapped up onto the sides of the rocky banks, uprooting trees, and anything in its path, pulling everything into the raging flood.

A few miles downstream, the tiny village of Rio Medina had barely any warning at all. Within two minutes of the wailing flood-warning siren, a forty-foot wall of water and debris completely overwhelmed the little village. The water swept through so fast no one had time to get to higher ground. Everything was uprooted and carried downstream in a tumbling, raging mass of foam, twisted metal, timber, and bawling livestock. The violent flood left nothing behind but lives scraped bare of all possessions, leaving only memories. Death and destruction were carried forward in the rolling waves, to crash and crush against roads, bridges, and structures downstream. Twisted, distorted fragments of cars, farm equipment, barns, and houses floated in the grisly, unstoppable, muddy, chaotic surge racing downstream.

At a place where the river course turns west above Rio Medina then loops back around to the south, the raging flood cut a new path right across Willie's Feed Store to rejoin the old riverbed along Highway 471. It made similar cuts all along the way, as the wall of churning water raced its way toward the unsuspecting town of Castroville, and the stream's confluence with the San Antonio River.

Rita scrambled on hands and knees to Jesse's lifeless body. Crying hysterically, she cradled him in her arms and rocked back and forth. It took some doing to get her to let him go so Tom could make an examination. Katie pulled her away, and physically restrained her while Tom checked Jesse. Tom placed Jesse on his back and listened to his chest. He was breathing.

"Is he alive?" Rita cried.

"Yes. He's alive. He's knocked out cold. Go get a wet cloth!"

Tom told Jake to bathe Jesse's face with the damp cloth, while Tom looked at Katie's arm. He peeled away the blood-soaked t-shirt from the deep wound on her arm. "Looks like it missed the major arteries," he observed. He wrapped her arm tightly with compression bandages. "If it soaks through, make sure you tell someone," he instructed as he wrapped tape around the bandage on her arm. Finally, Tom looked to his own wounds. He took bandages from the first aid kit, and asked Katie to wrap them tightly around his chest and abdomen. Katie was relieved to see that his guts were not poking through his wounds. By the time she was finished, Jesse was awake and looking around. Tom moved back to his side, "Can you sit up?"

"I think so," Jesse answered.

They pulled Jesse to a sitting position, and he looked around at the others. "Thank God you are alive," he said when he saw Rita. "Thank God you are alive," Rita repeated to him. She moved in to hug him, causing Jesse to wince at the pressure.

"He has a dislocated shoulder," Tom told her, "from his first encounter with the croc." Then to Jesse, "Can you get up?"

Jesse tried to rise, but screamed out in pain as he clutched his right leg below the knee. He fell back moaning. Tom immediately opened his pocketknife, and slit Jesse's jeans up to the thigh. Jesse's leg bent at an odd angle to the outside, and a huge purple knot bulged on the side of his calf. Tom gingerly prodded the purple and black mass. "That's not good," he said halfway to himself.

"What is it?" Rita asked.

"It's a hematoma, probably a fracture. That is from the blood, and maybe the bone, poking against the skin. We definitely do not want it to break through the skin. This is a bad break. It's broken sideways not front to back. That is going to make it even more difficult to transport him out of here. I can't set the bones here. It looks like the internal bleeding may have stopped, but I can't be sure. He won't be able to support any weight at all on that side. He can't even use a crutch because of his shoulder on the other side." He motioned to Jake, "Go find me something we can use to make a splint." He turned back to Jesse. "Jesse, can you hear me?"

"Yeah."

"You've got a broken leg, man. It's bad broke. The good news is it's not compound. Yet. It's going to hurt like hell, man. We're going to have to carry you out of here." He looked at Rita and Katie as if for the first time. He shook his head, "Who are you two and what are you doing here?"

"We're together, Jesse and I," she answered. "We came looking for all of you – to get you out of this cave."

Tom look confused. "How did you know we were stuck down here?"

Rita told him about the earthquake, and she was afraid the cave had collapsed on them.

"How did you even know where to find us?"

Rita directed her response at Jesse. "Jesse, you left your map of the cave behind at Enchanted Rock. Remember?"

"Yeah. I didn't know we were coming back in here," Jesse groaned.

"I took your map, plotted the location where you found that skin, and located the cave entrance on a topo. I thought you might be somewhere around that spot. Remember that hole in the cliff in Government Canyon that you thought it might be connected to Honey Creek?"

"Yeah," Jesse moaned.

"Well it is! We got in that way, and oriented in your direction trying to find you. It was sheer luck, but it was a calculated risk. It worked out, except for that thing!" She looked at Tom, "What in the hell was that thing?" she asked.

While Tom placed a splint on the moaning Jesse, Jake took over the conversation. "That? That was a crocodile – a big one! Professor Morrison identified the hide as an extinct, prehistoric crocodile; or, at least, it **was** extinct. He talked us into coming back in here to get evidence. It almost got us killed, like it did those poor guys back up in the cavern."

"What guys?" Katie asked shaking her head with eyes wide.

"The main party." Jake covered his face with his hands. He seemed to sob. Through his fingers he muttered, "There are eight dead guys further up in TC Passage." Removing his hands from his face he said, "The croc attacked the main cave party. Killed them all," he shook his head looking from Kate to Rita and back. "Then it attacked us just before you got here. We couldn't get out of the cave from the other side because the main tunnel collapsed, so we had to come back through here." He looked at Rita, "That's when we came upon you two being attacked, and here we are! Tell me you know the way back out of here," he pleaded.

"We marked a trail. We'll go out the way we came in," Rita assured him.

Tom looked relieved, "As soon as we get Jesse ready to travel, we need to get out of here before it comes back." He looked out on the dark, still water, with worried eyes.

Mike Hardesty waited for his cue at the end of the promo. The director counted down with his fingers and pointed right at Mike, as he announced, "'NewsLive9!' has the ONLY live reporter in downtown San Antonio. Parents: be warned: if you have small children, the accounts and descriptions of this tragic scene are graphic and violent. Please exercise discretion in viewing this report. We go now live, to our reporter on the scene, Carl Bellow. Carl are you with us?"

"I'm here Mike. I am standing in the heart of what was once a fabulous vacation destination city: downtown San Antonio. The scene has been one of utter panic and chaos here. My crew and I escaped injury, and have camped in our van parked on the street in front of the Alamo. Incredibly, the Alamo is one of the few structures still standing."

As he spoke, the camera panned around the area where he stood. "Communications are improving, with cellular service mostly restored throughout the area. Phone lines and utilities are still cut off. The streets around the famed River Walk have collapsed and fallen into the river. Bridges have collapsed. Buildings in the downtown district have folded into heaps of bricks and debris. A thick blanket of dust covers everything. At first, you could not see beyond a few feet in front of you. Visibility has continued to improve, and the sun is beginning to break through the dust-filled sky. Buildings still standing are in danger of collapsing at any moment. I have never seen such destruction, even in Iraq or Afghanistan. Fires that have been burning for two days still rage out of control. Bodies litter the ground on every street. The death toll is going to be in the thousands. Few police and emergency workers can be seen; they, themselves, have become victims."

"First-responders from outside, except those being dropped in by air, simply cannot reach the downtown area. The freeways collapsed and are not passable, and the streets and sidewalks around the River Walk crumpled into the river. A foul, grisly odor permeates everywhere, as ghastly scenes of death linger on the streets of San Antonio. Too often, there is no help."

"There is no place for shelter. From where I stand, I can see few buildings not damaged. There is no way in and no way out. I will continue to report as long as my batteries hold out. We've been charging them by running the van, but we're getting low on gasoline. There is no place to go anyway. Helicopters fly overhead, and continue to drop supplies and to airlift casualties out. We hear the Corps of Engineers will be using bulldozers and heavy equipment to open thoroughfares into the city soon, clearing the debris from collapsed freeways and overpasses. We are told to shelter in place, and to wait for the help they promise is on the way."

"Buildings have become so damaged they are a danger to anyone nearby. They could fall at any time. Survivors are staying in the open in streets and parks, away from buildings. They are afraid to go inside, yet those in the open feel defenseless and exposed."

"I have seen amazing reactions all across the city, Mike. We've seen scenes of abject terror and ugliness, and incidents of unbelievably heroic acts. Some survivors are attempting to aid the victims that still show signs of life. Survivors are attempting to become rescuers. Some of the actions I have seen here, Mike, have been truly heartwarming; people helping people. All we can count on is ourselves, and the response has been overwhelming. Reports of violence and looting are still coming in, but for the most part, it seems the realization we are all victims is beginning to dawn on everyone. Some of these pictures will haunt our dreams for years to come. Bodies are being stacked along the sidewalks, and makeshift hospitals are being set up in the open parks around the city. Supplies and materials are being taken from drugstores in the downtown area, and the huge Nix hospital is being raided for medical supplies to help whatever victims we can reach. Occasional wails and pleas for help come from mounds of debris as people try to move massive piles of rubble by hand. People, some still alive, are still being pulled from rubble piles and carried up from huge holes in the ground. The screams of the injured and dying, pleading for help, is overwhelming. The stench of death is everywhere and is absolutely unbearable in places. There is no one to help us, except ourselves."

"We are getting reports from west of the city, that animals, some presumably escaped from the zoo, are now roaming the countryside, plundering livestock and corpses. Some of these reports seem impossibly exaggerated. We will investigate as time becomes available. We are also getting reports of flooding west of the city. We do not know where the water is coming from, but we are hearing rumors that Medina dam ruptured. We need to get closer to those events out in the southwestern edge of the city.”

“After we conclude this report, Mike, we are packing up to move closer to Lackland AFB; if we can get through. We hear a large community of survivors have gathered in that area, around Wilford Hall Hospital. If we can get there, we may get a clearer picture of the rescue and recovery efforts underway by the military and local authorities. We will attempt to establish contact later this afternoon.”

“From downtown San Antonio, with continuing live coverage of the Great San Antonio Earthquake, this is Carl Bellow, ‘NewsLive9!’ Back to you Mike.”

Chapter 20

"JBSA02 Base! This is Locust Leader! Do you have a copy? Over," the radio crackled.

The controller at Joint Base San Antonio keyed his mike and answered, "Roger, Locust Leader. Go ahead. Over."

"Roger Base, we have a sighting of a threat target at coordinates 29.335034, -98-692702, SSW of Joint Base San Antonio Lackland/Medina Training Annex. Copy?"

"Roger, Locust Leader. Identify target. Over."

"Target appears to be a large reptile, possibly a lizard or alligator or something. Locust 4 has video downloading to you now along with heat imagery. The animal was reported attacking refugees fleeing from the flooded river. Over."

"Roger, Locust Leader, do you still have visual contact? Over."

"Negative, Base. It went into a wooded area on a cedar hilltop. We have it located inside a wooded perimeter, bound by Highway 90 and the Medina River. Over."

"Roger, Locust Leader. Have your unit maintain position and report any changes while we look at the film. Affirm."

"Roger, WILCO, Base. Locust standing by. Locust Leader out." The loud WHOOMP WHOOMP

WHOOMP of the helicopter engines could be heard over the radio until the pilot released the transmit button.

"Base out." Master Sergeant Rodney Logan rose from his seat and moved to the telemetry console across the room. He looked over the technician's shoulder as the pictures came inching down the screen. He took one look, swung halfway around, and barked, "Get Colonel Duncan in here right away," he ordered.

'Dutch' Duncan arrived within three minutes. "What have you got?"

"Sir, Locust reports seeing a huge animal, attacking flood survivors on the ground out near Lackland/Medina complex. It is becoming a serious threat to the recovery. We have images on console three."

The Colonel looked over the technician's shoulder and squinted at the computer screen. "What the hell is that?"

"We don't know, sir. Maybe an alligator escaped from the zoo."

"I've never seen any alligator in a zoo that big! That thing is huge! Show me the heat imagery screen." The technician tapped a button and a red and green screen appeared on his monitor. The Colonel bent forward and peered even closer, "Where is it?"

"Uh…, Sir. It's a cold blooded animal; we can't get a heat image." The Sergeant tried not to sound smug. "We've been using visual sightings. We can't pick anything up on sonar either."

The Colonel rubbed his chin in thought, "Locust, you say? Patch me through to the pilot."

"Yes, sir!"

The Colonel picked up the desk mike and held it in his hands as he perched on the edge of the desk. "Locust Leader, this is Operations Command, Colonel Duncan. Over!"

Over the sound of his rotor blades the pilot called, "Roger Ops, this is Locust Leader, sir. Over."

"Tell me what you see. Over."

"Yes, Sir. We had visual and photo imagery of a large animal harassing refugees fleeing the Medina River flood, sir. Over."

"Do you still have a visual?"

The pilot did not respond right away because Colonel Duncan forgot to say "over." Locust Leader was unsure if the Colonel had finished talking. Finally, the pilot keyed his mike, "No, sir, but we know where it is. We've got it pinned down on a hilltop in the southwest corner of the old Medina training complex. We do not have a visual right now, but we've surrounded the area. We saw it go beneath the cedars, and we know it has not come out. Over."

"Any civilian or ancillary presence there? Over."

"No, sir. No roads, houses, buildings or anything. There is a huge open field around this hilltop on the old training base. The hilltop is covered in cedar trees. Over."

"Are your ships carrying live ordinance? Over."

"No, sir. Over."

"Ok. Maintain your surveillance and notify Base at once of any change. We'll get back to you ASAP. Ops Command out."

"10-4, Ops. Locust Leader out."

The Colonel turned away from the monitors and barked, "Get me General Briggs on the land line." He turned to Sergeant Logan, "Get on the horn and prep four Apache attack ships loaded with 50s. Have them ready to join Locust on the perimeter of that hill, and to stand by for my orders."

"Yes, sir." The Sergeant went about his business as a nearby clerk called to the Colonel, "General Briggs on line 4 Colonel."

Duncan reached over and picked up the red phone. "General. This is Duncan."

The General was in a jovial mood. He laughed and warmly greeted the Colonel. "Hey. What's up, Dutch?"

"You're not going to believe this one, General. We've got a huge crocodile pinned down out on Medina JBSA."

"A crocodile, you say?"

"Yes, sir. A big one. It's causing one hell of a mess in the rescue and recovery down here! With the fires and the earthquake response, and now the Medina River flooding, the recovery is being severely impacted. This thing is attacking survivors and probably plundering the dead, too. I need a live-fire authorization for four Apache gunships to take this thing out right away."

The General laughed. "Four Apaches? Kind of overkill for a crocodile. Ain't it, Dutch?

"General, this is the biggest damned crocodile you ever saw! I swear it's almost as big as a bus! We've got the thing cornered in a remote area right now, and we need to take it out before it moves into a populated area."

"Got boots on the ground?"

"No, sir. No time to get them there. No roads run through that sector; they'd have to walk in. It's nearly a mile from any kind of road at all. We'd have to drop them in short of the tree line. By the time we marshalled a ground response, the thing might be gone. Besides, you are not going to take this thing out with small arms. We have a clear shot right now except for some trees. No other houses, buildings, or personnel are in the area. It has crawled up under a heavy tree cover. We don't have sonar or heat on the target; but we saw it go in there, and it hasn't come back out."

"You don't have a visual on the thing?"

"No, sir. It's under heavy cedar and brush coverage," the Colonel wondered if the General was even listening.

"Let me get this straight." The General, clearly listening, was no longer in a jovial mood. "You want me to authorize a live-fire on a target you don't have visual, sonar, or even heat imagery on?"

"Sir, it's a cold blooded animal; it doesn't give off heat." The Colonel intended to sound smug. If he could get Briggs fired up, he might get mad enough to authorize live fire. "I'm not sure why the sonar is not picking it up, but we know exactly where it is. Nothing else is in there. We could light up that hilltop and take it out with minimal risk."

"Dutch, how do you know no one else is on that hill?"

"It's fenced-in Federal property, sir. No trespassing. Part of an old Medina training field."

"Dutch," the General, still smarting from the 'heat image' put-down, tried to sound condescending, "with people fleeing a flood, don't you think a hilltop might be the first place they would go?"

"Yes sir, if it weren't for an eight-foot chain link fence with three feet of razor wire on top! There are other easier hilltops nearby for them to use for shelter. We don't see any sign of anyone in the sector, General. None."

The General paused to think. "How'd the crocodile get in there?"

"The river takes a wide sweep back to the west. It probably got swept into the low-lying field as the water made the turn. There is a lot of wood and flood debris littering that field. I think it was trying to make it back to the water, when it encountered that refugee group. So it turned south and took shelter on that hillside. It probably ate the fence for lunch! I'm telling you General, this damn thing is enormous!"

"All right, Dutch. Here's what I'm willing to do. I'll give you 387s, no 50s. You go pour some limited rounds on the perimeter around the top of that hill. Try to flush it out. One short burst. If no one pops up waving white flags, AND if you get a confirmed visual on the thing, fire away! But I'm telling you right here and now, Dutch, if you kill a civilian or take any collateral damage, this is on you! You make sure of your damned shot!"

"Target ammo?" the Colonel asked skeptically. "We need at least 388s."

"Uh-uh! Hell to the no! It's 7s or nothing, Dutch."

"Yes, sir, I'll take it." Colonel Duncan hung up the phone.

An unceasing stream of ambulances and helicopters were coming in and out of the Hill Country Medical Hospital. Where were they putting all the patients? Sara turned away from the window and checked Cody for the hundredth time that day. Since they had removed the machines, Cody was breathing without life support. It had been a day and a half since Thursday morning when they had taken Cody off life support. It had been a full week today, since his accident.

The hospital had put out a call for doctors in the community to come forward to help with care. Dr. Bryan was still away with his Army unit. A couple of new doctors checked on Cody, but no one had come by since yesterday morning – absolutely no one. No doctor, physician assistant, technician, nurse, clerk, or candy striper. No one! Sara even had to retrieve Cody's tray from the food cart in the hall herself. A couple of times she wandered out into the chaotic hall to get water or ice. She felt lonely and wanted to talk with someone, but no one had time. They hustled back and forth; literally running in and out of the nurses' center. Announcements kept coming over the PA system, calling teams to certain areas or rooms of the hospital. She walked down to the emergency room and found utter chaos. She read a large sign at the doors that said 'Hospital Closed for routine admissions". Only the helicopter and ambulance drivers, with their gurneys loaded with the injured, sick, and dying, moved past the guard at the door. She overheard one nurse tell an ambulance driver the hospital was full, and he should take his patient to Kyle or Austin if he could. When the ambulance driver objected, the nurse snapped and turned on him as she screamed, "If he's not bleeding to death, suffocating, or having a heart attack, he can't come in!" Seeing the pain on the patient's face, she softened, "Take him to the emergency field hospital outside Schertz out by Randolph. They'll help him there." The ambulance driver shook his head sadly, turned his gurney around, and rolled back to his unit.

Jesse felt the agonizing pain travel up his leg all the way to his head. Tom had wrapped his broken leg as tightly as possible to a makeshift splint. Both of his legs were tied together to provide as much support as possible. Any effort to move him or stand him up, resulted in screams and howls of excruciating agony. Tom gave him five more Tylenol and wished he had something stronger. The group gathered to try to figure out what they were going to do. "How far to the place where we can get out of this cave," Tom asked Rita.

"It's about six miles through these tunnels. And once we get out…" she paused.

"What?" Tom asked.

"We're in a remote section of Government Canyon. It's a state park with no paved roads. We have a truck, but it's still fifteen miles back out to a main highway. It's gonna be a rough ride."

"Once we get topside, can't we call for help?"

"Professor, you don't know this because you've been underground all this time, but there's been a major earthquake. Everything is in disaster mode. I don't think there's anyone to come get us. We'll have to drive ourselves out, at least as far as the main highway. Maybe we can find help then. But I don't know…" she trailed off.

Tom's eyes searched the campsite. "Anything here we can use for a travois?" he asked no one in particular. Jake circled the camp, poking around and came back with a kit bag. "Maybe we can empty this out and put him at least partly inside it," he offered.

"No," Tom said, "we can't put his legs in it. He won't be able to stand that. If we put his torso in it, his legs would drag. That won't work. Keep looking. We need a couple of poles. Think!" They looked through everything in the camp, but could not find anything like a pole they could use to make a travois or a stretcher. Not having anything else to use, Rita asked them to bring her all the rope they could locate. Rita took one of the ropes and uncoiled it. "I can't believe you guys don't know how to do this," she half-heartedly jabbed at the men. She laid the rope out on the cave floor in a series of snake-like s-turns of equal size. "What are you going to do with that?" Jake asked. "Just watch. Empty all those bags," Rita said.

Rita took a different rope and tied a clove hitch around the first switchback loop in the first rope. Then, six inches from the first, she did the same with the next loop. She went all the way up one side and down the other, doing the same. She made sure each clove knot sat exactly six inches from the preceding one, all the way around. She threaded a final rope through all of the loops formed by the slipknots, all the way around. She circled the entire assembly twice with the finishing rope. Finally, she pushed the clove hitches as tight as she could against the outside rope. She stepped back and looked at a square rope mattress, slightly larger than the length of Jesse's body.

"Put those empty bags on top and tie them in place." When finished they had a rope stretcher with handle holds at each corner. 'We'll put him on and carry him out feet first. Everyone gets a corner. Kate, take the left side because of your arm. Jake, you and Tom take the head which is the heavier end." Tom passed out rubber gloves from the first aid kit. "Here! Put these on. They will keep you from getting blisters. Double or triple up on them. Change them out when they break through."

With Jesse placed on the makeshift stretcher, Rita and Kate took the front and led the group down the tunnel toward the exit. "Follow me, boys," she tossed back over her shoulder. She gave a knowing look at Katie; she could not resist taking one more jab, making sure they could overhear her stage whisper, "Do I have to do everything around here?"

By the time Carl arrived on the outskirts of Lackland AFB, it was late afternoon. Along the way, he had fallen in behind a construction team of heavy bulldozers going from place to place, clearing paths beneath, over, or around all of the collapsed overpasses. Carl cautiously drove through a newly cleared pathway.

The last thing they needed was a flat tire. It took most of the day to reach the field hospital on Lackland. He interviewed as many as he could, recording each interview. He calculated he had barely enough juice to make one more telecast back to the station before he ran out of gas in the satellite truck.

Most of the victims he saw now were flood refugees. Reports of the Medina River out of its banks had been coming across the radio all day. Slowly, heavy equipment operators were opening up the inner city as rescue and recovery trucks, with flashing lights, hauled survivors out as quickly as possible. A steady stream of ambulances and helicopters were coming and going from the huge MASH-like tent hospital on the military base.

Now the sun sank low in the sky, and news time neared. The sky turned yellowish-red against the dust-laden sky. Carl moved his crew again, pushing further west trying to track down some of the incredible stories they had been hearing. He heard of entire houses, with families still inside, floating away down the roaring river. Incredible stories of heroism and sacrifice were repeated as rescue crews told of heroic life-saving efforts; some successful some not. He kept hearing of animal attacks. The size of the animal grew impossibly large with each retelling. He had to get closer. It was time to set up for the six o'clock news. Outside the old Medina Air Base, he stopped his truck, deployed his satellite equipment, and prepared to transmit.

As Carl was preparing to go live, a group of four Apache helicopters roared right over his head and flew off to the southwest. Carl watched as four other helicopters formed in a line to the west, as the Apache gunships broke formation and surrounded a heavily wooded hillside over a mile away. To his astonishment, the gunships suddenly unleased short bursts of gunfire into the open area around the summit of the hillside. The helicopters ceased firing and hovered in place all around the little hilltop. Carl called to Wanda in the truck, "Tell Hardesty to get us on live as soon as possible! Something big is going down right now!"

James positioned the camera to get Carl and the hilltop in the frame. He could not take his eyes away from the scene unfolding over Carl's shoulder. "What the hell? Have they got the entire Al Qaeda army cornered up there? Do we stay in place, or move back?'

"Keep rolling!" Carl shouted. "Make sure it's recording. Let me know when we go live!" Gunfire rang out again as Wanda shouted from the door of the truck, "Live in 3 – 2 – 1!" She pointed at Carl. The rapid fire of the guns sounded like a buzz saw in the distance.

"This is Carl Bellow for NewsLive9! reporting live outside Lackland Air Force Base. The sounds you hear behind me are four Apache attack helicopters pouring heavy gunfire into a brushy hilltop outside San Antonio! Four other Ranger helicopters are circling to the north around the perimeter of this hillside near the Medina training area."

Mike Hardesty at the station cut in, "Carl, what are they shooting at?"

"We have no idea whatsoever, Mike! As you can see, they are cutting those cedar breaks up pretty good. We have no official information on what is unfolding right before our eyes! I cannot imagine the Army firing live rounds amongst hundreds, if not thousands, of earthquake and flood survivors; but you can see and hear it for yourself. This is absolutely incredible!"

"What have you been hearing, Carl?"

"We've encountered hundreds of flood survivors swarming past all afternoon. They are telling us that Medina dam broke wide open, and flooded the entire Medina River Valley. The tiny town of Rio Medina is gone, and a good portion of Castroville is under water. We are hearing reports of the flood cresting forty feet at Castroville, but we cannot reach the river to confirm that. The water is rushing downstream to join the San Antonio River south of here; just beyond that hillside behind us that is now taking heavy fire from the U.S. Army."

Carl continued his report, "All day long, we've been getting outrageous reports of zoo animals plundering the dead and attacking survivors as they flee the flooded river bottoms. Some of these reports involve a crocodile of impossible proportions. The stress of the earthquake and the horror of the flood are clearly affecting the rationale of these survivors. We have heard reports of a crocodile-like animal as large as a semi-truck, Mike. Some are reporting a crocodile some forty feet long and over eight feet high! Clearly, the panic has upset their judgment and perception, as they run for their lives from what must be a hellish event!"

Hardesty cut back in with another question, "Could that be what the Army is shooting at, Carl?"

Carl Bellow stared dumbly into the camera lens with his mouth open. For the first time in his entire career, he had no words. Breaking all the laws of news reporting, he turned his back on the camera to stare toward the hillside as the camera panned past him, recording long white streaks of tracer rounds mixed with the hot shells chewing up the distant hillside. All he could think of to say was, "Reporting live from San Antonio, this is Carl Bellow for NewsLive9!"

Aquasaurus hunkered down, trying to shield its eyes from the harsh, blinding glare. With darkness quickly approaching, it became easier to see. The animal had no concept of being hunted, nor did it have any comprehension of the danger whistling through the air above its impromptu lair. It only knew it needed water soon. In the blinding light, it had no idea where water might be. After taking cover beneath the trees, it had settled down in the shade beneath a rocky outcropping in a dry drainage creek. The shady coolness under the ledge gave some relief to the crocodile, unaccustomed to the direct heat of the sun. It wallowed out a depression in the cool, damp soil beneath the rock, getting as close to the ground as possible. It hid in a drainage ditch that twisted down the side of the hill toward the river bottoms and emptied into the river. Obscured by the heavy leaf cover overhead and beneath a rock cliff, the animal was impossible to see from the air.

Instinctively, the crocodile knew water ran downhill. While it had rested, the sky had become dark and it was easier for the croc to see. It slowly slid out from under the rock overhang into the dry creek bottom. The sound and smell of water grew stronger. Heavy on the ground, the huge reptile sought the buoyancy of the water where movement would be less effort. The need to walk and crawl had taken a lot of energy and vigor from the animal. The harsh blinding light created halos and circles over blurred images. Practically blind, it navigated solely on the scent and sound of the water. Like water, it sought low-lying areas as it slid forward over the rocks and loose gravel of the creek bed. Its skin was dry and hot. It missed the protective shelter of the shade and longed to return to the quiet places inside the deep cave. It longed for the home it had somehow lost. There, it was quiet, and the soothing sounds of drips sliding down stalactites and cavern walls gave it peace. It related water to the cave, and it believed the cave was near the water. It desired the soothing coolness of the water. It wanted to leave the harsh, glaring, noisy world behind, to sink deeply once again into the black water. The humming and buzzing sounds on the summit of the hillside decreased as it moved further downhill.

The growing darkness was a relief and brought cooler temperatures. The scent of the water grew stronger; desire and need rose in the animal as it crawled toward the life-saving water it could now hear and smell.

Behind, the hillside erupted with noise like buzzing bees. It was a hostile environment. Helicopters swarmed the hillside like flies, flinging stinging darts earthward toward an unseen target. The chain guns chewed the trees to bits and scattered huge splinters, of hundred-year-old ash juniper trees. Sawdust and broken limbs chopped by the unrelenting gunfire littered the ground.

In the run-off wadi, out of sight of overhead eyes, Aquasaurus came to the bank of the swollen Medina River. A few miles downstream, the swollen Medina would join the San Antonio River. The animal plunged, at last, into the raging tide of the flood-ravaged river, and sank into the depths. It was satisfied to let the current wash it downstream, as it closed its eyes and rested. It floated, eyes and bulla barely above the surface, as the unrelenting and unstoppable flood carried it toward the Gulf of Mexico.

Chapter 21

The makeshift stretcher worked surprisingly well, considering it consisted only of rope without any solid support. It held Jesse off the ground, and the four of them could lift and carry him easily. Jesse lay inside what amounted to a hammock; his middle section sagged lower than his feet and head. At least it was an easier way to carry Jesse out of the cave. It was rough going, at first, until they got the hang of carrying the litter. Every little jolt or bump caused Jesse to cry out in pain, but he could not have walked out on his own. The bumps and jolts were painful for Katie and Tom too. Rita knew of no other way. Jesse tried to stay as quiet as possible, and did not complain. After a while, the carriers learned to match their steps, to make the transit as comfortable as possible. However, the rough, uneven floor of the cave made it extremely difficult to carry the stretcher smoothly.

Jesse held the light at first, but the pain soon grew so intense he could not keep it aimed in front. Katie and Rita used headlights strapped to their foreheads, which they salvaged from the left over kit bags. The problem with headlights is they illuminate the cave only in the direction their heads are turned. Therefore, they concentrated on looking straight ahead in order to best see where they were going. Rita could not help but think what might happen if the crocodile came upon them again from one of the side tunnels or from behind. Once, Rita thought she heard something down one of the dark side tunnels. She was so distracted she stumbled over a rock. As she struggled to keep her feet, she threw everyone else out of rhythm; and they all stumbled, spilling Jesse out onto the rough rock floor. His high-pitched screams of pain echoed off the walls. Jake's mind raced back to their dead friends screaming in the dark cave. The fall had not caused any additional injury to Jesse, and gradually his pain subsided enough for them to carry onward again. Rita made sure she did not stumble or trip again. She was not certain how much more pain or shock Jesse could stand.

Katie felt as though her arm would fall off. Her position in the front left allowed her to use her uninjured right arm. She could not switch with Rita because she could not lift from her left side. It would do no good to switch with one of the others in the back. Sometimes her arm ached so badly she had to call for a rest. In the back, they could switch sides, which eased their aching arms somewhat. Rita's arms were tired too; but because she had been climbing a long time, she still felt strong. She could hold up better and carry longer than Katie could. Whenever Katie asked for a stop, they would halt and rest. Rita wanted to make sure they did not drop Jesse again.

When they rested, they would share their stories. Katie told of Rita's crazy Mr. Toad-ride through the canyons in the dark of night. Tom and Jake told them a little of finding the main party, maimed and dead. Even though they left out some of the more graphic scenes, the women heard all they wanted to hear. "What are we going to do about them?" Katie asked.

"As soon as we get Jesse taken care of and turned over to the emergency responders, we'll report their location and assist a recovery team to go in after them. Jake or I may have to lead them in."

"I'm bringing a gun!" Jake promised.

Tom laughed at him, "You got a cannon?"

Rita tried to explain the problem with potential emergency response a little clearer. "Tom, when we get outside, you'll see what I mean. There is no emergency response. That earthquake? They are treating hundreds, if not thousands, of injured and dead. All of the emergency crews are dealing with the disaster. This earthquake is bigger than anything that has ever happened around here. We will have to get Jesse to the hospital on our own. There is no one else to help. And, we are going to have to hope we can find a hospital that can take him."

After sixteen hours, Rita called a halt at the base of a massive dark wall as they carefully and gladly laid the makeshift stretcher down. They were so tired they collapsed into a circle around Jessie. Jesse was quiet, though still in great pain. It appeared they were at a dead end at the base of the wall. No side tunnels led off in other directions. Their progress was clearly blocked.

"I thought we were never going to get here," Rita breathed deeply. "It was a long haul."

"Here?" Jake asked. "Here where? Where is the opening that leads out of the cave?"

Rita slowly raked her flashlight up the sheer rock wall towering four stories above them. She looked at Jake and pointed with her eyes, "Up there!"

Late Friday night, Sara sat by Cody's bed, crying. Five days had passed since Cody was injured and there was no sign when he might regain consciousness – if ever. Sara wondered if this nightmare might ever end. Tired of the continuous earthquake coverage on every television channel, she turned on the music channels in the room. She punched the remote control until she found some soft religious music. It calmed her and gave her some peace. Mentally, she counted her blessings, hoping to throw off the sense of hopelessness she felt so deeply.

She tried to call Pokey; but he was in some committee meeting somewhere, probably covering for her. She knew her absence was causing her to fall behind on several important issues. She had already missed the fracking vote. She decided if Cody needed full-time care when he recovered, she would resign from the legislature. They would have to understand Cody is her first priority. Realizing that she was sinking into negative thinking again, she went back to counting her blessings. Cody was alive. He was breathing on his own. The nurses had not come back in for another horrifying and painful "code blue." He did not seem to be in any immediate danger. Sometimes, he even moved a little, just small twitches and jerks; but it was movement. Everyone said that was a good sign. His color was better now. He just needed to wake up. Sara's clothes were clammy; she had brought nothing to change into. She was exhausted, and worried. It all comes back to the same place, she thought. No matter how hard she tried to put a good face on it, nothing is good when your son is comatose.

The warm room and the soothing music helped her relax enough to drift off into a restless, troubled sleep. Countless times, she searched her mind for something, anything she could do to end this suffering. Countless times, she came up with nothing. In her dreams, she could see her blonde-haired little boy running, playing, and catching butterflies or fishing on the pond. She remembered the bright sun playing in the highlights of his hair. She longed for those days. She wanted her son back. She was sick and tired of being sick and tired.

A sudden noise in the room broke her troubled dreams. She opened her eyes to see a man in a camouflage uniform laying a sheet and bedspread on the floor next to Cody's bed. He knelt with his back to her as he worked. Sara could not imagine what he was doing. He stood and fluffed a pillow, dropping it at the head of the pallet. She realized he was making a bed on the floor. As he turned toward her, she recognized Dr. Bryan!

"What … what are you doing?" She asked.

"Hi. Sorry I woke you. I'm going to get some sleep," he exclaimed. "I'm exhausted! Haven't slept in two days. I'm going to bed down here tonight. If Cody needs anything, wake me up. I'm dead on my feet!" He dropped onto the pallet and scrunched the pillow beneath his head. He had not even taken off his boots.

"I'm so happy to see you!" Sara cried. "No one has checked on him in over a day!"

"I just checked him, and he seems to be doing fine. Yes, he is unconscious; but the body has a way of healing itself sometimes. I read about the code blue, but don't let it worry you," he reassured her. "He seems to have gotten through it without any more damage," he yawned. "I'll be here in case anything happens."

Sara went to the door and turned off the room light. It did not seem to matter to Dr. Bryan, already still and breathing heavily. Sara went into the hall and walked to the nurses' station. "Can I have a blanket for Dr. Bryan?" she asked.

"Dr. Bryan?" the nurse looked at her blankly.

"Yes," Sara answered. "Dr. Bryan."

"Honey, Dr. Bryan isn't here. He was deployed to the emergency evacuation center down by San Antonio. Weren't you told? He won't be back for several days, if then. We have temporary doctors who will take over your son's care. You should have a visit from a local San Marcos doctor in the morning." She checked her sheet, "It will be … Dr. Thompson," she said cheerily. "He's good. You will like him. We have called in as many local doctors as we could get to volunteer here at the hospital. He is one of the best."

This time it was Sara, who looked at the nurse blankly. Obviously, she did not know Dr. Bryan was currently making a pallet in Cody's room. "Can I have a blanket, please?"

Sara took the blanket back to the room. In her absence, Dr. Bryan had removed his boots and heavy uniform shirt. She saw even his undershirt was camouflaged. Why would you need to camouflage your undershirt? She laughed to herself, thinking that if he dropped it in the woods he might never find it. Were his undershorts camouflaged? She arched her eyes at the image of him walking around nude in the woods looking for his camouflaged clothing. She snapped back to reality. She must really be tired. Dr. Bryan slept soundly without snoring. Point for Dr. Bryan, she thought. Sara carefully laid the soft blanket over him. He stirred in his sleep, bunching the soft blanket under his chin. Sara looked at his kind face. She wondered if he came back just to check on Cody. Otherwise, wouldn't the hospital have known he was here? What did that mean? Anything? However, just having him here gave Sara a great sense of comfort and security. She returned to her chair, as the soft music played on the darkened TV. Exhausted herself, she fell into a deep, peaceful sleep. The troubled dreams did not return.

A few hours later, Sara suddenly jerked awake. Something had made a noise. She looked to her left and saw the door closing. She always kept the door open so she could see who walked past. Next to Cody's bed, Dr. Bryan's pallet was gone. Her watch said 5:38 in the morning. Well, that was good while it lasted, she thought. She wished he had awakened her to say goodbye. Sara saw something taped to the mirror. She pulled off an envelope with her name on it. Inside she found a handwritten note reading:

> "I didn't want to wake you – you were sleeping so soundly. I want you to know we are doing everything we can do to help Cody. I've read all of the reports, and I don't see anything too alarming. In fact, things look pretty good right now. I know! What's good about him being in a coma? Right? If Cody doesn't have any more events, he shouldn't be in any immediate danger. I know it looks bad – hopeless. But don't give up hope. I've seen dozens of these cases end well.

> I have to go back now. I don't know when I can come again, but I promise I will. Keep doing what you are doing, and I think we will have a good result. I wouldn't be surprised if he wakes up before I get back. Hang in there. My personal cell phone is 512-555-4975. If I can't answer, leave a message. Try not to worry. I'll see you soon.

> Colton."

Sara was still disappointed he had left before they could talk, but she was happy he cared enough to leave her a note. She checked on Cody and sat back down in her chair. It was a puzzle. Why would he come all the way back here to check on Cody, as exhausted as he was? Why would he spend his downtime checking on a boy he barely knew? Why would he give up sleep to make sure she and Cody were doing well? Was he showing professional courtesy; or, did he truly care? She tried to remember the times he had been in to see Cody before, but she drew a blank. She remembered he seemed rushed and distracted. He had been kind, but busy. She had felt like Dr. Bryan considered Cody just another case, another checkmark he had to make on his daily rounds sheet. Now she thought differently. He was a kind man, as well as a doctor. She drifted off to sleep, strangely comforted by the knowledge Dr. Bryan – Colton – honestly seemed to care about them. Colton. Such a nice name for such a nice doctor. Colton and Cody – the names complimented each other. Maybe one day Cody could be a great doctor, too. She drifted to a place where peaceful sea-green waters flowed past palm trees. She sat in a rattan chair near a large four-poster bed, as the soft sea breezes blew the gossamer white curtains out toward the sea, only to draw them softly back into the room. So peaceful. So quiet. The white, sheer curtains through which she could see the green sunlit sea… so comforting …

Chapter 22

Inside the tumbling waters of the flooded San Antonio River, Aquasaurus swam in its own element. The flooded riverbed made excellent cover, and the flowing current greatly increased the distance it could travel. The millions of acre-feet of water, raging headlong downstream, contained abundant food. Hundreds of head of cattle were drowned and decaying along with livestock of all sorts. Scattered here and there, especially along the muddy banks, were tangled brush piles of downed trees and limbs jammed onto the slimy banks by the force of the water, and dumped high above the normal water line. Bits of cloth, clothing, and paper flapped and fluttered in the wind; caught in barbed wire fences all along the river. Toys and personal effects, and even one television, dangled from the high branches of a tree. Scrubby oaks and cedar caught and held the floating wreckage and detritus from a hundred homes. Within and beneath the piles of rubble were rotting human corpses. The buzzards were already circling overhead. The tree-lined river bottom provided ample cover from above and to the side. Floating southward in the deep, deadly night, the crocodile could rest and travel at the same time.

Armed soldiers in battle fatigues bailed from UH-53 helicopters on Medina Base, to form a battle line facing the hill. The order came to "move out!" They stepped off toward the last known location of the target, the summit. Not knowing what to expect, they were locked-and-loaded. Other helicopters in the sky lit the field from above, but it was still very dark on the ground. The battle line entered deep grass where it was impossible to see even a few feet ahead. A ragged pale quarter moon began to rise, but did little to light the field. The soldiers could not help but think that at any minute the beast might come charging out of the grass and attack. The officers had not relayed the enormity of the animal to the units, believing they were over-exaggerated. They believed they were looking for a normal crocodile escaped from the zoo. Their job was to find, not to kill the animal. Find it, and flush it out into the open. Parks service personnel were on-hand to try to capture the endangered animal. The soldiers carped about having to hump it through the wild Texas terrain in the middle of the night. It was a hazardous occupation.

Not only did they have to worry about grass burrs and cacti, but also other hazards lurked in the weeds. Sergeant Massy stumbled across the first snake while still in the LZ. He lifted it with the barrel of his M-16 and waved it around the rest of the troops until the First Sergeant told him to throw it aside. The grassy hillside writhed with snakes. Some of them were poisonous. Before the troops had gone a quarter-mile, they had found at least a dozen large ones. They buzzed and struck at the men's leather-covered boots. Terrified soldiers had trampled more than one snake to death. It is hard to maintain order when you are walking on snakes. Several men, who had been in hot war-zones a number of times, panicked and broke ranks when they heard the unmistakable rattling buzz. The officers had not given the order to fire, so the soldiers could not shoot the coiling, writhing things. In their panic, they may have shot each other.

The company reached the summit of the hill safely, which, by some estimations, was a miracle in itself. No one looked forward to the trek back down to the LZ. Their Lieutenant made several requests to relocate the extraction point to the other side of the hill where it was rocky and probably had fewer snakes. At least, it would be easier to see them on the rocks than to spot them in the high grass. Command had still not made the decision by the time they arrived on top of the hill. They were amazed at the damage the helicopter guns had done to the cedars and oaks on the hilltop. They searched every hole and every nook and cranny trying to flush out the crocodile. After forty minutes, they determined there was no crocodile on the summit. They radioed word back to the command center. It seemed apparent the animal had escaped the hill through a dry creek that meandered down the slope toward the river.

A Captain sent a platoon with a tracker squad down the dry creek bed to follow and locate the crocodile. Halfway down the dry creek bed, they suffered their first casualty. A rock rolled under a soldier's boot, and he twisted his ankle. Medical corpsmen stabilized the sprain as well as they could. They offered to carry the grunt back to the helicopters and lift him out. "Back through those snakes?" he asked. "Yeah," the medic nodded. "Hell no! Give me that stick over there and I'll catch up with my squad!" With his makeshift crutch, he hobbled down the creek bed to catch up with his team.

The dry creek emptied into the Medina River, two miles from its confluence with the San Antonio River. The GIs stood on the edge of the swollen river and examined the tracks and signs. They were confident the animal had entered the water at least a couple of hours before they arrived at the site. They reported to the battalion commander that the crocodile had escaped into the flooded river.

Two hundred miles southeast, the San Antonio River joined the Guadalupe River near the estuary above San Antonio Bay on the Gulf of Mexico. The river ran through five counties before it merged with the sea. Unlike most rivers, it did not flow directly into the Gulf. It flowed into a marshy, boggy estuary, and spread out on the flat plain in a confusing matrix of canals and shallow lakes. The estuary is a mix of fresh and briny water, growing saltier the closer to the bay it flows. Slow and lazy, the estuary forms a natural filter, catching and removing many of the contaminants from the water before it mixes with the sea. Low and marshy, it is a natural habitat for alligators and crocodiles. The low lying swamps provided important habitat and cover for a wide range of creatures. Favoring the briny water, Aquasaurus moved further downstream toward the sea.

The coast guard cruiser received the call just after daybreak. A fishing boat sent out a 'mayday' before dawn. Scanning the calculated location, a seaman called out. "Sighting. Thirty degrees off the bow – 1 o'clock! Approximately three nautical miles. Craft appears to be capsized, Captain."

The pilot turned the forty-seven foot cruiser slightly to the right and throttled up. As they neared the site, they backed the engine off to idle and allowed their forward momentum to bring them in closer to the upturned boat. They spotted the first body floating off their starboard side. Soon they saw several more men floating near the capsized shrimping boat. None of the floaters were struggling or trying to get their attention. It was a bad sign. When the seamen were finished, they had pulled eight waterlogged bodies from the water. The lifeboat circled the shrimp boat several times searching for more. The crew made loud announcements over the speakers, but no other shrimpers responded. The mate blew the ship air horn three times. There was no response from the wreck. It appeared all of the fishermen were dead. Some of the recovered bodies were in bad condition, which surprised the captain. The ship had not exploded; no fire or smoke was present. The bodies had not been in the water long, yet they were mangled and broken. Sharks?

"Captain, this one is alive!" a medic called to the captain. The seamen moved the injured man forward. He was an Asian, probably Vietnamese. His heavily accented English was difficult to understand, and no one on board the Coast Guard boat spoke his language. Gradually they pieced together enough information to understand what had happened. Eight men were on board the shrimp boat. The mate matched that number to the recovered bodies and reported that all of the shrimpers were accounted for. All were dead, except this one. The mate radioed the coordinates of the disabled boat to a rescue helicopter. Meanwhile, no Vietnamese speakers could be located back at the base. All of the Viet Nam veterans were retired from the service.

While they waited for the evacuation chopper, they tended the fisherman as well as they could. His name was Gnu. It is a common name pronounced with a silent 'g'. As Mr. Gnu regained strength, he tried to explain what had happened. Although in great pain, he kept putting his arms in front of his body, spreading them apart, and then slamming them back together, like huge jaws. "What's he trying to say? It looks like an alligator, but no alligator would be big enough to attack a shrimp boat. Besides, in this briny water, it would have to be a crocodile; but no crocodiles live anywhere near here, and it probably wouldn't be big enough either. Is he trying to say his boat was attacked by a crocodile?"

"Captain!" the watch sounded, pointing. "Off the port side, something is in the water."

The captain picked up his binoculars. "Mother … that's one hell of huge crocodile! And it's headed this way! Turnabout, full speed! The damned thing's going to try to ram us!" Captain ordered battle stations as three seamen manned the aft guns. The Captain did not give the command to fire as the coast guard cruiser quickly outran the animal. After they were a safe distance away, they cut the engines and looked for the animal through the glasses. "Sir, that thing never showed up on the radar! We never got a reading on it. Not a single blip. We don't know where it is now." The captain peered out on the water through his binoculars. "Keep trying to get eyes on it," the captain ordered. "It's around here somewhere. Did you see the size of that thing?"

Meanwhile the mate keyed the radio and called the incident in to the command center, along with their current coordinates for the rescue helicopter. Command told them to maintain a distance from the animal, but not to shoot unless they were in grave danger. They were to stand by for further instructions. Everyone scanned water, but no one saw any sign of the crocodile. They floated – waiting. No giant crocodile could be seen in the choppy waves.

Eventually the call with their orders came through. They were not, at all, what the Captain was expecting. "You will turn your injured and dead over to Sea Dog 3, which should be arriving at your location in three minutes." They could hear the helicopter engines in the distance. "Then, you are to maintain surveillance of the capsized fishing vessel until a recovery crew arrives. When relieved, return to your assigned patrol route. Over."

"Sir," the captain spoke again, "are you aware there is a crocodile in these waters that is a threat to small craft in the area? Over."

"Yes, Captain. We are aware. Go to secure channel, please. Shore Command out."

The radio operator on board switched to a secure channel and regained connection with command. On the secure channel, Command could communicate over a handset, which looked like a normal telephone, without the conversation being overheard. "Captain, the Air Force has been tracking this creature since yesterday. With your sighting, we now know where it is. Good work! The Navy will seek out and deal with the animal. You are to return to your assigned patrol once the recovery team arrives and you have turned over your casualties."

Sir," the captain spoke again, "Are you also aware this beast cannot be tracked by radar? We have been unable to get a position on it. We are trying to regain a visual but without results."

The radio went silent for several moments. "We are aware. That is why the Army and the Air Force lost the animal in the first place. We do not know why or how, but it seems to be immune to radar or heat imaging. However, our operations are stretched too thin; so the Navy is taking command of this situation. You are to maintain your position at the accident scene. Report any further sightings, but do not pursue the animal. Do not fire unless you are in clear and imminent danger. I repeat: make way for naval operations, and do not interfere. Be prepared to assist if needed. The Coast Guard is ordered to stand down, Captain. Our mission is to make the waterways safe for small craft. Other Coast Guard units are en route to your location to guard smaller vessels in the vicinity. This information is confidential at this time, and no general warning has been issued. Be alert, and protect and defend. Do not seek and destroy. Understood?"

"Aye, sir!" the captain turned to his men watching the rescue helicopter land on the water nearby. He turned his back on the salty spray the giant helicopter rotors kicked into the air. "Head back to the capsized fishing boat," he ordered the steersman. He turned to the first mate, "The Navy is taking over the search for the crocodile."

"Skipper," the mate said over the noise of the airship, "if it is a crocodile, it won't go to sea. It will hang around the edge of the estuaries and swampy shores. The Navy won't find it out there; they will be too far out to see it."

The Captain knew his mate was right but simply muttered, "We've got our orders."

"Aye, sir." The mate turned back to supervise the crew as it off-loaded casualties to the waiting helicopter floating nearby.

Jake looked up from the base of the sheer wall to the top. "How in the world are we going to get Jesse all the way up this rock wall?" Jake asked. "He can't climb!"

"We are going to lift him out," Rita assured him. "First, scramble up this wall. See that anchor rope just to the left here. See it?"

"I see it. Then what?"

"If you need it, use it to ascend this cliff. Once you get up there, find me two stiff poles, and lower them down along with a couple of lengths of rope. You'll find some in the gear bag near the truck. It's parked across the creek to the east. We'll go from there." Rita watched him make his ascent of the cliff. An experienced climber, Jake had no trouble quickly reaching the top. He peered over the ledge, gave Rita a 'thumbs up' in the spot of her light, and left to go look for the equipment. Below, they waited for his return.

Rita turned to Katie, "Can you climb?"

"I don't know."

Katie had her good right arm, and strong legs. She could hold on to the cliff; but without three points of contact, she could not advance up the face. Every time she let go of her right handhold, she fell back off the rock. She would need at least one strong foothold to climb with one arm, and it was not likely she would find strong footholds every step of the way to the top. "Ok, stop." Rita said. "We'll go to plan B."

"You got more than one plan?" Katie asked.

"We could send Jake for help," Tom offered.

"He may not find any – remember the earthquake? We're climbing this wall, and we're getting out of this cave. Whatever it takes," Rita assured him.

Soon, Jake appeared at the top of the wall and lowered down the items Rita had requested. "Got it!"

she called up. "Now, anchor a safety rope to something nearby, and lower the end to me. Make sure it is a long one. We need at least fifty feet." She gave the poles to Tom. "Slide these through the loops on each side of the stretcher for stability." Then, she attached the loose rope dangling from the cliff to Katie's safety belt. "Katie, Jake is going to keep tension on this rope to keep you from falling and to provide you an anchor as you move from grip to grip. Climb with your legs and keep on the rope. Use your ascender." The ascender is a metal tool, which loops around an anchor rope. Its shape provides a strong handhold. If you have a solid base, you can slide the ascender up the rope; but it will not slide back down unless you take the tension off. The idea is to find a solid foothold, slide the ascender up the anchor rope, and then pull yourself upwards all the way to the top. If Katie fell, the safety rope would keep her from falling all the way to the bottom.

"Jake, keep the tension on her line. She's coming up!"

Rita stood beneath Katie to help break her fall if necessary. She watched as Katie gained the summit. Satisfied that Katie was safely on top, Rita turned her attention to Tom and Jesse. "Tom, do you think you can make it up there?"

"Yeah, I think I can. I've got use of my arms and legs."

"Have you done any climbing?"

"Not really. I've done some, but not much," he admitted.

"Ok. We'll put the safety rope on you, too, when it's your turn to go up. Let's get Jesse ready." She examined the poles on each side of Jesse's stretcher.

"What are you going to do?" Jesse asked. "Just stay quiet and be still. We're going to lift you out of here."

She showed Tom how to rig the sling. Each corner rope must be exactly the same length to keep the stretcher from tilting. They were going to tie Jesse in, but it would be better, and less painful for Jesse, if the stretcher went up level. Once they had everything set up, Rita revealed the rest of her plan to Tom. "We're going to get you up top, where you can help Jake pull Jesse up. I'll stay down here below to steady him as the stretcher goes up the face, and to free it if it snags on a rock. "Once we get him topside, I'll climb the rest of the way up and we can get out of here. It is less than a mile to the cave opening. With those poles, it will be easier to carry him out once we get up there."

She tied the safety rope around Tom's waist and called Jake to keep the slack out again. Using Rita's ascender, Tom climbed the rock just as Katie had, but at a much slower pace. Once he arrived on top, she called for him to drop the ascender tool back down. She stood out of the way to keep it from bonging her on the head as it fell and bounced across the cave floor. She tied the anchor rope to the apex of the rigged sling on Jesse's stretcher. With no other rope, she would free-climb the face beneath Jesse's stretcher. "Ok! Pull him up – slowly!" she called and watched as Jesse's stretcher slowly inched up the wall. It rose straight and level. Once the stretcher rose above her head, she started up the rock wall without a safety. A couple of times, the stretcher hung up on a projection; but she reached up and pulled it free from the wall. Foot by foot, the stretcher rose up the cliff face with Rita just below. If the stretcher broke loose and fell, it would carry Jesse and Rita to their deaths on the cave floor below. Finally, the stretcher reached the summit. Rita watched as arms reached out to drag Jesse's stretcher to the top of the ledge. She climbed over the lip of the cliff, and joined them on top. They were only a short distance from the opening now as they lifted the stretcher and moved off into the darkness.

Thirty minutes later, they were pulling Jesse and his stretcher through the narrow opening to the outside. The air smelled so fresh and clean. The golden sun rose just over the treetops, flooding the creek bed with warm spring sunshine. Free of the cave at last, they stood in a circle around Jesse and group-hugged. Bandaged and bruised, dirty and exhausted, they looked exactly like what they were – bedraggled survivors from a war.

Sara awoke with a start. The sun shone brightly behind the gossamer white curtains of her dream. Awake now, the white curtains still gently waved back and forth in the breeze. She could not recall curtains in the room, she realized. She felt awake, but she must be dreaming. She looked up to see the face of her son, the light making a golden halo around his head. 'My son has become an angel,' she thought as she looked at him in awe. How peaceful and radiant he looked. She could see his thin body through his heavenly gown. Soft, soothing, celestial music flooded the air around him. Cody floated over her as she gazed up from her chair.

'Wait a minute,' she thought. 'An angel with an IV?' Her mind a whirl, she traced the plastic tubes back to the still beeping machine. Confused, she looked back into the glowing face of her angelic son.

"Mom," he said, "I'm hungry!"

Chapter 23

Hootie waited in the parking lot of Katie's apartment for two days. Except for quick trips to eat, he had not left for more than a few minutes. He called her number dozens of times, but got no answer. He knew he could not leave a message on the phone; he had to tell her in person. Hootie had knocked on her door every few hours or so, in case he may have missed her return to her apartment. No answer. He would not leave until he had taken care of this. He felt like he owed it to Clint. If he had to wait a week, he needed to see it through. He dreaded what he had to tell her, knowing it would be hard, but she deserved to hear it in person. Clint would want it that way.

He sat in his truck just after sunset on the second day. He had finished a book and listened to all of his CDs by then. Behind the seat were piles of Styrofoam cups, and wads of empty hamburger bags. It smelled like onion inside the cab. It had not been bad at first, but now it had gotten rank.

He looked up from a newspaper, and saw Katie outside her apartment. She had her left arm in a sling. She slowly climbed the stairs, one at a time. She looked like she had been in a fight. Her clothes were torn; and her bloodstained t-shirt hung limply on her body, barely covering her. 'Maybe she got caught in the earthquake,' he thought. He watched as she unlocked the door and let herself in. The light next to the window came on, and he saw the blue flicker of the TV set. Hootie decided to give her a little time; he could wait for her to take a shower before he dropped the news on her. He was not ready yet, anyway.

For the next half-hour, he went over in his mind what he had to say. How do you tell someone her father is dead? He had never had to do that before. Even though he had sat thinking about it over the past couple of days, he still did not know what he would say or how. What if she freaks out? What if she goes all to pieces? What would he do? How would he handle that? How could he comfort her when his own heart was breaking inside? Once again, he searched for the magic words to make the situation go away. Magic words do not exist.

Wearily, he climbed the cold steel steps to her apartment. He saw the TV flickering through the curtains as he gently rapped on the door. Three knocks. He waited. He wished she would not answer, but then he would still be waiting around to tell her. Soon he heard her bump something inside, so he rapped again. Three raps. "Who is it?" she called from behind the wooden door.

"Hootie," he answered.

The door swung open, and Hootie saw Katie standing in the doorway with a towel wrapped around her head. Suddenly, he wished he had waited until morning. He wished he had given her a chance to get some rest. She stood looking at him with her bruised face and her arm in a white plaster cast. "Mr. Johnson?" she asked eyes wide.

He shrugged and mumbled, "Hootie." He looked
at her, wishing he had some other way to tell her. He
looked down at his boots and coughed. When he looked
back at her face, he could not stop the tears welling up in
his eyes.

She knew. Suddenly, without him having to say
a word, she knew.

He caught her as she sagged to the floor and
helped her to the sofa. No words would come. As if,
there were words that would help, anyway. She cried for
hours. Eventually, she fell off into exhausted sleep as
Hootie held her and rocked her in his arms. The door to
her apartment still hung open.

The doctor said Jesse got off lucky. He would
recover in time. After they got him cleaned up, they
found no concussion; but his hip and leg were broken.
His arm was back in its socket, but he would have lots
of pain for some time. They pumped him so full of pain
medicine; he was not going to feel anything for a few
hours. Jesse would not be climbing or going back into
caves for a few weeks. After the doctor patched Jesse
up, Rita rolled his wheelchair out to her car. She
struggled to get him into the passenger seat, but finally
got him belted in. Heavily medicated, he rambled on
about different things and changed subject in mid-
sentence several times. Rita felt relieved that he had
suffered no permanent damage. Once, he asked where
they were going. "Home," she simply said. He wondered
aloud about his car, his equipment, and his keys. She let
him ramble as she drove to her apartment.

By the time she pulled into her parking space, Jesse was sleeping soundly in a drug-induced stupor. She pulled the hospital wheelchair from the back seat and spread it open. When she got him seated, they rolled to the first-floor door of her apartment. She propped opened the front door and rolled him inside. She left him sitting in the chair as she gathered the spare clothes he had left at her place. She helped him into fresh shorts and a baggy t-shirt. Then, she pulled back the bed covers and got him beneath the sheets. She arranged his pillow, turned off the lamp near the bed, and went into the bathroom.

The hot water felt so good. She felt like she had not showered for a week. Sticky brown stuff clung to her hair. After her shower, she checked on Jesse once more and then came back to brush her teeth. After rinsing her mouth, she looked into the mirror. Was she older? She felt and looked older; harder somehow. She felt lucky to have escaped from the crocodile and the dark cave without injury. It was bad enough that Jesse was hurt. She thought of Katie as toothpaste swirled down the basin drain. A crocodile tooth, one of the smaller ones, had sliced almost through her arm. Luckily, she would recover with no loss of movement. That thing could have snapped her whole arm off. The doctor had released Katie about an hour before Jesse, and she was probably in bed asleep by now. Rita would call her in the morning. Finally, Rita realized how tired she was; she needed sleep badly.

She stood in the bathroom door, and looked at Jesse lying in the darkened room. He lay sleeping on his side with a pillow propping up the cast on his leg, as the doctor instructed. As she had always known, she realized Jesse was 'the one'. She just hoped that she was 'the one' for him. When he woke up, she intended to make sure he got that message loud and clear. She did not go down in caves for just anyone. With a contented smile on her face, she reached out and turned off the light, crossed the dark room, and got into bed.

Hundreds of partiers danced on the warm sandy beach of Padre Island. The night glowed brightly from bonfires stacked on the beach as high as could be reached. The loud music mixed with the laughs and screams of the joyful partiers. It was the last Saturday night of Spring Break. Sunday, they were going back home and back to school. In various stages of undress, they danced and jumped to the loud music. The party ramped up to full swing. Beer and spirits flowed freely, and the mob danced long into the night without a care in the world.

Barely a hundred yards offshore, firelight from the beach party flickered and reflected in cold yellow eyes floating just above the surface of the water. The sliver of a moon peeked from behind swirling clouds to reveal a grisly scene. The moon glistened across the bottom of a capsized boat, its metal hull crumpled and bent. Draped across the keel were three bodies; blood streamed in channels down the cold aluminum hull into the sea. Nearby, two other motionless bodies bobbed up and down in the dark waves. Debris lapped against the shore nearby; pushed in, then pulled back out by the waves. Unseen by the dancers on the beach, the crocodile waited. It opened its bloody mouth, and roared loudly, almost in triumph, as it swung its massive tail from side-to-side and silently swam ashore.

The end.